SATAN'S SHOPKEEPER

EVAN CLOUSE

COVER IMAGE ILLUSTRATED BY
ARPIT MEHTA

Library of Congress Control Number: Pending

ISBN: Softcover 978-1-961210-20-2

eBook 978-1-961210-21-9

Rev. date:

CONTENTS

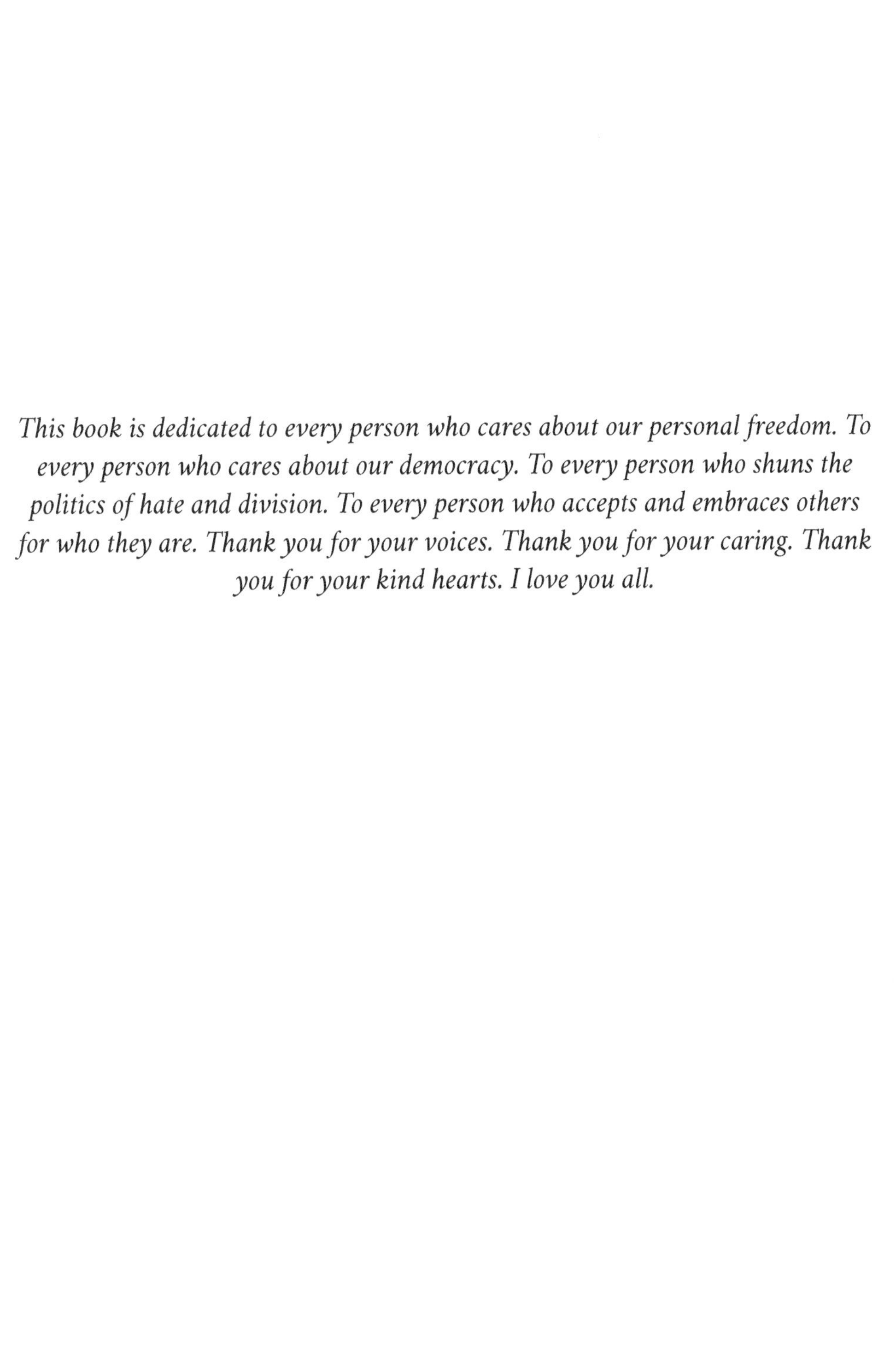
This book is dedicated to every person who cares about our personal freedom. To every person who cares about our democracy. To every person who shuns the politics of hate and division. To every person who accepts and embraces others for who they are. Thank you for your voices. Thank you for your caring. Thank you for your kind hearts. I love you all.

Acknowledgments

I would like to thank every person who has supported me and understands just how important this work is to me. Thank you for reading. Thank you for your input. Thank you for caring. You know who you are.

CHAPTER 1

SALESMANSHIP

Alexander Picklesbee rubbed the weariness from his damned eyes as he approached the metal security gate on his convenience shop. There was a slight creak in his back as he reached down and inserted the key into the lock. He remained in a hunched over position for a moment while lamenting his next task. He deeply inhaled, closed his black eyes, and grasped the bottom of the gate. His perpetually fifty-year-old tender hands fried on the white-hot metal as he flung the gate upward as quickly as possible. He looked down upon his blistered hands and quietly said to himself, "Every morning and every evening my hands are scorched on this gate. Every morning, I take my place behind this counter and every evening I lock up for the night. And each time, my hands are burned. My hands, which were previously used for such marvelous, meticulous operations, are burned and scarred over and over. This has happened every day since December 23, 1888. My, it has been one-hundred-thirty-six years since my passing.

"One-hundred-thirty-six years of tending to this shop and burning my hands. And it shall be so for all of eternity. This is my lot in life. Well, in death, actually. Ah well. It could be much worse for me. At least I'm not constantly pushing a boulder up a mountain or having my intestines eaten by demons in perpetuity or even having a red-hot poker getting thrust up my posterior. No, a few seconds of burning hands twice a day and tending to my convenience store so that the demons can have their snack foods, magazines, and soft drinks. Not a bad situation, um, *comparatively* speaking. Plus, the rowdiness has subsided quite a bit since I lost my liquor license. Our liege made sure of *that* after a group of young demons bought a case of beer here, got drunk, and drove their jalopy over his mailbox. Now, *they* have to build new mailboxes all over hell for eternity and the more *responsible* demons must purchase their libations at the package store all the way over on the bad side of town. And I get to enjoy a bit less anxiety on Friday and Saturday nights."

He began whistling as he put his white apron on and looked at himself in the glass of the cigar display behind the counter. His silver, slick-backed hair reflected the flames from across the street. He delicately brushed his light grey pencil mustache that rested just above his thin upper lip before straightening the apron on his tall, lanky frame and smiling at his reflection. "Perfect," he said just as the front door buzzer alerted him of an entering customer. "And right on time. I do need to get the coffee started."

He turned and looked at the approaching customer and enthusiastically said, "Why, good *morning* my liege." The seven-foot customer raised his red, horned head as his wagging thin, pointy tail knocked over cans of soup and bottles of ketchup onto the floor. He opened his mouth, showing his jagged, pure-white teeth as his purple forked tongue slithered over them. "What's so fucking good about it, Alexander?" a forlorn Satan responded as items continued to haphazardly crash off of the shelves behind him.

Alexander continued to smile as he responded in a bubbly tone, "Why, the weather, my liege. Isn't it the most wonderful day? It's a perfectly cozy 444.6 degrees. And doesn't the fire and brimstone look absolutely *beautiful* with its glowing reds, yellows, and oranges?"

Satan leaned up against the counter and replied, "Yeah, but the fire and brimstone is *always* beautiful and it's *always* the perfect temperature. I dunno what's wrong with me. Maybe I'm entering my mid-life crisis or something. All I know is that I'm bored. Same temperature. Same sulphury smell. Same torture. Over and over. I need a new kick."

"Well," the ever-smiling Alexander gleefully responded. "I think I have *just* the thing to turn that frown upside down, my lord. Would you like whipped cream and extra cinnamon on your cappuccino this morning? And perhaps a cherry on top?"

"Yeah, that'll be fine, I suppose," Satan replied in a disinterested tone. "I do like extra cinnamon. But that's just another example, Alexander. I have that same fucking drink every morning. I torture the same souls every day. Move those flaming hot boulders over there. Now move them over there, and so on. Here's my fiery spade up your perverted ass for the umpteenth-millionth time. Oh, yawn. Keep pulling out your intestines over and over and over. How gauche. It all seems so pointless somehow. I mean, what am I actually accomplishing? Why can't *I* have some *real* fun like those goody-goodies up in Heaven? Partying, fucking virgins, listening to live performances from some of the greatest musicians in the world, shooting paper wads through their stupid fucking halos, using their wings to fly around drunk on wine. And they have a never-ending supply of wine too! If they run out, they just have God's fucking brat kid turn water into it! Why can't *I* fucking do that? I gotta have *my* shit delivered from Kalamazoo. And Kalamazoo isn't exactly known for its wine! It's bullshit, Alexander. It really is."

"Oh, I agree, sire," Alexander sympathetically responded while wiping spilled whipped cream from the glistening countertop. "But what about those mean girl cheerleaders that recently arrived? They're fun, aren't they?"

"Recently arrived?" Satan roared back. "That was like *forty fucking years* ago! I mean, *yeah,* they were fun for a *time,* but even *their* excruciating screams while I'm stretching them out with my impossibly large cock has grown tiresome. Tiresome? Hell, they've become downright annoying. Always talking about each other behind their backs and making up shit. And that fucking gum snapping! Jesus fucking Christ that's off-putting! Alexander, stop selling those little bitches' chewing gum, got it?"

"It would be my pleasure, sire," Alexander joyfully replied. "I must admit, I am a bit tired of cleaning up their graffiti from the bathroom walls."

"They do that?" a surprised Satan asked. "Man, does anybody have any respect for *anything* anymore? I mean, look at you. Hard working every day. Pleasant to the customers. Then, those little twats just strut their tight little asses in here and make more work for you. Times have changed, Alexander. I think that we both remember a time when the banished demons respected other demons' property and privacy. And didn't snap their fucking gum during dinner!"

"Yes, it truly is a sad day in hell, my lord," Alexander replied before displaying a mischievous little grin. "I *really* shouldn't tell you this, but they left a message on the wall last night that I haven't had a chance to clean up."

"They did? I wanna see!" Satan roared before stomping down the hallway, past the supply closet to the women's restroom. Alexander heard his hoofs approaching once again. "Um, Alexander?" he inquired. "May I please have the key to the ladies' room?"

"Of course, sire," Alexander answered as he handed over a small key that was attached to a rusted tire rim. "Just please bring that back, my lord."

"I know. I will," Satan dutifully replied. Alexander's whistling was suddenly interrupted by Satan's booming voice. "Why those little *bitches*! I can't make a girl cum? Oh reeeeeaaally? Well, *those* little skanks are in for a workout tonight! Fuck them! I'm going to fuck them so hard that they won't be able to walk for a century! And they're going to spend eternity writing 'Satan is the greatest fuck ever!' on every fucking bathroom wall in hell until their arms fall off! Plus, no more chewing gum!" His thunderous stride came back to the counter as he said, "Here's the key back. Thanks."

"You are most welcome, my lord," Alexander replied as the tire rim clanged on the stone floor. "I must say, my liege, that it is quite unsettling seeing you in such a state." "Yeah, I know," Satan responded while looking down at his clawed, shuffling feet. "I didn't mean to put my troubles onto you. Sorry to be such a Debbie-downer. But it isn't just the boredom, Alexander. I don't like the trends that I'm seeing. There are *way* more souls going to heaven than our little slice of heav...um...I mean, hell.

"And do you know why? Oh man, this'll make you laugh, Alexander. It's because more and more people are turning away from organized religion! That's right! The more people who realize that they don't need Daddy's Big Book-O-Bullshit to lead moral lives, the more fucking souls go to heaven! How counter-intuitive is *that*? How the fuck do you square *that* circle? I've built an entire career out of persuading people to leave their flocks. My natural assumption was that they'd then follow *me* and sin and shit. But that's not what is happening! People are realizing *on their own* that most of the leaders in organized religion are simply manipulating and brainwashing their congregations for their own benefit!

"Yup, they're figuring out that a bunch of these so-called holy men, and I do mean *men*, are doing this shit for their own greed, or power, or so they can fuck innocent kids. Well, that's mostly the Catholics, but there are perverted motherfuckers in every religion, Alexander. Don't kid yourself about that."

"Oh, I'm quite sure there are, my liege. And *you* would most certainly know," Alexander replied while picking up jars of pickles from the floor and placing them back on the shelf in a perfectly straight line. "Fuck yeah, I *do* know. I've done a deep analysis recently and it showed that people who turn away from organized religion aren't turning to me or to sin. Oh sure, they still fuck around and shit, but they don't *really* sin. They don't do *really* cruel things to their neighbors. They've figured out that they can just naturally be kind to other people without some robe-wearing jerk-off telling them what to do. And judging them. They've figured out that the organized religions who proclaim to be speaking God's word are no more than a bunch of judgy fucking hens bitching about the coleslaw that the new 'brown' family brought and shit like that.

"Did you know, Alexander, that more innocent people have died over religion than anything else? I mean, I've done *all kinds* of plagues and shit on the Earth and *my* shit doesn't hold a *candle* to all the times that some golden fucking calf orders his dullard troops into a war against people that they hate for no fucking reason. They say they are doing it for God's glory, so they kill a bunch of innocent fuckers without giving it any thought. And do you know what's *really* fucking unfair here? Heaven gets all of those innocent souls, and I don't get shit! Oh, you would *think* that I'd get the so-called pious fuckers who are actually evil and engage in the wars, but *nooooooo*. I don't! God says, 'Well, they thought that they were doing it for a good cause and thought they were doing it in my name, so I guess we shouldn't send them to hell, blah, blah, blah, puke.' What an egotistical panty waste. No, *those* fuckers go to Purgatory and get to purify their souls or some shit until they can be reincarnated into some little baby. They get a fucking *do-over*! Not fair, man. Not fucking fair. They did cruel, evil shit. Their souls should be mine.

"So, all of these people realize how judgmental and toxic and hate filled most organized religions are and say, 'Fuck that noise!,' but are good anyway, so they get to go to heaven. Because they've *also* figured out that it doesn't matter what, *if any*, religion you belong to in order to enter their fucking pearly gates and party it up for eternity. It's how you lived and treated other people on Earth. That's it. You're a decent person who never intentionally did anything to harm anyone? Heaven. No fucking questions asked. Saint Peter could give a fuck less how you spent your Sundays, or whatever fucking day is supposedly holy. You're an asshole who does fucked up and hurtful shit to others? You go to hell, and I'm a happy fucking man. But you're an asshole who does fucked up and hurtful things to others in the *name of God*? Fucking Purgatory and do-over. Absolute bullshit! So, God gets to fortify his numbers in heaven and *I'm* sitting here with the same damned fuckers that I've had for eons. Including those fucking mean girl cheerleaders. Man, am I pissed at them."

Alexander's wheels began turning in his advantageous mind as he listened to Satan's lament. He thought about how he could turn this situation in his favor. He drew upon his vast experience as a shopkeeper to find the words to make the sale on his dastardly epiphany.

"You are so correct sire," he began nonchalantly. "It is quite unfair. All of the time and energy that you have spent corrupting souls. All of the possessions. The manipulations. The sitting on somebody's shoulder and whispering in their ear. All of it, for what? Just so that you can watch God's army grow in numbers and your army grow old and stale. It is a travesty, sire. Blasphemous, in fact. Here. Let me refill your cappuccino. Wouldn't want our lord to be drinking tepid coffee. Yes, and I believe he is laughing at you, sire. He is sitting up in heaven right now with all of his newly arrived angels and laughing. All of them are. They are laughing at you because they do not believe that you have any recourse. If only there was a way to turn the tables. If only there was a way that you could expedite your recruitment of blackened souls and send them here to you before their predestined arrival date. If only. But I suppose it is impossible. I feel for you sire, but I just don't know how you might be able to get the upper…hey. Wait a minute. I may have an idea, lord. Now please, have some patience and hear me out."

"Okay, I'm up for anything. What do ya have?" an intrigued Satan responded.

"Well, how about addition by subtraction?" the devious Alexander answered. "What if you were to let one of *your* souls go back to Earth?"

"How the fuck does *that* help?" Satan yelled back.

"Please, please, my lord," Alexander continued in a smooth voice. "Please let me finish. If you were to allow one of *your* souls to leave and go to Earth, then *that* soul could recruit for you. He could look for blackened souls who are destined to come to you but arrange it so that they arrive sooner than expected. Now, we can't simply *kill* these souls. At best, they would be pitied by God and sent to Purgatory to await their do-over. No, they would need to be coaxed into doing *themselves* in. They would need to be undone by their *own* sinful actions. What do you think?"

Satan rubbed his wide, red chin and said while peering suspiciously at Alexander, "I'm intrigued. But just *who* would we send?"

"Well," a slightly chuckling Alexander replied. "I'm not one to *boast*, sire, but *I* believe that *I* may be of service to you in this capacity. If you would allow me immortality on Earth, I could find these dark souls, take a job as a local shopkeeper, and entice them into purchasing possessed items that I could turn against them. Their lust, or greed, or pride, or envy, or wrath, or gluttony, or sloth, would lead them to purchasing ordinary household goods that would be the cause of their ultimate demise. And then they would be led to *you*. Our dark lord. Oh, just think of all of the fun you could have playing with your new toys. All that I ask for is immortality. And the freedom to do your bidding as I see fit. Deal?"

Satan continued stroking his broad chin while contemplating the offer. "Huh, well, it might be worth a try. But don't do that shit that got you put down here in the first place! That'll piss me off and I'll have no choice but to drag your ass back down here. And *this* time, your sentence will be a helluva lot worse than burning your hands every day. Got it?"

"But of course, sire," a beaming Alexander replied. "I most certainly will never do *that* again. You have my word as your humble servant and as a gentleman." Satan smiled broadly, placed his enormous hand in Alexander's, and the pair shook on the deal. Satan then said, "So, you got any ideas on where you'd like to start?"

"Oh, my yes, sire," Alexander gleefully answered. "I've *always* wanted to work in a candy shop."

CHAPTER 2

LICORICE

Fifteen-year-old Veronica sprung out of her canopy bed and rushed into the shower. She hastily dried herself and put on her latest pair of designer jeans and a cute pink top. As she brushed her lush blonde locks, she stared at herself in the mirror. Her piercing blue eyes glimmered and her petite lips were turned upward in a devilish little smile. She threw open her bedroom door and yelled out in her "innocent" sing-song voice, "Daaaaaady! Are you ready? It's time to go get my sixteenth birthday presents!"

"In just a moment," her father answered in a defeated tone from his study. His eyes darted back and forth between his checkbook ledger and the stack of bills on his desk. He solemnly began sifting through the envelopes. *Second Notice. Third Notice. Final Notice. We have to cut back somehow. I simply can't do this anymore. I'm at the end of my rope. But how?* he thought to himself. *Our club membership? No, of course not. We have to keep up appearances, after all. Lay off the maid? Then who would do the cleaning around here? How about some of the streaming channels? No. The memberships to the symphony? Veronica's credit card? Her cell? Her acting classes? Her modeling classes? Her vocal lessons? No. My little girl deserves the best. Ah, here's one. My wife's tennis lessons.*

His thoughts were interrupted by a demanding voice from outside of his study. "Daddy! I want to go *now*! And where's Mommy? Isn't she coming along?"

"Uh, no dearest," her father replied in an attempted cheerful tone. "She has another…*ahem*…tennis lesson." His face turned beet red as he crushed the bill from the tennis club and threw it onto the floor, missing the waste bin.

He pasted a fake smile on his face and opened the heavy mahogany study door. "Okay, my princess. Let's go pick out your present. It will be a special day for my special girl."

"*Present?*" Veronica replied in a snide tone. "Oh no Daddy. I'm turning *sixteen*. It is the most *special* birthday for a beautiful, talented girl like me. You mean *presents*. Here's my list of everywhere we are going to go. And we are *going* to go…*now!*"

The father began sweating profusely as he looked at all the stores that his daughter had planned to go to. Sweat poured from his forehead when he saw the name of a luxury car dealership. He allowed himself a slight smile when he read the final stop on her list. "Ye Ol' Candy Shop? Why, we haven't been there in years. Why on earth do you want to go there, princess?"

"Because, Daddy," Veronica replied with a faux sweetness. "We used to go there *all the time* when I was a little girl. And I'm about to enter *womanhood,* so I thought I'd give you one last time to celebrate my youthful innocence and buy me *all* the candy that I want."

"W-what do you mean womanhood?" her confused father asked. "Sixteen is still a child. Don't rush growing up. It will come fast enough. Adulthood comes with a great many pressures that you aren't aware of. You still have some time for youthful innocence, so hold onto that for as long as you can."

He was unable to hear his daughter's devious voice say under her breath, "Yeah, well tell that to the varsity football team, heh, heh, heh."

As the pair were driving to the first shop, Veronica said, "Daddy, while we're at the car dealership, you should get a new car too. I mean, its sooooo embarrassing when you drop me off in this thing that's three years old! My friends' fathers get a new car *every year*. Really, Daddy. Get with the times."

"Um, well we'll see," the father replied before trying to change the subject. "How about a little music?"

He turned on the radio and the latest top 40 computer generated drivel came thundering out of the speakers. "Oh yay!" Veronica squealed. "This my favorite jam!" She then began singing along at the top of her lungs. Her shrill, off-key voice penetrated her father's eardrums as he began thinking of one possible financial deduction. Upon the song's conclusion, her father asked, "So, just how long have you been taking those vocal lessons, princess? My, you're so good *now* that I bet that they can't teach you another thing."

"What are you saying Daddy?" Veronica shot back with folded arms. "Are you wanting to deprive me of my vocal lessons? What's next? My acting lessons? My modeling lessons? Are you going to deprive your daughter of being Beyonce, Daddy? Is that what you are saying? Because I am *going* to be Beyonce Daddy! Or maybe one of the Kardashians with a tighter ass. Or Lady Gaga. I haven't decided yet *exactly* what I'm going to be when I grow up. But I *will* be famous! And rich! Are you saying you want to deny your little girl her dreams, Daddy? Are you?"

"W-well, of course not, princess," her father replied meekly as his forehead once again began sweating. "I-it was just a suggestion. I'm sure you will be the biggest star of them all and…oh good. We're at the shopping center."

Veronica began bouncing from store to store. She purchased bag after bag of designer dresses. And tops. And jeans. And shoes. And handbags. And jewelry. And make-up. Veronica's father would stand there and watch this teenage blur enthusiastically jet from rack to rack and shop to shop while his mind calculated the costs. Each time he would attempt to protest a purchase he would be greeted with, "But don't I look *pretty* in this Daddy? Are you saying that I don't *deserve* to look pretty? Are you saying that I'm not *special*? Well, Daddy? Am I or am I *not* your special little girl?"

"O-of course, you are my princess," the defeated father would reply.

"You are my *most* special little girl. Of course, you may have it." At each store, an additional credit card would be declined. "Oh my God, Daddy!" Veronica would declare. "This is sooooo embarrassing!"

"Um, it's just a little accounting mix-up, princess," he would say to his daughter before digging deeper into his wallet, pulling out another high interest piece of plastic and handing it over to the haughty salesclerk. "H-here. Try this one," he would say sheepishly.

The father's mind was racing as the pair pulled into the luxury car dealership. In an effort to reduce his anxiety he suggested delicately, "Okay princess. Here we are. We will get your first car. But just remember dear. This is your *first* car. And you, *of course*, don't have a family and won't need much space. Just a nice little car to get you from point A to point B. Right?"

"Well, of course Daddy," Veronica's sweet voice replied. "I don't need anything *too* fancy. Just something with a really big back seat to, um, y'know take all my friends around town. And it has to have all of the latest safety equipment. You want me to be safe, don't you Daddy? And a kick-ass stereo! And navigation system! And leather interior with wood trim! And the body has to be a metallic blue to match my beautiful eyes. That's all I want, Daddy. All I want is that!" Veronica concluded as she pointed to the ultra-deluxe SUV sitting behind the showroom windows.

Veronica was giggling and bouncing with joy as her father looked at the price sticker. He looked away from his daughter to hide his tears. He also had to look away from the sticker that read *$133,855.*

The twenty-something salesman came floating in like a shark in bloody water. He looked at the shocked expression on the father's face. Starting at her feet, he eventually looked at the delight on the attractive young woman's face. And he plotted his attack.

"Well, hello folks," the smarmy salesman began. "How can we help you today?"

"W-well, you see," the father began, "it is my daughter's sixteenth birthday soon and we are here to pick out her first car."

"Sixteen, you say?" the salesman said in a slithery sneer. "You don't say. I would have thought that you were at least twenty, miss…" He extended his hand as his eyes toured her female frame once again.

"V-veronica," Veronica answered as she shook his hand while trying to hide her blushing face.

"Veronica. What a beautiful name for such a beautiful girl," the salesman replied in a seductive voice. He then turned to the father and said, "And what great taste in vehicles. Yes, you have picked out the perfect first car for such a charming young lady. Just think of how stylish your daughter will look as she drives around town in this! You do want your daughter to look stylish don't you, sir?"

"Yeah, you want me to look stylish don't you, Daddy?" Veronica echoed.

"W-w-why, of course, princess, but…" the father attempted to answer.

"And this vehicle has all the most advanced safety features! We all know how young drivers can be. You want your precious daughter to be safe, don't you, sir?"

"Yeah, Daddy. You want me to be safe, don't you?" Veronica repeated.

"And just look at the space!" the salesman continued. "Look at all the room in this back seat. It would be perfect for, um, *entertaining*."

"Yeah, Daddy. You know how many friends I have. I must have something that I can, um, entertain in," Veronica parroted.

"W-well, of course, dear, but, um, it's just that it's a bit, um, pricey," the father stammered.

"I see, I see," the salesman countered. "Well, of course there are financial considerations. I totally understand that. But, if I had a daughter as special as *this* one, well, I guess *money* wouldn't be much of a consideration for me. My daughter's *happiness* would be. But, sure, we can look at something…cheaper."

"Daddy!" Veronica yelled out. "Don't you want me to be happy? To be stylish? To be safe? Are you saying that money is more important than your daughter's happiness? Are you saying that I'm not *special* Daddy? That I don't *deserve* this car?" Tears began welling up in Veronica's deep, blue eyes as she finished her plea with, "are you saying that you don't love me anymore?"

"No, no, no!" the father immediately blurted out. "Of course, I love you, princess. Yes, if this is the car that my little girl wants, then this is the car that she will have. Draw up the papers, young man."

An hour later, the father's shaking hand was signing the finance papers. "Very good!" The salesman exclaimed. "We will have this beauty all wrapped up and ready to go for you tomorrow."

Veronica squealed and hugged her father as she said, "Thank you, Daddy! You have made me sooooo happy!" She then went over to the salesman and hugged him tightly. "And thank *you*, Mister Salesman! I don't know how I can *ever* repay you for being such a joy to work with!"

"I have an idea," the lecherous salesman whispered into Veronica's ear. "How about we test out your backseat Saturday night?"

The near-hyperventilating Veronica whispered back, "Yeah. That'll be fun. We'll talk about it tomorrow when I pick up my new car."

The father was nearing a nervous breakdown as he parked his three-year-old luxury sedan in front of Ye Ol' Candy Shop. Veronica ran into the shop, causing the bell on the front door to clang rapidly. She looked around in youthful, gluttonous awe at the explosion of colors of the sweet delights resting on shelves in bright packages or glass cannisters. Her eyes then fell upon the kindly looking shopkeeper. He looked exactly as he should have looked. Silver, slick-back hair. A light grey pencil mustache resting just above his thin upper lip. On his tall, lanky frame he wore a crisp, white apron. She smiled at him. The shopkeeper's gaze averted briefly to the beleaguered looking father. He then looked again at Veronica and smiled at her. "Here is a basket, my dear. Get anything that you would like," the shopkeeper said in a kind voice. "I'll bet that it is almost your birthday. Treat yourself, my dear. It is my pleasure to give you what you deserve."

Veronica shrieked with glee and proceeded to fill her basket with the sugary treats. She took voluminous handfuls of everything in the shop until the bags in her basket were nearly bursting. She greedily took a second basket, then third. Her beaming face stood at the counter as her embarrassed father stood next to her. "I-I'm so sorry," the father stated. "You have been so kind to us, and I believe we may have gone a bit, um, overboard."

"Oh, think nothing of it," the kindly shopkeeper responded. "She is a *very* special girl. I hope that she enjoys her candy."

Veronica's eyes then gazed upon a golden package of black licorice. "Oooooo, I want that too!" she demanded.

"Oh, my dear," the shopkeeper answered. "I'm so sorry, but that is a very special licorice. It is my last package, and it is reserved for someone else. You see, this special licorice has the ability to give the person who eats it whatever it is that they deserve. I'm sorry dear, but it isn't for you."

"But I *want* it! *Give* it to me! Daddy! Tell the old man to *give* it to me!" Veronica screamed.

"Oh, very well," the shopkeeper stated with a sigh of resignation as he pulled the golden package from the shelf and handed it to the pacified Veronica. "But be careful with this my dear. Always remember. We are *all* deserving of special things. But we do not deserve *everything* that we might desire in this life. Appreciate what you *do* have and do not worry about what you do not. Appreciate the warmth of your home. The food on your table. The love of your family. Take some time to appreciate that because *those* are the most important things in your life. Then, the special treats, like this licorice, will be even *more* enjoyable for you. Because you will appreciate it and not take it for granted. So, eat this in moderation, my dear. Appreciate the licorice and it will appreciate you. The licorice will know what you deserve by how you eat it. Have a wonderful birthday, my dear."

"Okay, whatever," Veronica replied dismissively. "C'mon Daddy! Let's go! I want to go home and try on all my new clothes and eat my candy!"

As he watched the father and daughter leave his store, the kindly old shopkeeper's face darkened and contorted into a twisted little grin as he said to himself, "Yes, my dear. Have a *wonderful* birthday. In *hell*, heh, heh, heh."

The father heard his daughter squealing with joy from her bedroom as she was emptying her bags of gifts. He then heard her shout out, "Oh,

Daddy! This is the most delicious licorice that I have ever eaten!" The father went up to his daughter's room and found her sitting on her bed in a wrinkled heap of expensive newly bought designer clothes. Her new shoes and purses were strewn haphazardly on the floor and her jewelry was tossed in a tangled pile on her dresser. She was shoveling the licorice into her greedy little mouth which was oozing black drool over her $300 pink top.

"May I have a bite, princess?" the father meekly inquired.

"No! It's mine!" Veronica shrieked back.

"Please, Veronica," the father asked again. "Please. Just one bite for your loving father?"

Veronica looked up at her father with disdain and said through her full mouth, "Oh, fine. But just one bite!"

The father placed the licorice into his mouth and bit into it. He began chewing and his tastebuds exploded with sensory delight. "Oh, my!" He cried out. "I have *never* tasted anything so sweet. So absolutely wonderful. This truly *is* a treat to be appreciated. To be eaten on special occasions. Veronica, dear. Save some for later. Save some so that you can appreciate it over a long period of time."

"No!" Veronica defiantly yelled back causing black spittle to shower her father's face. Her expression then turned from gluttonous rapture to one of pain. "Oh, I don't feel so good," she lamented. The father could only stand in shocked silence as he witnessed long strands of black licorice slide out of his daughter's mouth, nostrils, and ears. Veronica emitted a torturous scream as the bloody licorice twisted itself around her neck. It then crawled up the bedposts of her canopy bed and wrapped itself around a wooden beam in the ceiling. Veronica was screaming in agony as her body was lifted off the bed until she was hanging two feet above her mattress. The licorice continued to tighten its grip around her neck and Veronica's face turned from bright red to purple. The pressure continued and caused her entire head to swell. Finally, Veronica forced out one final tortured scream just before her brilliant blue eyes popped out of their sockets and landed at the feet of her dismayed father.

The father looked up at his unrecognizable, deceased daughter. He looked down at her bloody, blue eyeballs laying at his feet. He looked at the half-eaten bag of licorice on the bed. He picked up the piece of licorice that his daughter had dropped and took one more small bite. His face darkened and contorted into a twisted little grin as he said to himself, "I wonder if her *mother* would care for some licorice?"

Veronica's shrieking soul was being pulled down into a pitch-black portal by eternally long and bloody strings of licorice. Her body poured out sweat as the temperature rapidly increased. Her sweat and blood-soaked frame finally came to an abrupt and violent thud on the scorching ground. The confused and frightened gluttonous teen looked around and began weeping as plumes of flames shot up around her.

A large, smiling crimson demon appeared before her. His seven-foot-muscular frame peered down at her through glowing red eyes. His long horns were dripping with blood as he opened his mouth and said in an ominous voice, "My, my, my, Alexander didn't waste any time in providing me with a special treat now, did he? Hello there, my dearest Veronica. Welcome to your new home. Welcome to your own personal hell. I am so looking forward to this new adventure. It is always so much fun to think of new ways to torture the souls of the damned. But what to do with you?"

Veronica's hands were blistering on the searing stone ground while she attempted to crawl backwards away from the embodiment of pure evil. A geyser of flames shot out of the ground and blocked her escape with each move. She cried out for her father. He was not there. He could not save her. He could not pacify her every whim. He could not protect her any longer. He was much too busy planning her funeral. And that of her mother.

"Yes, what to do," Satan continued while stroking his chin. "Oh, I know. You never could get enough, could you my dear? You never could get enough material things, or food, or attention. Nothing was ever enough to satiate your never-ending greed. Well, I think that you're going to like it here. You will eat and eat and eat. For eternity, you will eat and for eternity you will finally feel full. You will feel so full that your internal organs will strain against your frame. You will want to vomit, but you won't be able to. You will want to shit, but you won't be able to. For eternity you shall continue to eat and pray for your body to purge waste from your body. But your prayers will go unanswered. So why don't we get started. Here my dear. Open wide. Have a piece of licorice."

Chapter 3

Toolbelt

Alexander Picklesbee was sweating as he ascended a crickety wooden ladder. He carefully placed a large, metal toolbox on the top display shelf and smiled. *Perfectly centered*, he thought to himself while wiping his damp hands on his pure white apron. The bell on the front door of the small, local hardware store began ringing. Alexander peered over the shelves and saw a large man wearing a construction hat enter. As Alexander watched him from his lofty perch, he began searching for the man's soul. He stared at the man's brawny frame as he went from aisle to aisle and tossed miscellaneous items into his short shopping cart. Alexander then smiled as he was encompassed by a wave of frigid blackness. "Why *yes*," Alexander whispered to himself in a morbid voice. "Yes, I think that *you'll* do just fine. But why? What is it that you have done? Why is it that your soul is irredeemable? You look to be so friendly. Ah, I see it now. Naughty, naughty, my good man. My lord certainly does enjoy playing with *your* type."

Alexader's thoughts were interrupted by the customer's voice. "Um, I said *excuse* me?" "Oh my, I am so sorry," Alexander responded to the smiling customer who was looking up at him. "As I age, my mind *does* seem to wander a bit. Yes, kind sir, how may I assist you?"

"Oh, that's all right," the smiling patron answered as Alexander's black wingtips touched the old, stained linoleum floor. "I can get a little lost in the forest myself from time to time. I was just wondering…" He was interrupted by a second customer entering. "Why, hey there Cliff!" the newly arrived man yelled out. "Great to see you!" The man approached and firmly shook Cliff's calloused hand. "Great to see you too, Herb!" the beaming Cliff responded. "So, when are you gonna come over and watch a game with me? I cleaned the basement out of my ex's stuff and made it into a really cool man-cave. Yeah, now that I don't have *that* ol' ball and chain around my wallet, I finally have some money to spend on the important things in life. I've put in a wet bar, a couple pinball machines and you should see all of the cool memorabilia that I've got. Now, I know you're not much of a Baltimore fan, but that's okay. God'll forgive ya. And I think you'll really enjoy looking at all of the vintage pennants and signed balls and old programs. Maybe it'll convert ya."

Herb chuckled and said, "Not likely, my friend. I'm a true-blue New York fan. Always have been and always will be. But that really does sound fun. How 'bout tonight for the LA, Cleveland game? I'll bring over some pizza and scotch. And I know you're enjoying your freedom, but I really am sorry about your marriage. She just took off with some younger guy, huh? Wow. What a bitch."

"Yeah, well, I guess that things just didn't work out for her with me. That's alright. I hope she's happy, wherever she might be. Heard she may have gone to Alaska, but who cares? She now has her life, and I have mine. And I think that we're both better off for it. And we're *definitely* on for tonight. Get a large from Alotini's and make it *loaded*. Don't worry about the scotch. I have a special blend that I'd love to share with you."

"Wow," Herb replied. "You sure are taking this better than I would have. If my wife had just up and left me, I don't think I'd be able to get out of bed for a month. She's my entire world. But hey. That's just me. I'm glad that this is a healthy move for you. So, how's the new project coming along? When is our little burg going to finally get that nice hotel that you're building?"

"Twenty-two floors down, one to go," Cliff answered. "Yep, just put up the iron work for the twenty-third floor. We're right on schedule for the start of next year's tourist season. Well, unless that dumbass kicks all of my workers out of the country. Then I'm screwed. As is the entire construction industry. But I'm sure that was just a bunch of campaign mumbo-jumbo. Anyone in his right mind would know that mass deportations would collapse our economy."

"Yeah, I'm sure that won't happen," Herb agreed. "That hotel is going to be so great for this town. Now, instead of people just coming to the lake for a day then driving off to stay in the city, they can stay right *here*. Eat here. Shop here. Drink here. This town is gonna be bustling, man. Anyway, I'll let you get to it, and I'll see ya tonight. Say, Mister shopkeeper, could I get a package of those D cell batteries? I'm restocking all of my emergency kits. Y'know. Just in case he *does* upend our country. But I'm sure that won't happen. Just like Cliff said. Campaign mumbo-jumbo."

Herb left the shop and Alexander once again turned his attention to Cliff. "Now, I believe that you were about to ask me something before your friend arrived. How may I help you?"

"Yeah, well, I'm looking for a new toolbelt. A really heavy one. Preferably with a big buckle, but I didn't see any back there. Are you out? I'd really like to get a new one. My old one is a bit, um, worn out." Alexander's thin lips turned upward in a serpentine smile while he focused for a moment. He lifted his head and joyfully stated, "Why yes, I do believe that I have just the thing. In fact, a shipment just came in. It's an…um… *import*. Come, come. I have just what you are looking for behind the counter." Alexander reached under the counter and pulled out a heavy brown leather toolbelt with an impossibly large, brass buckle.

"That's perfect!" Cliff exclaimed. "I'll take it. Oh, and these zip ties. I like to strap things down when I'm working. Wouldn't want to lose anything, y'know?"

"Oh, how I *know*," Alexander replied as he rang up the man's order. "We do need to tie down those things that are most important to us, now, don't we? Yes, we wouldn't want them to get away. And are you sure you want to pay with a credit card? Perhaps cash would be a bit more appropriate for this particular purchase. We can't take it with us now, can we?"

A smiling Cliff exited the store just as a young blonde woman was entering. A startled Alexander looked upon her pretty face. She had brilliant blue eyes, full, red lips and the smooth, pale complexion of a porcelain doll. His face turned ashen, and his eyes widened as he softly said to himself, "Noooo. It *can't* be her. Why, she has been deceased for well over one-hundred years. But she looks just *like* her. Absolutely identical. Her face. Her figure. Even her posture. Oh, dear Satan, why are you tempting me? Why did you send me this angel that looks just like my…"

Cliff got into his white pickup and started the engine. He took the toolbelt from his bag and smelled it. "Yeah, I do love the smell of new leather. I have a feeling *this* toolbelt might get worn out *too*. That reminds me. I better finish sound proofing that room before Herb gets there tonight, heh, heh, heh."

Cliff was twenty-three stories above his beloved town. The leaves in the trees below were just beginning to turn from their lush green to vibrant reds, yellows, and oranges. He tested the clamp on his toolbelt to ensure his safety cable was secure before shouting out orders to the industrious men who were feverishly welding, screwing, hammering, and wiring. He smiled at his workforce that were the lifeblood of his prosperity before looking down to survey the blueprints. There was a sudden gust of icy wind. Cliff's hard hat flew off of his head and the blueprints fluttered from his grip. He desperately lunged for them and took a misstep. His large body succumbed to gravity as he plummeted towards the unforgiving ground. His sure demise was abruptly halted as the clamp on his toolbelt strained to hold him by its attached safety cable. Frantic brown faces looked down then began pulling him up from the three floors that he had fallen.

"Wow, thanks boys," Cliff stated while his relieved heart pounded in his chest. "Man, good thing I bought this new belt today. I think my old one would have given out. Plus, I didn't drop one tool. Nope, not one. I got my hammer, screwdrivers, pliers, utility knife, yep, everything.

Alright, I think that I've had enough excitement for one day. Hector, have the boys finish up what they're working on then you fellas go get yourself a well-earned beer. I know *I'm* going to have one. Besides, I have a little home improvement project that I need to finish. See you boys in the morning."

Cliff walked down the stairs of his basement and turned on the overhead track lights. He looked at the covered walls and marveled at all of the latest additions to his vast collection of sports memorabilia. He went behind the bar and opened a new bottle of scotch. He held the glass under his nose and took in the enticing fragrance before taking a sip. "Yeah, Herb's gonna love this. And he's gonna love this old program on the wall too. Yeah, this was Baltimore's greatest win over his pansy-ass team, heh, heh, heh. Ah well. Not everyone can get into heaven. Not that being a New York fan is a sin. Nope. Just a really big character flaw. But not a sin. Not like having an affair with some young stud. An affair in my bedroom. An affair in the bed that I paid for. No, being a New York fan is forgivable. But betraying me? Well, that isn't. I'd better finish this soundproofing and jump in the shower. Man, I'm looking forward to that pizza."

Cliff approached the far wall of the basement. He looked adoringly at the framed autographed eight-by-tens of some of his masculine heroes. He reached around for the corner of the wall. There was a slight 'click' before he lifted the three-foot section revealing a wooden door behind the wall. He began chuckling as he fiddled with the lock. "Yeah, gotta finish the soundproofing. My new toolbelt is going to get a workout too, heh, heh, heh."

Herb pulled into Cliff's driveway and parked behind his white truck. The seasoned scents of pepperoni and melted cheese wafted from his open car door. He bounced up the stairs and rang the bell. He waited a few moments before ringing it again. After several minutes of ringing and knocking, he said to himself, "Huh. Well, I know he's home. His truck's there and all the lights are on. Maybe he had to work late and is in the shower. Screw it. The pizza's getting cold. Front door's unlocked. Hope he doesn't shoot me."

Herb cautiously opened the heavy oak front door and peered in. "Hey Cliff! I'm here with the pizza! Cliff? Where are ya buddy?" His eyes darted around the foyer until they rested on the cracked opening that led to the basement. He opened the door and looked down into the brightly lit cavern. "Wow," he stated in amazement as he descended into the marvel of a man-cave. "Jesus, how much did he spend on all of this shit?" he said aloud as he toured the subterranean museum. "I mean, is that *his* authentic signature? That had to be mid-four figures. And wow. Look at these pennants. Amazing they've lasted all these decades. And this old program. Why it's…oh, real cute. Yeah, *that's* not something for a New York fan to be proud of," he stated before rolling his eyes and shouting out, "Nice one, asshole! It sure would be a shame if someone spilled a drink on this old program! Get your ass down here! The pizza's getting cold and the game's about to start! And I'm about to dive headfirst into this open bottle of scotch!"

He placed the pizza on the counter of the bar, got a fresh glass and poured himself two fingers of the tempting brown elixir. "Wow, that is smoooooth," Herb said as the first sip slid down his throat and his body immediately warmed. "Hmmmm, what's this?" he asked aloud as his eyes fell upon a cracked-open wooden door behind a removed portion of wall. "Um, Cliff? You in there, buddy?" he called out as he slowly approached. He placed his hand over his mouth and nose to try to cover the foul stench that poured out of the opening. He was about to leave to call for help when he heard a weak, female voice saying, "Heeeelp meeee. Pleeease. Heeeelp meeee."

"What the hell?" Herb exclaimed before he instinctively pulled an autographed baseball bat from the wall and threw the door open. There was the sound of his glass of scotch breaking on the hard, stone floor as a horrified Herb fell to his knees in dismay. Laying directly in front of him was the zip-tied corpse of a young man. His skin was pale blue, and his phallus had been removed and was sticking out from between his purple lips. In the corner of the small, macabre space was the frail, viciously beaten, and shaking body of Cliff's wife. Her pleading eyes were sunken, and her bound flesh was covered from head to toe in dark blue and black welts, many of which resembled a buckle. Laying in front of her was a menacingly blood-stained, well-worn toolbelt.

A drop of liquid fell upon Herb's forehead. His shaking hand wiped it away and he stared down at the crimson streak on his saturated palm. He looked up and screamed. Directly overhead was his friend Cliff. His new toolbelt was looped over an overhead rafter and around his blue neck. The hammer from the toolbelt was embedded in Cliff's skull and two screwdrivers jutted out from his bleeding eye sockets. Hanging off of his protruding, bloated tongue was his pliers. The rest of his dangling, stiff body was covered in carpenter's nails, making him look like a bloody, grotesque cactus.

Herb got up and willed his shocked body over to Cliff's wife. He pulled a utility knife from Cliff's abdomen and used it to cut the desperate woman's zip ties from her wrists and ankles. Her feces and urine covered naked form collapsed against his. He took off his jacket, wrapped it around her shivering body and held her tightly as they both wept.

"Well, hey there Cliff ol buddy!" an excited Satan exclaimed as he slapped the back of his latest sweaty and confused damned soul. "I bet you thought that you were going to die by falling off that building, now, didn't you? Yeah, I bet you thought that your possessed toolbelt was gonna give out and you were gonna crash into the ground. But naw. I wanted to drag your demise out a little bit. Plus, the chapter was running too short, and we needed another scene, and it seemed more fun for your friend to discover you. *And* for him to discover what an evil little fucker you are. And don't worry about your wife. Once your pussy friend got done crying like a little bitch, he called the cops and shit. She's in the hospital. She'll be fucked in the head for the rest of her life, but she'll make it. Good job on her boyfriend though. That was some twisted shit you did to him. Got you a one-way ticket to me!

"But hey! Welcome aboard buddy! Boy, have I got a destiny for you. Right up your ally. Since you really like working on tall buildings, I've got a job for you. Just look up there. See that fiftieth floor at the tippety-top of my casino? Well, we have a few loose screws up there that I'm going to need you to tighten. And don't worry. You'll have a safety cable attached to your toolbelt, just in case you fall. Oh, who am I kidding? Just *in case* you fall? Well, *of course* you are going to fall! And when you fall, that toolbelt is going to give way and you're going to keep falling faster and faster and faster for fifty floors until SPLAT! Your body is going to explode all over the fucking place! Pretty fun, right?

"Now come with me and look here, at the base of the building. See all these big squares with numbers on them? Well, that's what we're going to use to place our bets! Because, you see, you are going to fall and splat and fall and splat for all of eternity. The same grisly death is going to happen to you over and over and over again! But what *won't* be the same is where your body parts land after they catapult out of you. See? So just before you fall, we'll all be taking bets. For example, I might put fifty bucks on your kidney landing on number twenty-three! Or somebody else might say that your spleen will land on number eight! Or whatever. You get the point. Now, get to climbing. Those screws aren't gonna tighten themselves and daddy needs a new pair of shoes."

Following Cliff's one-hundred-and-forty-seventh "mishap," a dismayed Satan roared, "What the fuck is going on! I was *sure* his gall-bladder would land on number sixty-eight. It's landed there over half the time! Motherfucker! I don't know how, but you motherfuckers have rigged this somehow and…yeah, here's your fucking fifty dollars you fucking bitches. Go get yourself some new pom-poms. And stop snapping that fucking gum in my ear!"

Chapter 4

Toy Soldiers

Alexander's eyes were darting under his thin eyelids as his dreaming mind was obsessed by the vision of beauty he had seen at the hardware store. He recalled every inch of her blue-jean, baggy T-shirted frame. He began to drool slightly as he once again gazed into her brilliant blue eyes which were perfectly framed by her porcelain skin and flowing golden locks. He watched intently as she glided through the shop. Then, before he had an opportunity to approach her, she had abruptly left. He had stood at the front window and watched her delicate body bounce down the sidewalk while holding hands with a formidably built man.

Her blue jeans and T-shirt suddenly changed to a flowing, blue, Victorian gown. Her blonde hair became wrapped in a tight bun with elegant pearl accents. He felt his twenty-five-year-old former self prance up from behind her as he called out her name. "Virgina! Here I am my darling!"

The nineteen-year-old Virgina Smith twirled around causing the long hem of her expensive dress to rise slightly. "Alexander, my love!" she called out in her upscale, Received Pronunciation British accent. The pair's arms, eyes, and lips locked in a loving embrace. "This campus is just so large, I thought that I might never find you, my love."

"Yes, yes, it is quite expansive," Alexander agreed. "But how nice it is for you to visit me. What a lovely break from the never-ending drudgery of my studies."

"I know that you dislike your studies," Virgina countered. "But you are so gifted at them. You are going to be quite famous one day. I am quite sure of it. Mummy and Daddy think so too."

"Yes, well, perhaps," a blushing Alexander replied. "No, not perhaps. My professors tell me that I have unique skills and that I may very well be the most natural surgeon that they have ever encountered. Only two more years and I will have my license to practice, my love. Two more years and I shall fulfill the dreams of my overbearing father and dreadful mother. And then I shall have my freedom from them. We both shall. I shall have the freedom from the constant criticism. The constant judgement. And from my loving mother, the constant lashings.

"I know that I shouldn't say so, but I just abhor them. I have never been good enough in their eyes. Even now, with my exceptional marks, they keep pushing me and pushing me to do more. They even criticize my involvement with you, my love. My boorish mother said that there will be plenty of time for playthings once my studies are complete and that you are an unwanted distraction. You, the love of my life, may be a distraction, but it is a most welcome one. You may have saved me, my darling. Saved me from the poison that my mother had instilled in me since birth. Saved me from the belief that all women were brutal and self-serving. That they use their feminine wiles to tempt men and entrap them. That they were unscrupulous and cruel. I held that belief, my love. I thought that all women were simply evil. I believed that because I had the perfect example of such trash raising me.

"And then I met you a year ago and I realized that women were *not* evil. That any given woman was no more evil than any given man. Your beauty and kindness towards me changed me forever. And although I loathed it, I decided to double-down on my studies and work towards being the greatest surgeon of our time. But I was no longer doing it for *them*. I was doing it for *us*. For *our* freedom. For *our* future. Which leads me to a question that I would like to ask you, my darling."

Alexander fished in his pocket and retrieved a small box. He got down on one knee and his tearful eyes gazed upward into her intoxicating blue pools. His uncharacteristically shaking hands slowly opened the velvet box. "Oh, Alexander," an astonished Virginia stated. "Please, wait, my love. There is something that I must tell you."

"Nooooooo!" Alexander wailed as he abruptly sat upright in his bed. His pinstriped, white pajamas were saturated in sweat. And tears. He rubbed his swollen eyes and said to himself, "My. It has been decades since I dreamed of her. Yes, I thought that she was finally out of my mind forever. Then *she* came into the store and revived my memories. Who could she be? Why does she look so much like my Virginia? Ah well. Another trivial story for another time. Perhaps after work I will try to find out a bit more about our mystery lady. Just out of curiosity, of course. Not for *that*. I promised my lord that I would not do *that* again, so perish the thought. Yes, after work. I must begin to get ready. I do not want to be late for my first day at Goody's Toy Emporium."

The five-year-old boy was beaming with anticipation as he looked up at the kindly old shopkeeper who was delicately placing his latest treasures into a plain brown bag. The tall, lanky shopkeeper smiled at the boy as he placed the bag into his awaiting hands and said, "Here you are, my fine lad. Enjoy your toy soldiers. I am sure that they will give you hours upon hours of fun. But just remember. Only use these soldiers when you absolutely must and only against outside threats. They are *never* to be used for your own self-enrichment and must *never* be used against their own people. These are *patriotic* toy soldiers who have taken an oath to protect their country. They have not taken an oath to you, and I am now placing them in your trust. I now trust that they will be used by you to protect our freedom and that they will *never* be used against innocent people. Do you understand?"

"Yes," the boy responded. "I understand. I pledge to you, mister shopkeeper, that my soldiers will only be used against bad people. I promise. People like you, right? You don't talk like us. Is it alright to use my soldiers against people who don't talk like us?"

"Oh, I think not," a chuckling Alexander answered in his heavy

British accent. "Just because someone does not talk the same or look the same or even come from the same country is not a reason to turn your toy soldiers against them. There are all sorts of people who may be different from you, but who are your friends. No, my dear lad, do not turn your toy soldiers against your friends. Use them only against those who truly mean us harm. Alright?" Alexander patted the boy on his head, smiled, and said, "Good boy. You protect the dignity of these soldiers and of the oath that they took, and they will, in turn, protect you."

Alexander watched the boy and his father leave the shop and said under his breath as his eyes darkened, "But if you *betray* their dignity, a price will be paid. Yes, we can tell so much about what a boy will become when he grows into manhood by how he plays with his toys, heh, heh, heh. Now, time to close up shop and walk about the neighborhood a bit. Or perhaps the neighborhood near the hardware store. It is only three bus exchanges away, after all."

The boy raced up the winding staircase of his mansion. He threw open his playroom door and dumped his large bag of four-inch plastic soldiers upon the floor. He got down on his knees and began lining the plastic green men in position. Their tiny guns were pointed toward an area of the room that contained an eclectic assortment of stuffed animals, board games, action figures, and other random childhood playthings.

The boy looked across the room at the discarded toy menagerie and said with an evil sneer, "Alright assholes. I now have my army. And they will do anything that I say. Just look at them. Standing proudly and pointing their guns at you. You toys that I never wanted here. You toys that invaded my playroom every birthday, Easter, and Christmas. I never asked for you. You are boring and stupid, and I hate you because you do nothing for me. And if you do nothing for me, then I have no use for you. All you do is take up space in my playroom. Well, I am now going to take care of that. My soldiers are going to lock you away until we can find a place to put you."

The toy soldiers stood in frozen silence, awaiting their orders as the boy exited the room. A small trail of liquid green plastic dripped from one of the soldier's eyes when the boy returned with a small playpen. The boy set the playpen up next to the window which he immediately opened, allowing a gust of cold air to enter. "This is where you will stay. And you won't get any blankets, either," the boy sneered as he picked up two of his soldiers and marched them across the floor toward the pile of toys. "Now, are you going to get in this playpen, or do my soldiers have to shoot you?" he said as he strategically placed the additional toy soldiers around the unwanted toys. He looked around the room and saw a toy robot sitting on the shelf. "I think that I'll start with you," the boy haughtily stated as he grabbed one of the toy soldiers, walked across the room, and positioned the soldier to point his plastic muzzle at the robot.

"Yes, you will be the first," he said. "You were one of my favorites. I was so excited to get you last Christmas. You always did what I wanted you to do. All I had to do was put batteries in you and press the buttons on the remote and you did exactly what I told you to do. But then you broke. Your arms won't lift anymore, and your wheels get stuck, and you don't do what I tell you to do anymore. You betrayed me, so in the playpen you go."

He picked up the robot and marched him across the room with the dutiful toy soldier still pointing his muzzle at the forlorn, metal toy. The boy cackled as he dropped the robot into the playpen. "Now, who's next? Yeah, you. Stuffed donkey. All you did was sit there and judge me. You're definitely out of here." The donkey was marched into the playpen by the boy holding a toy soldier.

One by one, all of the undesirable toys were rounded up by the toy soldiers. One by one they were thrown into the playpen. One by one they internally wept as they powerlessly awaited their dastardly fate. The boy threw the final toy into the playpen and began laughing while placing his toy soldiers around its perimeter. "Yeah, this is great. Finally, all you useless toys are in one place where I can keep you under the watch of my toy soldiers. And if any of you try to escape, my soldiers will shoot you. But wait. They are still in my playroom. They are still taking up space and I still have to look at their stupid faces. No, I can keep you here for a while, but you're still poisoning my playroom. Okay soldiers. Just guard these stupid toys tonight. I know just what to do with them. Tomorrow, we'll put them on my big toy train, and we'll take them to the basement. But wait. Then they'll be taking up space there. No, just holding them won't do. They need to go into the furnace. Then my entire house will be rid of these stupid toys who have done nothing for me, and I will be left with only the toys that do what I want. Then, this will be the greatest house ever!"

"This is fuckin' bullshit," one of the toy soldiers whispered to another as the boy's loud snoring was heard from the adjacent bedroom. "I mean, what in the hell are we doing? We took an oath to defend freedom, not be the lethal personal police force of some spoiled brat who gets rid of any toy that he doesn't like. I mean, they're just toys. Just like us. They have the same dreams of being loved and played with. What was their infraction? Being bought as a present for some unappreciative little asshole who is unable to see how all these toys contribute into making this playroom a more joyful place? They're just toys. Just like us. And if this little bastard can turn on them, he sure as hell can turn on us too. We could be next. Just like he did to that poor robot."

"Yeah, he'll definitely turn on us too unless we do every twisted thing that he wants," another toy soldier replied. "If we don't do things that violate our oath and basic sense of humanity, then he'll just buy bigger toy soldiers and march *us* into the furnace too. Plus, if this is how he treats toys, how in the hell is he going to treat actual human beings when he gets older? Man, have mercy on the people if this little asshole ever gets any power. So, what should we do Sarge?"

"Well, the way I see it," the first toy soldier began answering. "Is we took an oath to protect all of the toys in this playroom, regardless of where that toy came from. We did not take an oath to this boy and this boy has betrayed all of these unfortunate toys and us. He has committed treason. And there's just one fitting punishment for that."

The boy woke up sitting in a chair. He began frantically struggling against the yo-yo strings and sharp, metal slinky rings that bound him.

His sweaty face looked around his playroom. The eyes of all of his toys were staring at him with morbid, anticipatory glee. He heard several loud clicks of rifles being cocked directly in front of him. His toy soldiers were all lined up with their tiny plastic guns pointed at him. One of the toy soldiers yelled out, "Fire!"

"Well, well, well," Satan cheerfully stated as the black soul of the boy fell upon the blistering brimstone. "Wow. Alexander's fuckin' good. I wasn't expecting you for about eighty years. He prevented a lot of needless suffering and bloodshed too. I was actually kinda looking forward to seeing all that, but hey! Now that you won't be around to kill them off, maybe I've got a chance to corrupt their souls! Yeah, if you had killed them off, they'd get a one-way ticket to heaven! But now that the future's been altered, I have a shot at tens of thousands more souls. Damn if this isn't a great plan. Anyway, welcome to hell. Let me show you around a little bit. We don't get too many kids down here. Even the blackest of kid's souls at least get Purgatory and a fuckin' do-over. But not *you*. *You're* a special case. One way ticket to fuckin' paradise, kid!

"Now, now, don't cry. I know you miss your daddy. Don't worry. He'll join you here soon enough. So, just turn that frown upside down and…hey! Stop looking at those fucking cheerleaders! They're too old for you and…wow. That's ironic. Anyway, take a look at this pamphlet. It'll give you all the basics about living here."

The boy took the charred pamphlet, wiped tears from his eyes and began reading.

CONGRATULATIONS ON MAKING IT TO HELL!

On behalf of our lord, Satan, we would like to thank you for being a damned soul and choosing, through your Earthly actions, to reside in Hell. We are most pleased that you committed such abhorrent atrocities that the Universe banished you here for all eternity.

While here, which will be forever, please feel free to enjoy our wide variety of amenities that are designed to cater to your every whim. Whether it be horseback riding, fine dining, relaxing by the pool, or having a fun night out singing karaoke with friends, we have it all here for you. Oh wait. I had you going there, didn't I? Just a little harmless fib from one damned soul to another. Let me start again. Welcome home. This is hell. You are fucked. The End.

"Okay kid, have you read the pamphlet? Pretty self-explanatory, right?" Satan stated. "Okay, so now you know that you're a damned soul that is going to be punished for all of eternity, Now what to do? Oh right! Your eternal punishment! Fuck, sorry. I've just had so much on my mind lately and…" Satan's voice trailed off for a moment as he looked over at the mean girl cheerleaders. "And their fucking gum-snapping is distracting! Knock that shit off, bitches! Where in the hell are you getting your gum? Seriously. Where in hell are you getting your fucking gum? Oh, never mind. Bigger fish to fry. Now, what to do with this kid? Oh yeah. I think that'll do.

"Alright kid, here's what we're going to do. What's the one thing that you love more than anything? Attention, right? A relentless stream of adoration from your brainwashed followers. So, I don't think that I'll cause you any physical harm. That shit's so overdone anyway. No, from now on, you're going to stand in that corner over there naked. And everybody that walks by you is going to stop and point and laugh at you. Over and over and over for all eternity you are going to bathe in embarrassment and low self-esteem. You are going to absolutely hate yourself because you will come face to face with how people *really* feel about you and you are going to understand what a worthless piece of shit you truly are. You are going to get the unvarnished truth from everybody! And that shit's not gonna be pretty, let me tell ya because everybody, and I mean *everybody*, thinks you're an asshole. Yes. An eternity of self-loathing and shame seems to be what is needed in this moment. And if I get bored with that, there's always the eternal hot poker up the ass. But let's start here and see how this works out for a while, alright? Now if you would please disrobe."

CHAPTER 5

STIRRINGS

Melissa Bartlesworth leapt from her bed and shouted, "Oh shit! I'm late!" Her tangled blonde mane went flying into the bathroom and she hastily turned on the shower. From over the beading water she heard her fiancé, Robert Jackson saying, "What's the big deal, babe? You run the place. Who cares if you're a little late?"

"I'll tell you who cares," Melissa yelled back as she was soaping her perfectly pale skin. "My father! I may be the general manager, but my father still owns the joint! And he has always said that people in leadership positions must set an example for their employees! That the rules apply to everyone, regardless of your position! If I'm even one second late, he'll write me up! Just like he would for *any* of our employees! Man, for a child of the seventies, he sure has become an old prude. But that's true of the entire lineage of Bartlesworth men dating back to my great-great-great-great grandfather. They built this company up from scratch and have run it like a tight ship ever since. And I'm the first woman since my great-great-great-great grandmother to be in position to take over! I know my father loves me, but he's the only Bartlesworth in six generations who didn't have a son and a namesake. I can't screw this up, babe!"

The shower was turned off and there was bustling activity in the bathroom as Melissa rapidly toweled off, put on a light coat of makeup and her form-fitting business suit. She ran out of the restroom, planted a light kiss on her fiancé's tan lips, and jetted out the door. Robert chuckled to himself while rubbing his short afro. "Wow. Well, she *is* a Bartlesworth. Smart. Attractive. And unbelievably driven to succeed. But tight ship? The Bartlesworths are known for their corruption. At least she and her father don't pull the same shit as the previous generations. They've cleaned up their name pretty well. I think I'll grab her a breakfast sandwich on my way to the office and surprise her with it. She's got to be starving."

Melissa launched herself down the stairs of her brownstone, quickly turned right, and ran into the back of an older man. "Oh, my lord! I'm so sorry!" she stated through her embarrassment. "Are you okay?" The older man turned around and looked at her with kind eyes. He had silver, slicked back hair, and wore an inviting smile under his thin mustache. His sharp, light grey pinstriped suit reflected the rising morning sun as he delicately placed his hand upon her shoulder and said softly. "Why yes, my dear. I am quite all right. No harm done at all. Now, where are you running off to my dear? Surely nothing can be so important."

Melissa chuckled and said, "Yeah, you're right about that. Being on time for work isn't important enough to mow down an innocent pedestrian. I am so sorry about that." "Tut, tut," the kindly older man replied. "Think nothing of it. Why, if I were a younger man I would have welcomed the opportunity to be meet such a beautiful young woman in such a fashion. But you mentioned you were running late for work. That is quite important. Yes, one must always be on time for work. May I walk with you my dear? I may be able to run a bit of interference for you through these crowds. And I do crave a bit of conversation this morning."

"Why, that is so nice of you," Melissa replied. "Yes, I would welcome a chaperone this morning." The pair began walking and the older man asked, "So tell me about yourself, my dear." Her answer took considerably longer than the question.

"Oh wow, where do I start?" Melissa began. "I guess I'll start at the beginning. A long time ago. My great, great, great, great, um, how many is that? Four? Yep, that's right. My great, great, great, great grandfather inherited a clothier shop after my great, great, great, great grandmother's father passed away. He was the one who originally started the shop. Anyway, my great, great, great, great, grandfather renamed the clothier to what it is now and has been for over one-hundred-fifty-years. And every generation has produced exactly one son. For generation after generation the clothier has been passed down to son after son. My father now owns it. He is Thomas the VI. I, um, am not. Obviously. Yes, every generation has produced a son until I came along. Much to my father's disappointment, I suppose. Which is why I mustn't be late. Every day I must prove myself to my father that I am capable of taking over when he retires. And here we are. My family's clothier. I'm Melissa, by the way."

The kindly older man looked up at the twelve-foot red scripted letters on the building's façade which read 'Bartlesworth's Fine Clothing. Providing New York's Finest With The Finest Since 1865.' The older man's face turned ashen as he looked down at the tender face of his companion. "*You* are Melissa *Bartlesworth?*"

"Why, yes," Melissa replied. "Why? Have we met before?" "Um, no," the older man replied as his face began to redden. "No, I do not believe that we have. At least, not in *this* lifetime. Well, it was lovely chatting with you, young lady, and I do hope you have arrived at work on time. And speaking of time, I'm afraid I must be off. I just remembered an important, um, *engagement* that I had forgotten about. I do hope we see each other again, my dear. Perhaps we could have a spot of tea."

Melissa watched the man briskly turn and march down the sidewalk through the throngs of people. She chuckled slightly and said through a mimicking British accent, "A spot of tea, heh, heh, heh. My, what a sweet man. Yes, I believe that I would enjoy having a spot of tea with him sometime. And now, to face my father." She opened the grand front door and yelled out, "Daddy! I'm here! I'm so sorry I'm a bit late! Please don't be cross with me!"

Alexander Picklesbee knew exactly where he needed to go. As his long, slender legs strode toward the public library, his mind wandered back once again to the year 1863. The twenty-five-year old's expression changed from romantic hopefulness to confusion as he heard his beloved say, "Oh, Alexander, please, wait, my love. There is something that I must tell you." He once again felt the same lump of trepidation in his throat while listening to her explanation.

"Oh, my darling, please stand up and put that box away. Please, my love. Now is not the time. But it will be. I promise you. Please, keep that precious symbol of our love and future union in that box until we are ready. I do so want to answer the question that were about to ask me, but now is not the time. I have some news, my beloved. It may not seem like good news at first, but it soon will be. It will be the most wonderful news, my love. We *will* have a future together, but not here. Our future lies in America!"

"America?" a befuddled and slightly heart-broken Alexander exclaimed. "What on earth are you speaking about, my dear?" "Well," Virginia continued. "I was not supposed to tell anyone about this until everything was settled, but Mummy, Daddy, and I are emigrating to America! New York, in fact! Isn't it the most exciting news?"

"Why would your family emigrate to America *now*?" an exasperated Alexander inquired. "Why, they are a country that is being torn apart. Their Southern states are fighting to secede from the union. And it is quite a bloody battle if the news accounts are to be believed. There is so much uncertainty there, my love. Why is your family going there and taking you with them?"

"Well," Virginia began again. "Daddy believes that this is the perfect opportunity to start his clothier business in the New World. There is just so much competition here, and he has struggled so. He has just signed a contract with the United States to manufacture uniforms for them. He will be even more successful than he has been here, in London. He already has hired the laborers and ordered the materials and purchased the most elegant brownstone for us to live in. And I simply *must* go along, my darling. I *must* be there to help my family as they build their business."

"But, but," Alexander began stammering. "But, what, what about *us?*

Our future together? I simply cannot live without you, my love." "Nor I you," Virginia countered. "But it will be for only a brief time. While I am helping my family build our grand business, *you* can finish medical school *here*. It will only be two years, my love, and by that time daddy will have built our business and we shall live like royalty in America. Daddy has assured me that he will be able to bring you over once you have completed your studies. And what better land for the most gifted surgeon the world has ever seen than in a war-torn country? You will be able to establish yourself as America's most distinguished surgeon and I shall be so proud of you as I walk into gala events upon your steady arm. And I will write to you every day, my love. I promise you that."

The bitter-sweet words fell upon Alexander's disappointed heart as he mournfully replied, "And I shall write you every day as well, my darling." And he did. He wrote Virginia every day. There was no detail trivial enough to not mention. He told her what he had eaten that day, the marks he was receiving in his studies, the temperature outside his barren walls, and the color of the leaves each morning. And she, in turn, wrote to him. He relished reading her daily letters about her father's thriving business, details about the war, and the splendid activities that she was engaged in in New York. By the time he finished reading, the letters would be soggy from his tears of love, joy, and longing. He would place each elegantly scripted correspondence into its envelope, kiss it lightly, and gently place it in a wooden box. Right next to the small velvet box that was waiting to be opened after she would finally say 'yes' to him.

He wrote her daily. After six months, Virginia's correspondence became less frequent and considerably more brief. Her daily letters became three times a week. Then twice. Following a month of another disappointing trip to his postal box, he finally received a letter from her. His hands shook as he tore open the flimsy paper that contained the most recent news of his beloved Virginia. His eyes welled with tears once again as he read the perfectly written words. Tears flowed down his twenty-six-year-old face as he turned bright red and balled the paper in his clenched fist. He walked back to his quarters in a disillusioned daze as the words she had written pounded in his brain.

Alexander,

It is with the heaviest of hearts that I write to you and there is no easy way to say this. I must tell you that I have met another man. He is a most wonderful man, Alexander. He has been such a help to daddy in his business and has just been promoted to run our clothier while daddy travels this vast land to sign new contracts. We met and he has simply swept me off of my feet. I adore him so. I know that this must come as a disappointment to you, but you are a fine man, and I know that there is a fine woman in London who will be just as supportive and proud of you as I would have been. A future between you and I was simply not meant to be. I am sorry for any hurt that I may have caused you. Please respect my wishes and do not write me back. My husband, Thomas Bartlesworth, would not care for such an intrusion. I wish you well.

Virginia Bartlesworth

Alexander Picklesbee wiped fresh tears from his eyes as he entered the cold, stone library. He politely asked the librarian for the area that housed the archived records. He entered a dusty, dingy area of the library, pulled up a hard wooden chair and opened the first musty volume. For hours, he poured over the yellowed pages to find the connection that he hoped he would not find.

"Ah yes, here it is. The date that my Virginia and her family entered this nation. Articles about her father's clothier business. And here, the damned wedding announcement. Why am I doing this to myself? Every word provides yet another dagger to my broken heart. Oh, but this lightens the mood a bit. The announcement of her father's death in 1865. Only two years after they came to this land and one year after their blasphemous union. Cause of death unknown. Suspected food poisoning. But I can feel it, Mister Thomas Bartlesworth. Through this paper and through all these years I can sense your treachery. I can sense it as clearly as I can sense the foulness of one of my damned customers. Yes, you poisoned her father, didn't you? You didn't marry her out of love. You married her out of ambition. Out of greed. You never gave her what I could have. But perhaps that's just as well. I hope that she learned about what kind of man you were. I hope she dreamed about what her life would have been with me. And I hope it haunted her until her dying breath.

"Yes, quite the lineage we have here. He and Virginia had a son, Thomas II. My, three years in prison for tax evasion? Not enough as far as I'm concerned. That must have sent my Virginia over the edge. She took her own life by hanging, right after her husband died of a heart attack. Good. Rot in hell, bitch. Although I never saw her there, nor her husband, or any of their bastard descendants. But hell *is* a rather large place. I'm sure they are all there somewhere. Burning. Oh yes, Thomas III. You *must* be there. The authorities may not have been able to convict you, but I can feel what you did. Serial rapists always find their way south. And Thomas IV. Using your government contracts as leverage with foreign governments? I see. An unloving *and* unpatriotic lot. Nothing on Thomas V? Really? Oh, here it is. Mafia ties. I was wondering when that would come up. And finally, Thomas VI. Melissa's father. And he is, um, what is *this*? He has written a *memoir*? About his entire family? Exposing all of their treachery and ill-gotten gains? Well, that would have saved some time. And I can feel it in him. He is the one Bartlesworth who doesn't seem corrupt. In fact, he went public about his family's rather unfortunate past. Yes, he may actually possess a pure soul. And his daughter may, as well. His daughter, Melissa. His daughter who looks and sounds *exactly* like my Virginia. My Virginia who betrayed me. Lied to me. Slept with another man when she was betrothed to me. My Virginia who destroyed everything that I had built. My Virginia who turned me into…no. Snap out of it Picklesbee. Calm down. That was quite some time ago and Melissa is *not* Virginia. She is her own person. She is a *good* person. She is *not* the type of person that I was sent here for. No, I must stay away from her now. Let bygones be bygones. She is not responsible for the actions of her ancestor."

Alexander got up from the ancient wood table, dusted his pinstriped trousers and proceeded to the exit. As he climbed the stone steps his face darkened and he wore an evil little grin as he said in a low, sinister growl, "But all of this *has* stirred distant memories and feelings. I must cope with them somehow, mustn't I? Yes, I believe that I require a small nip. Just a taste to calm my nerves. And perhaps the warmth of a lady of the evening. And I *definitely* will need some surgical instruments, heh, heh, heh."

CHAPTER 6

SCALPEL

The thick scent of cheap perfume still hung in Alexander's modest New York flat while he wiped spilled gin from a worn, wooden bedside table. "My she was quite the little lush," he said to himself. "Yes, well, we all have our vices now, don't we? And all of that expensive gin does serve to drown out the pain. And she certainly had plenty of *that* last night, so who am I to judge." He stripped the bed of its soiled linens and found a pair of wadded red lace panties. "Ah, I see we left something behind. I have never been one to keep souvenirs, but these are just so lovely. I think that I'll just pack these away in case she returns for them. Oh, who am I kidding? I will never see that poor woman again. At least not here, heh, heh, heh." He placed fresh sheets and blankets on the bed and stretched them around the frame until they were as taught as a drumhead. "Perfect. Now how about some music before I go on my next excursion?" He fumbled with a small transistor radio until he found the 'on' dial. "My, such newfangled devices. I don't know if I will ever get acclimated to these wonders of ingenuity. Music flowing through the airwaves that come out of this little box. Simply marvelous."

There was a light 'click' as he turned the radio on. He continued to twist the dial until he arrived at the desired volume. "*...was found last* *night in a back alley in Queens. The victim's identity has yet to be released but she is suspected to be a local, um, escort. One detective is quoted as saying that he has never witnessed such a gruesome scene and that it may take days to piece her face and body together so that they can establish her identity. Another officer on the scene stated that the condition of the remains reminded him of old pictures that he had seen from the Jack the Ri..."*

"Oh my, what a pity," Alexander solemnly stated as he turned the radio off. "Yes, another soul gone from this world. But I certainly do appreciate the homage from the constables. It does put a spring in my step to receive such recognition. But enough of these trivialities. I have more important things to do, like my next assignment. What was it that I was wanting to do next? Oh, yes. In fact, that news is quite fitting. What a lovely trip down memory lane. Surgical tools. Now, where might I find a damned soul who would be shopping at a medical supply store? Concentrate now, Alexander. Let your blackened soul reach out to others. Where are you, my new friend? *Who* are you? Aaaaah. I believe I have found the place. Boise, Idaho. Interesting. Perhaps I will fit in better there. Perhaps the world isn't quite so advanced in the American West. I do long to sit astride an elegant beast once again. Now concentrate, Alexander. Let us go to Boise, heh, heh, heh."

Alexander shook his head in frustration as his pin-striped suited body appeared suddenly on a deserted side street in Boise. He looked down the lane and saw cars zooming to and fro on the adjacent main artery. "How disappointing," he said to himself. "Just more of these motorized vehicles bustling about. Not one horse in sight. Ah well. Mustn't be late for my new job."

"Yeah! Be right with ya!" the manager of the medical supply store yelled out to Alexander as he walked into the antiseptic, bright white shop. Alexander's anticipatory black heart began beating rapidly as he perused the glistening scalpels, saws, clamps, and other devices that were to be used for the salvation of life. Or damnation of it.

The somewhat pudgy thirty-something manager came up to Alexander and said, "Sorry about that. Shipment day. How may I help you?" Alexander smiled at the sweaty man and his eyes turned black as he stared into the manager's soul. "Oh, my good man," Alexander began in his cordial British accent. "It isn't what *you* can do for *me*. It is what *I* am here to do for *you*. Yes, I am here to assist you today. You will hire me to be your shopkeeper. I shall tend to your store. At no charge to you, my good man. Do not worry about a thing. I shall care for your wonderful shop as though it were my very own. Now, why don't you just toddle off home, now? You deserve a day off. Immerse your weary body in a hot soak. Read a good book. I have heard quite a few good things about the *Hanging Chads* series by Evan Clouse. Why, it is even available on your Kindle device right now. All you need to do is go on your electronic keypad and order it from the amazon. I do not know why they sell books from a tropical rainforest, but there are many things about this world that I do not understand. Then, have a nice dinner and fall into a well-earned deep slumber. When you return to your sparkling boutique tomorrow, you will find everything in perfect order. And you will not remember that we have ever met. Now, off with you my good man. But before you go, where do you keep your aprons?"

The mesmerized manager pointed to the counter, nodded, and silently walked out the door. "Works every time, heh, heh, heh," Alexander commented. "If only I could do that to everyone in every situation. Oh my, what fun I could have. But alas, I cannot. I can only place a temporary spell upon those that I need for my hellish mission. Ah well. Do not look a gift horse in the mouth, as the saying goes. A small price to pay for immortality on this Earth. Well, as long as I do not continue my dastardly deeds that sent me to hell in the first place. No, Satan was very clear on that. I must curb my inner stirrings and resist my more, um, violent impulses. I do hope that he won't be too cross about what I did with that call girl last night. Surely, he of all demons must understand that men have their follies. Yes, I'm quite sure an indiscretion every now and then will be fine. And what a fine, crisp white apron. Oh, I believe that I am going to enjoy my brief time here."

"How disappointing," Alexander lamented as the sun was beginning to set behind the cityscape of Boise. "I was quite sure that I had felt darkness from this place and now it is time to close up shop. Oh, I've had many customers and engaged in many delightful conversations throughout the day, but none of them were appropriate. Sinners? Sure. But just run of the mill sins. A gambling habit here, an affair there. Certainly not the type of stock that would be appropriate for my lord's sultry accommodations." Just as he was about to insert the shop's key in the front lock, his heart leapt with joy.

"I'm so sorry," the mustached man with a bad combover stated as he stormed through the front door. "Are you still open? Please tell me that you're still open. I just received word that I have a last-minute appointment and I simply must have some new tools. My others are a bit, um, worn down. And stained. Please? I promise, I won't be long. Really. I know where everything is at."

Alexander grinned at the man while the screams of innocent young women pounded in his brain. In an instant, Alexander could see every horrid indiscretion that had been committed by this heinous creature. And he could sense that this so-called physician's macabre business had been booming. Ever since America's Supreme Court had voted to strip constitutional protections and autonomy from women in the first step of many to make them second class citizens, the young women of Idaho increasingly turned to back-alley butchers out of desperation.

These women had become impregnated and no longer had the right of self-determination of their reproductive healthcare. Some women were the victims of rape. Some welcomed the joyous news only to find that their body was not capable of carrying the growing ball of goo to term. Some learned that their very lives were at stake should they attempt to do so. And some were simply the victims of bad choices committed in the heat of passion who knew that they did not have the financial viability to raise a child or did not wish to shame their family. Or perhaps did not wish to bring their father's or uncle's or cousin's incestuous bastard into the world. Regardless of the origin of their current condition, they were prevented by law from making decisions about their own body and their own lives. America was great again. Especially for vile men whose sadism was unleashed upon the innocent. 'Great' was *not* the word that the innocent would use to describe this period of human history, however. They might use much more appropriate terms such as 'humiliating,' 'insufferable,' 'torturous,' or perhaps 'lethal.'

The hopelessness of their situation drove some of these innocent young women into the awaiting arms of this ruthless creature who now unknowingly stood in front of a servant of Satan. This "doctor's" contact information had been passed from woman to woman in hushed tones throughout college campuses, high school restrooms, bars, and restaurants. He would open a large metal door in the middle of a dark alley and welcome them into his seemingly sterile world of renewed feminine freedom. He would speak to them in a kind-hearted manner while holding their shaking hands or gently wiping their fearful tears away with a soft tissue. He would smile at them as he would delicately describe the simple procedure. His smile would broaden as he took their money, watched as they changed into a putrid green gown, and lay upon the frigid metal slab. His smile would turn from kindness to torturous rapture as he strapped them down, pulled out a filthy, blood-stained scalpel and say in a deep, morbid voice, "I would like to tell you that this won't hurt, my dear. But at this point, I think we *both* know better than that, now don't we. Let's get started. This is going to take a while. My, you remind me of my estranged daughter. In fact, *all* of you do. Yes, I'm going to take my time and savor every moment of this. Now, open up and say 'Aaaaah,' you little whore."

Alexander mentally wiped the streaks of blood from his mind and re-engaged with his customer. "Why yes sir, we *are* still open. Especially for *you*. I do admire a man with such talents as yours. I admire them a great deal. Why, I myself used to practice such…um…well that was a long time ago. Here, I may have just what you are looking for behind the counter. I just have a feeling that you may be in the market for a new razor-sharp scalpel. Am I right?"

The customer left the store wearing an evil grin. "Yes, I am right," the darkened voice of Alexander stated as he clicked the door lock and turned out the overhead florescent lights. "I'm *always* right. Enjoy this operation, my good man. And hold on to that scalpel and use it with care. You certainly don't want it to end up in the wrong hands, heh, heh, heh."

"Scream all you like, my dear," the demented physician stated as his latest victim struggled against the burlap straps of the blood-stained steel slab. "No one can hear you. And pray all that you like as well. Little whores like you won't be heard by our lord and savior. Little whores like you who tempt us men into sinful thoughts. Walking around in your little shorts or dresses or skirts. Showing off your slender legs. Bending over so that we can see the outline of your panties that cover your petite little bottoms. And then you wonder why you were raped outside of that bar. You cried and cried on my shoulder while you described how horrific it was to be held down by those three men. How much pain you felt between your temptress legs as they took turns with you. Oh, boo hoo. How can you blame them, looking like you do. You flirted with them, didn't you? Accepted their drinks? Winked at them? Perhaps allowed a little light brushing against your breasts? What is a man to do? The pain you experienced is *nothing* like what *we* experience every day having to watch your feminine forms wiggle down the sidewalk. You're all just like my daughter. Tempting us. And then, when we act upon our God-given impulses, we're the bad guys? No. You little tramps are the evil ones. You little tramps are the ones who will never find salvation. So go ahead and pray while you can, my dear. Because you won't be able to once I cut out your serpent's tongue."

The young woman's screams continued as the man lumbered toward her. All that she could focus on were the dark red splotches from count-less others on his scrubs. And his glistening new scalpel. He laughed softly as he pried her lips apart. His laughing intensified as he began to insert the scalpel into her wailing mouth. His right hand suddenly lurched toward her left wrist. "W-what the hell is going on?" he bellowed as his right hand began sawing through the woman's restraint. His shock continued as he unwillingly used the scalpel to release her other hand. Then her feet. The frenzied young woman kicked the man in his nose, and she ran toward the ominous metal door. She heard a clinking sound on the concrete floor and turned around. Laying there was the scalpel. It began to glow, and she slowly approached it. She felt as though this maniacal tool was beckoning to her.

"You little bitch!" the man yelled out as blood gushed from his broken nose. The young woman instinctively reached down, grabbed the scalpel, and sliced through the man's approaching thigh. She was in a daze as she looked at the bleeding doctor's body that was strapped down on the metal slab. She smiled slightly as the scalpel compelled her left hand toward the whimpering man's scrotum. With a slight flick of her wrist, the sharpened scalpel easily sliced through his ball sack, creating a grotesque mixture of testicles, blood, and semen which oozed out from between his legs and dripped off the edge of the metal slab. She watched with mesmerized glee while he slowly bled out and his pleas for mercy were finally silenced. He had been wrong. Her lord and savior had heard her prayers. And she had become an instrument of his retribution. As had her scalpel.

The young woman hastily dressed and took one last look at the macabre corpse. She spat at him, opened the large metal door, and raced down the dark alleyway. Her frightened mind was racing as she contemplated what she was to do next. Her fear suddenly turned into a surprised calm as a tall, slender gentleman dressed in a grey pin-stripe suit stepped in front of her from out of a doorway.

"Good evening, my dear," the stranger said in a kind, British voice. "Tut, tut, don't be frightened. I am here to help you. Take this envelope. Inside you will find a new identity, enough money to get you on your feet, and a one-way bus ticket to Oregon. Take this and go now. You are going to a better place. Unlike that horrid worm that you just disposed of. No, you are definitely going to different places. You, my dear, are going to Oregon. While his lifeless form is trapped forever in the oppressive hellscape known as Idaho. You are going to do great things with your life, my dear. I can sense it. Good for you. Now go. And my dear? Keep that scalpel handy. You never know when you may need it."

"Sonofabitch, another delivery from Alexander!" Satan yelled out with glee. "Oh wow. You really are a sadistic motherfucker aren't you? And I think that I have just the thing for your eternal damnation. Yeah, kill two birds with one stone. Or five. Where are those four fuckin' mean girl cheerleaders? Oh, there they are. I can hear their fucking snapping gum. Alright bitches, here's what we're going to do. This motherfucker thinks that women are his personal plaything and that he has the right to do anything he wants to them just because they turn him on? Well, boy-howdy is he gonna have fun with this. For eternity, he's gonna be tied down on that cold, metal slab over there. Well, maybe not cold. Can't even have fuckin' iced tea in this fuckin' sauna. Okay, take two. He's gonna be tied to that infernal wall of brimstone over there and he's gonna have to watch you four bitches dance all suggestive like in your little cheerleader outfits. He's gonna get the biggest, baddest case of blue balls in fucking eternity! And his balls are just gonna continue to grow and grow and grow until SPLAT! They fuckin' explode and his cum flies everywhere! Fun, huh? Then, once you bitches have made his balls explode, we'll send in some other group of sexy little sinners. And we'll just keep doing this for eternity. Dance, SPLAT! Dance, SPLAT! Dance, SPLAT! The clean-ups gonna be a bitch, though. Oh, what am I saying? We'll just get him a straw and make him suck up his own cum, then strap him back up again. Plus, he'll get some protein that way. You're welcome, motherfucker. Alright girls. Go put on your sexiest cheerleader outfits. You're on first shift. After that, I'm not sure. I'll have to put together a schedule and get it to ya. I'll put it up on the billboard. Alright, doc. Time for your scrotum to open up and say 'Aaaaaah', heh, heh, heh."

CHAPTER 7

VINYL RECORD

The dazed record store manager put on his battered denim jacket and silently exited his shop. He immediately turned right and proceeded to walk to his Queens home for an unplanned day off.

"Enjoy your day of leisure, my good man," Alexander said after him while putting on his bright white apron over his pin-striped suit. He smiled as he looked around at the piles of dusty bins of vinyl albums. "Oh, my, this place could use a bit of cleaning. And organization." His smile faded into a grimace as he continued. "And…and…what in the gates of hell is that infernal racket?" He went behind the counter and looked down at the shop's turntable. A heavy piece of black vinyl was spinning and emitting thunderous drums under an ear-splitting electric guitar solo. He scowled at the origin of his recently acquired headache, clicked the turntable off, and gently placed the record back into its sleeve.

"Now, where do you belong?" he said as he searched for the record's home. "You certainly do not belong in anyone's eardrums, that's for certain. Such barbarism. Ah, well. Everyone has their own tastes, I suppose. Or lack thereof, in this tripe's case. Ah, here you are. In bin number twenty-three. Now, how about something a bit more refined?"

Alexander sauntered around the small shop until he found the section he was looking for. "Now, why would all of these wonderful works be buried in the back of the shop? Hmmm, what might just inspire this shop's patrons to broaden their cultural horizon's? Yes. Perfect. Absolutely perfect. Especially for one in the business of soul gathering, heh, heh, heh."

Alexander grinned from ear to ear as he delicately placed the stylus upon the sheen vinyl and pressed play. "I must admit, this is much easier than having to manually crank as I had to do in my day. And just listen to this. Hi-fidelity indeed. The soaring violins. The ominous harmony of this majestic choir. Yes, this is simply morbidly wonderful." He found a duster underneath the counter and began swaying to the majestic chords while playing conductor to an invisible orchestra. A black tear fell from his eye while unsettled dust began flying about. Alexander frequently coughed from breathing in the dust particles that he and his duster were sending through the air. He looked toward the window. A brilliant ray of sunshine came bursting into the shop, illuminating the dust particles which appeared to be dancing in midair to the intoxicating sonic intricacies. His smile broadened and his heart swelled as his first customer entered.

"Well, we meet again," Melissa Bartlesworth stated. "I come in here all the time. I didn't know *you* worked here. And I'm so sorry, but I didn't catch your name the other morning."

The shocked and swooning Alexander struggled with his response for a moment before he said, "Oh, that is all right my dear. My name is Alexander. Alexander Picklesbee. It is so lovely to see you again. I did so enjoy our chat the other morning. You are so very lovely that you literally put a spring in this old man's step."

Melissa struggled to keep herself from blushing at the dashing gentleman's compliment. "Oh, um, well, um, the pleasure was mine. It's not every day that I get the pleasure of the company as someone as refined as yourself. But, like I said, I come in here all the time looking for new music to play in our clothier store. Well, and while I'm at it, I usually look for a little something for myself, but don't tell my dad, okay? Anyway, when did you start working here?"

"Well," a beaming Alexander answered as familiar urges crept into his heart. "It is quite fortuitous that you came in today, my dear. This will probably be my only time in this fine shop. You see, I'm a bit of a temporary employee. Yes, I tend to shops that are in need of my services. You might say that going from shop to shop to take care of their patrons is my calling. I do so enjoy meeting so many new souls and giving them what they deserve. Just like you." Alexander paused for a moment while the conflicting feelings of unbridled love and torturous heartbreak battled each other in his psyche. "What is it that I can help *you* with, my dear? What enticing sounds does *your* soul deserve?"

"Well, like I said, I'm looking for something to play at our store. Perhaps something in the fitting rooms. I just adore what you are playing right now. It's almost like I'm drawn to yo…I mean, it. So elegant. So refined. So, um, *dark*. It stirs something up in me. Please, tell me what it is. I simply must have it."

Alexander's heart simultaneously swelled and broke as he looked upon the perfect face of his lost love's descendent. "My, beautiful face and beautiful taste in music. Perhaps we are kindred spirits of a sort. Perhaps we were meant to meet once again in this shop. This, my dear, is Mozart's *Requiem in D Minor*. Enchanting, isn't it?"

"Yes, enchanting is the word for it," Melissa replied as she stared at the spinning vinyl behind the counter. "Enchanting and morbid. Like death itself. It perfectly captures the blackness that we will all experience upon death's final embrace. But, upon our death, our souls are free. We are free from the pain and humiliation. Free from all of the petty conflicts. Free from the persecution and manipulation and exploitation. So many of us are exploited by others in this world. I wish that I could free all of their souls so that they could be free from that. I wish to offer them a more enchanting existence. Yes, this music is just perfect. Perhaps not for the store, but for my personal use. I have been looking for something that relates to my current mood. Something that I can be absorbed by while I'm, um, thinking about the less fortunate. I will take it, Mr. Picklesbee."

"Oh, no need for such formalities, my dear. Alexander will be just fine," a devilishly grinning Alexander replied as he regretfully lifted the vinyl from its table and placed it into its protective sleeve. He concentrated for a moment on his past love. He concentrated on how his heart had been shattered by this woman's ancestor. He concentrated on how she had ruined his life and damned his soul. The album glowed for a moment before he placed it into a plain, brown, bag. "Yes, I sense that this album is for you. It is *exactly* what you deserve. I could not have picked out anything more perfect for you."

Melissa paid for the record and lifted the brown bag from off of the counter. She blushed once again before saying, "Um, listen. I don't know what it is about you, but I just find you, um, interesting. I was just wondering if you would like to have, as you would say, a spot of tea, sometime?"

"Um, um," Alexander uncharacteristically stammered. The battle that was raging in his heart had been won. At least, for the moment. "Why yes. That would be quite lovely. Almost as lovely as that faux-British accent that you use to imitate me. Spot of tea, indeed. It is quite humorous. I do believe that I would welcome the opportunity to get to know you better. Perhaps tonight after we both get off work? I could come down to your store and we could go from there. But, oh my, I do believe that I have forgotten to give you your receipt. Please, my dear, give me that bag. You must have your receipt."

"Oh, it's okay Alexander," Melissa replied. "I'm not planning on returning it or claiming it for my taxes or anything. It's fine. I don't need it." Alexander's mind raced while beads of sweat began forming above his silver brow. He had to save her from the curse that he had just placed into her hands and upon her soul. And the only way to do that was to hold the poisoned record in his hands once again. "I am sorry, my dear," he retorted. "But I simply must insist. The manager would be quite cross with me if I did not give a receipt to every customer. He was quite clear on that. Please. Give me the bag. A moment is all that I need."

"Well, okay, here you go," Melissa answered as she handed the bag over. Alexander hastily grabbed the brown bag and turned around. He concentrated once again. But this time, he concentrated on how this young woman's attention made him feel. The exhilaration he felt from the attention of a vibrant young woman caused the bag to glow once again. He turned toward the cash register, printed out the receipt, and placed it into the bag alongside the harmless record. "Thank you so much for your understanding, my dear. And I shall see you at…"

"How about six?" Melissa interrupted to complete his thought. "Six it is then," the smiling Alexander agreed. "It will be delightful. Enjoy that recording, my dear. I am quite happy to have introduced you to something that you deserve."

Melissa was blushing as she left the store. She was nearly bowled over by an entering teenage ruffian. "Hey! Watch where you're going, asshole!" Melissa screamed out. The boy yelled after her, "Fuck off, bitch! You don't own everything!" Alexander's pulse began to quicken as he felt this young man's desired atrocities in his black soul. He chuckled with a menacing darkness as the teenager turned toward him. He chortled a bit louder as he surveyed the young man's greasy black hair, pimply complexion, and beaten leather jacket that was covered with hand-drawn pentagrams and other miscellaneous hellish images.

"What's so funny old man?" the young man stated. "Listen. You probably don't have a fuckin' clue, but I need something loud. Something fast. Something that will raise holy fuckin' hell. Something that will get me noticed by my lord. Drums. Guitars. Bass. Hot chicks in fishnets on the cover with a bunch of blood. I'm talkin' metal, man! The heaviest fuckin' metal that you've got!"

Alexander exhaled as his heart rejoiced. "Why yes, young man. I do understand what you are looking for. In fact, I may have a better understanding of what you seek than *you* do. You want something to listen to while performing your ritual, don't you? Yes, something quite violent but that is a bit of a toe-tapper. Something that will cause your lord to view you in a positive light while you chant and do other, um, unseemly things. Yes, I believe I have just what you are looking for under the counter. This just, um, came in. It is quite new. Look upon this, my young friend. Is this what you seek? Is this what your soul deserves?"

"Oh, fuck yeah!" the young man exclaimed as he took the album into his shaking hands. His cynical face twisted into a macabre smile as he looked upon the images of blood soaked, scantily clad women using axe-shaped guitars to decapitate white swans. "This is perfect! Yeah, maybe you're alright old man. Here's my money. Keep the change."

"Oh, I'm quite all right," Alexander stated as his face darkened while the young man exited the shop. "Yes, I understand what you seek better than *you* do. And I understand that you will get what you have asked for. You wanted an invitation to meet Satan? Well, I have just given it to you. Play that record with care, my young friend. You may just want to be careful what you wish for, heh, heh, heh."

The young man flew down the suburban stairs of the basement of his mother's home. He went to the back of the basement and unlocked a door. Immediately upon its opening the cries from thirteen caged cats filled the air. "Shut the fuck up!" he yelled at them. "Oh, gonna keep crying, huh? Oh, I'm gonna give you motherfuckers something to cry about. Today's the day. Today, I am going to sacrifice you on my altar to my lord, Satan." He pulled back a black curtain revealing an altar constructed of a flattened cardboard box that sat upon several black-painted milk crates. Posters of cartoonish, hellish-looking metal bands adorned the walls. He went over to a small, rickety shelf and lifted the top of his suitcase record player. He lit the black candles that surrounded the interned felines and said, "But first, let's listen to *this* shit. Then I'm going to slash your fucking throats and drink your blood."

He had an evil little laugh as he placed the record on the turntable. The insipid drivel started, and he cranked the volume. Tinny sounds came whimpering out of the tiny built-in speaker. "Fuck, this thing sucks," the young man lamented. "Can't hardly hear it. I need to ask Mom for a new stereo this Christmas. Oh well, let's start the incantation."

He stood at the head of the altar, picked up a kitchen knife, and began reciting something in Latin. Or some other language that he didn't understand but had found in some "cool" book. As his chanting continued the drums, bass, and guitars became louder. "Fuck, yeah," the young man stated. "Maybe this thing just has a short in it. Let's get loud!" The small turntable did not disappoint as the tedious screeching vocals and thundering drums blared throughout the room. The altar began to shake and tumbled over in a heap.

"Fuck!" he yelled out. "My altar! Shit! Why is this so loud? Why can't I turn it down?" Out of frustration, he pulled the plug of the turntable from the adjacent outlet. The "music" continued to intensify. "What in the hell is going on?" "An appropriate question," the shopkeeper's cackling voice stated through the speakers. "What in the hell, indeed? This is what you wanted. This is what you asked for. This is what your soul deserves, heh, heh, heh."

The boy ran toward the door. He began weeping as he tried to pry the door open while blood dripped out of his punished ears. He then heard the snapping of the locks on the cages and the slight creaks of metal doors being opened. He turned around and thirteen growling cats were staring at him from their perch on the remnants of his altar. He screamed for his mommy as the cats pounced upon him. Multiple colors and textures of fur became entangled in the shrieking boy's blood as the cats sliced his skin open with their sharpened claws and chewed through the flesh on his face.

The boy's shrill cries harmonized perfectly with the satanic lyrics while two felines batted one of his eyeballs around the floor and four others played tug-of-war with his gnarled intestines. The music grew louder, and the basement window finally succumbed and shattered from the piercing sounds just as the boy finally succumbed to the merciless feline onslaught. The cats felt the fresh air and scurried through the open window to freedom just as the vinyl record stopped spinning.

The boy's mother yelled down the stairs. "Johnny! Thank God you finally turned that racket off! Do you have any laundry for me dear? Johnny, are you down here? Are you in this back room? Are you...oh my God! Johnny!"

"What is wrong with you little fuckers?" an angry Satan asked to

Johnny's damned soul. "Why do all of you assholes think I'm into torturing helpless animals? That's not my thing. In fact, it's pretty much the last refuge of little piss-ants who have daddy issues, or a small prick, or some other fucked up, meaningless thing. I don't want to hear your fucking lame-ass excuses. The bottom line is that you just like to watch living things suffer and that makes you a little pussy. No, hurting animals doesn't endear you to me. It just pisses me off. And not just because they're innocent and cute and shit. It's also because their souls now go to heaven and the fuckin' angels have more little furballs to play with. Don't you see? Sacrificing animals in *my name* only plays into the fucking angel's hands! Goddammit! I fucking hate it when you fuckers do this shit in my name. You should see all the mocking postcards I get! Here's one. Listen to this shit. Roses are red. Violets are blue. Your followers are a bunch of kitten killing ass-wipes. And so are you. Nice, huh? I just got that one from a dead nun. A fucking *nun* called *me* an ass-wipe and accused *me* of killing kittens! That's fucking *slander*! And all because of dickwads like you.

"Alright, you've had your fun, now I'm going to have mine. You know that album Alexander gave you? Well, that was recorded right here in hell by the only four metal musicians who were *actually* Satanists. All the rest of those spandex-wearing pansies are just *posers*. It's all an *act* to sell records to dipshits like you! You knew that, right? Jesus H., gullible much? I mean, they go on stage every night and bathe in blood, and "sacrifice" shit, and praise me, and a bunch of other stupid shit while there's fucking laser lights and explosions and black-leather dancing bitches. Then, they go back to their hotel rooms and hang out with their wives and change their fucking kids' diapers. They go grocery shopping. They play softball and golf. Seriously. Of all the so-called Satanic metal musicians there were only four who were true believers. And those four aren't really all that good. They just ripped off Iron Maiden and Black Sabbath. Poorly, at that. And you, my dumbass new friend, bought their only fucking album. Congratulations on fucking that up too.

"So, here's what we're gonna do. You get a front row seat at their concert. Yep, right in front of the speaker stack. For eternity your fucking ears are going to bleed while they play the same simplistic guitar solo over and over and over. You're going to have to listen to the same high-pitched screams of the singer over and over and over. The drums and bass will shake you to your core. By the end of the first song, you're going to beg for them to shut the fuck up! Yeah, you're going to be *begging* for some pussy Yacht Rock! Oh, and cats are going to be constantly eating your internal organs. Almost forgot that part. So, enjoy the show kid! It's gonna be fucking killer!"

Chapter 8

Blossoming

"Oh, this is quite ridiculous," Alexander said to himself as he straightened his grey tie and tucked it under his pin-striped suit. "What in the hell do I think I'm doing with this girl? Why, her face stirs up such complex feelings, I nearly killed her earlier today by placing a curse on the record she purchased. Then, just a bit of attention from a young beauty and I'm right back to being that manipulated boy that I was in college. Head over heels, hook, line, and sinker, and Cupid's arrow right through my heart. I've had well over a century to purge any feelings for my Virgina, and here is her descendant dredging them all up again. The rapture. The anxiety. The utter silliness of it all. Even if I were truly alive, which I am not, I would be far too old for her. Why, it would be positively scandalous. But seeing as how I'm a deceased damned soul of, let's see here, I died in 1888 at the age of fifty so that makes me…heh…one-hundred-and eighty-seven years old. Yes, quite scandalous indeed.

"But what harm does a spot of tea with a vivacious young woman do? Oh sure, perhaps I acted a tad impulsively earlier today, but I righted that wrong now, didn't I? Why, I haven't even peered into her soul to determine what fate may hold for her upon her passing. Will it be Heaven or Hell? I do not know, nor do I wish to find out. Her final breath will not be at my hands. Nor will I pursue anything more than a friendship with her. Yes, I believe that I deserve that. A friendship with my lost love's descendent. That is all. This shall be quite the fine test that I shall give myself. Being a friend to someone who looks identical to the woman who broke my heart and shattered my life. The woman who drove me into a bottle and out of medical school and ruined me. The woman who made me hate all women and made me do things to them. Vile, disgusting, bloody things that landed me in hell! A woman who… no! Just stop this Alexander, this instant. Suppress your anger. Suppress your hurt. That was Virginia, not your friend Melissa. And now, it is nearly six. Time for our spot of tea. And that is all. Just some nice conversation. And a spot of tea. So, I suppose I won't need this bag of utensils that I picked up at the medical supply store. No, I won't be needing them tonight. Although, it *is* always best to be prepared. Yes, I'll take them along. Just in case they are needed for, um, self-defense."

Alexander sauntered down the bustling Queens street humming Mozart. He casually glanced at the passers-by and would briefly peer into their souls. *Naughty, naughty,* he thought to himself. *Oh my. Quite the torrid affair, sir. But it's consensual, so who am I to judge? A compulsive liar. Oh, yawn. A neighborhood gossip. Annoying but certainly not purely sinful. Just boring little sinners with boring little sins. Certainly not the type of stock that would end up with my lord. Ah, what is this? A perfumery. Well, perhaps a bit behind her perfectly petite ears is what this evening calls for. And it will make a lovely gift for my new friend.*

Alexander entered the brightly lit establishment and looked at all of the glass bottles that were reflecting the pink and white neon lights. He approached the manager and said, "Hello, my good man. I am looking for a lovely perfume for a friend. Yes, she is just a friend, so nothing with a name with romantic overtures. Just a lovely little scent to put a spring in her step. Yes! That's it! Spring! Something that conjures up images of lovely wildflowers blowing in a warm Spring breeze. Do you have anything like that?"

"Sure do," the manager replied. "Come over here and take *this* in. Do you think that she would like that?" Alexander inhaled deeply. His smile broadened as the delicately textured aroma swept over his olfactory nerves. He peered at the label on the curved glass. "Ah, yes. 'Blossoming Anew.' What a perfect name for a most perfect scent for a most perfect young lady." He paused for a moment and listened to the immature guffawing of a pair of twenty-something men. Their meticulously manicured facial hair was identical as were the spiked locks on their heads. They both wore expensive athletic wear with gaudy gold chains wrapped around their muscular necks.

"Hey Bro," one of them was saying. "That old dude just said, 'young lady.' Probably more like a young tranny, Bro." "Yeah, totally Bro," the other agreed. "That old dude is totally into chicks with dicks, Bro." The pair then turned their attention to a young Black woman who was working behind the counter. "Hey baby. Wanna have some fun tonight?" "Yeah, wanna hang with us? We'll show you a real good time. You ever had two white bros at the same time? We'll rock your world, right Bro?" "Oh, totally, Bro. Come on baby. We're in the mood for a little dark meat. If you play your cards right, we might even buy you dinner, right Bro?"

The young woman glared at the pair while an intrigued Alexander looked on. She smiled demurely, suggestively licked her lips, and said seductively, "Yeah, that might be fun. I'm in the mood for a little white meat. I bet you boys would like to slide some between my full, pouty lips, wouldn't you? Mmmmmm, I bet you taste sooooo gooood. Especially your blood dripping down my throat after I bite your little peckers off. So yeah, I'm interested. You sexist…little…pricks."

"Whoa, Bro!" one of the loathsome men exclaimed. "This little bitch has claws! Hey baby, haven't you heard? You aren't people anymore. You don't have any rights. You're property. *Our* property. Especially (derogatory term omitted) bitches like you. Your body, our choice, right, Bro?" "Oh, yeah, totally Bro," the other stated. "Listen bitch. We can do this the easy way, or the hard way. But either way we're going to fuck you. Hard. Maybe not tonight, maybe not tomorrow, but soon. We can get to you. We're men, right, Bro? We can do anything that we want to stuck up bitches like you. We do it every night to stupid bitches who flaunt their shit all over the place. Just one little drop in their drink, and out they go.

And in *we* go, right, Bro? It's officially a man's world, so get with the program, lay back, and spread those black legs for us, 'cause we're gonna get it whether you like it or not, right, Bro?" "Yeah, right, Bro. And you'll *like it*, bitch. We'll *make* you like it. And hey, if you get knocked up, not our problem. Have fun raising our kids on your pathetic salary here, bitch. Right, Bro?"

Alexander smiled as pangs of excitement swept throughout his soul. He could feel the anger rising in the belittled young woman. He could feel her hurt. He could feel her embarrassment. And he could sense her conflict as she suppressed her urges to violently lash out at this arrogant pair of self-entitled and oppressive worms.

"Gentlemen, gentlemen," a devilishly grinning Alexander said before staring into the eyes of the manager. The manager glazed over and stood motionless in a trance while Alexander performed the same bit of trickery upon the young woman. "My, my gentlemen, you do have fine taste in women. Yes, she is quite beautiful. But you are missing something. Yes, you are missing something to attract the beautiful bees to your honey. A new cologne. I just happen to be working here tomorrow, isn't that right, Mister Manager?"

The manager replied in a robotic voice, "Yes. I'll give you a set of keys before you leave. I believe I and my employee need a day off. Yes, you may work here tomorrow." "Splendid!" Alexander exclaimed as he clapped his hands together. "Yes, gentlemen, I will be working here tomorrow, and I just happen to know that there is a special shipment arriving. A most wonderful scent that I guarantee will attract the most beautiful women in the world to you. So, why don't you come back tomorrow and see me, hmmmm? I'll even give you a bit of a discount. What do you say? Deal?"

The pair looked at one another for a moment before saying, "Yeah, alright. What do you think, Bro?" "Yeah, I don't know what a (derogatory term omitted) would know about picking up bitches, but what the hell, Bro? We'll give it a shot. See ya tomorrow morning, there Nancy. Come on, Bro. We'll do this mouthy bitch later."

Alexander chuckled to himself as his face darkened and his eyes turned black. "Oh, my fine friends. I know more about women than you could ever imagine. Yes, you might say that I know *all* of their ins and outs. And soon *you* will *too*." Alexander shook his head, and his face turned back to its natural pale grey. "Oh, now where was I? Oh, yes, this wonderful perfume. How much, my good man?" The manager came out of his trance and said, "That'll be fifty-six-forty-eight. And thank you for taking care of my shop tomorrow. I've been needing a day off. Here are the keys."

"Think nothing of it, my good man," Alexander replied as he picked up the keys and pink paper bag. "Think nothing of it at all. In fact, after tomorrow you will never think of me again. Nor will you, young lady. You two have a lovely evening and a lovely day off. Ta, ta."

"Alexander!" Melissa cried out as she saw her new friend enter the café. "It's just so lovely to see you. Here, I have found us a table. What is in your brown leather bag? Are you going on a trip?"

"No, no, nothing like that," a blushing Alexander answered. "No, this is just a little bag of essentials that I sometimes carry with me. Just in case. There is nothing for *you* in here, my dear. No, nothing. What is in this bag is not for you. Yet. I mean, and yet I have *another* bag that *is* for you my dear. Here. Just a trifle to celebrate our new friendship."

"Oh, Alexander, it's positively lovely!" Melissa exclaimed as she sprayed a bit of perfume upon her wrists. Alexander's pulse quickened as she stretched her lithe neck and rubbed her scented wrist upon it. "Mmmmm, yes lovely. Thank you. I absolutely love it."

"As I'm sure your *boyfriend* will, as well," Alexander probed. "Oh, yeah, him," Melissa replied dismissively. "Robert. Yeah, maybe. I really don't know what gets his attention anymore. But enough about me. I want to know about you. Alexander Picklesbee. What an interesting name. It has an elegance but is also rather fun. So, what is a Brit doing across the pond? Especially now. Come to watch firsthand the collapse of our nation?"

"Yes, well there is that isn't there?" a chuckling Alexander replied. "Yes, a wise man once said, 'ignorance and apathy breeds tyranny.' And how true that is turning out to be. A once proud nation that has turned against itself out of greed and perceived self-importance. Too many shun education and common sense and have turned their souls over to the darkness of lies and manipulation. All for cheaper eggs. It is all quite sad. And silly. But do not fret. Their souls will not be here forever, my dear. Yes, there will come a time that they no longer walk amongst us. And the fun part will be that their God that they professed allegiance to will abandon them. Yes, all of these pious worshippers shall be turned away from the pearly gates and will get a one-way ticket down to visit their *true* lord. All of them. Each and every one of them are going to burn for their hypocrisy and blasphemy. Yes, God truly is a stickler about that whole 'idolizing false prophets' thing. Quite a stickler, indeed."

"Well, from your mouth to God's ears," a laughing Melisa replied. "Indeed," an amused Alexander stated. "Perhaps not God's ears, but… anyway. Where were we? Oh yes. My history. Well, that truly is a quite long and sordid tale."

"Sordid?" a confused Melissa inquired. "I can hardly imagine a man as distinguished as yourself being involved in anything sordid."

"Oh, my dear," Alexander answered. "You are so young. You may be surprised at what men are capable of." Alexander's ears perked up when he heard Melissa say under her breath, "Or women."

"Actually, there's not that much to tell, my dear. I studied medicine for a time. Although I was becoming quite the skilled surgeon, I was really only doing it to appease my boorish father and overbearing mother. My heart simply wasn't in it. And then, I had a bit of a heart-break and decided to end my studies. Yes, the love of my life found another and broke off our engagement. In a letter."

"You quit school over a *woman?*" Melissa asked. "Why? Why would you throw years of education away just because some bitch dumped you? And she didn't even have the decency to tell you to your face? You must have had it really bad for her, Alexander. I'm so sorry. You should not have been treated that way. *I* never would have treated you that way. Women can be so cruel sometimes."

Melissa placed her pale, smooth hand over his and smiled at him. Alexander's heart began pounding in his chest as he could feel the sweat from her palm become absorbed by his flesh. He gazed into the glistening blue eyes of his original heartache. He abruptly pulled his hand away, reached for his cloth napkin, and wiped beads of sweat from his brow.

"Yes, yes they can," Alexander stammered as he tried to compose himself. "Quite cruel indeed. I believe that I may imbibe in something a bit stronger. Would you like to join me for a gin?"

The pair entered a darkened pub and sat in a round, red vinyl booth. Melissa took a lighter from her purse and lit the red candle in the middle of the table. Yellow flames flickered about her alluring face causing Alexander to clutch his brown leather medical bag. He cleared his throat, awkwardly smiled, and said, "Ah yes, a spot of tea is good, but a sip of gin is required for my current mood."

"Well, nice try," a laughing Melissa stated. "I mean, it *kinda* rhymed. And yes, I believe that I will have a gin as well. It is my favorite. It helps me become…inspired."

"Oh, me as well, my dear," Alexander said as he placed his leather bag on the seat next to him and gave it a loving pat. "Me as well. Sometimes a spot of gin is all that is required to make me feel a bit, um, *adventurous* shall we say. Which brings me back to my story. Yes, my heart was broken, and I ended my studies. I bounced around as a traveling salesman for a time. In fact, I did that until my, um, retirement. My last employment was in White Chapel. Yes, that job was quite the death of me. After that, I retired to a place, um, with a rather warm climate. But my old trade beckoned, and I found myself here, assisting shopkeepers whenever they might require my services. I am quite gifted in finding the most perfect item that my customers deserve. And that, my dear, is the story of Alexander Picklesbee. Former surgical student. Tradesman. Shopkeeper. And I am a bit embarrassed to say, hopeless romantic."

Melissa's eyes fell into his as she said in a breathy one, "Fascinating. I like you, Alexander Picklesbee. I think that we may have a long friendship together. I, um, propose that we have a standing date, um, I mean, you know, a regular night for us to get together and talk. Just talk. I could listen to your voice for hours. And I have a feeling that you have some amazing stories. Yes, I simply must know everything about my new friend, Alexander Picklesbee."

Alexander laughed nervously before responding. "Well, that sounds quite lovely, my dear. Yes, I believe that we may be kindred spirits of a sort. But perhaps you do not need to know *everything* about me. Every relationship requires just a bit of mystery, now, doesn't it?"

"Yes," Melissa agreed. "We will get to know one another, Alexander. But not *too* much. I will allow you to keep *your* secrets. And *I* shall keep *mine*."

The pair hugged cordially and went their separate ways down the cracked sidewalk. Alexander's eyes darted around his dimly lit surroundings. They finally rested upon a bright neon liquor store sign that illuminated the curvy figure of a working girl. *Perhaps this evening isn't quite over,* Alexander thought to himself as sweat from his palm absorbed into the handle of his medical bag. *No, perhaps I require a bottle of gin. And a bit of female companionship. But I mustn't stay up too late. I have an engagement at the perfumery tomorrow. But one bottle and one little indiscretion shouldn't take me too long. No, I can do this quite efficiently. I've had a great deal of practice, heh, heh, heh.*

Alexander Picklesbee, a swooning Melissa thought as she walked back toward her home. *Now why does that name sound familiar? Oh, and what am I going to pick Robert up for dinner? Oh, who cares. He can fend for himself for once. Alexander Picklesbee. Who are you, really? And why do I feel so drawn to you?*

CHAPTER 9

COLOGNE

Alexander had just finished slicking back his silver hair when he heard a knock on his apartment door. "Oh dear, who could that be?" he said to himself as a more determined knock echoed throughout his room. "I'm coming, I'm coming, just one moment," he said. "Just please stop knocking. I have a bit of a headache." He looked at the table that held his empty bottle of gin and shook his head regretfully before opening the door.

He was greeted by two cheap-suited men. "Yes, hello gentlemen," he greeted. "To what do I owe this pleasure?"

"Yeah, hey pal," the pudgier of the men answered while flashing a badge. "I'm Detective Anderson, and this is Detective Biggs. Could we ask you a few questions?"

"Why of course, detectives. Won't you please come in?" Alexander replied cordially. The detectives immediately glanced around the room and noticed an empty bottle of gin on a well-worn wooden table. And a pair of panties on the floor. "Have a party here last night, didja?" Biggs inquired as his cop's eyes scanned every tick on Alexander's slightly wrinkled face. "Maybe a little female companionship?"

Alexander chuckled slightly and said, "Well, I do not know if I would call it a party. Just a nip of gin and well, yes, I did have a female caller.

And yes, well, I suppose that is why you are here. Before you ask, my name is Alexander Picklesbee. But this morning, I suppose you can just call me John. Yes, I did have a female with me last night and yes, she performed a service for me in exchange for a bit of money. But detectives, it was all quite harmless and kept to the confines of my little abode here. I made sure that she wasn't too, um, boisterous. We had a consensual rendezvous and then she left."

"Uh, huh," Anderson said suspiciously. "So, this female companion, does she look anything like this?" The detective walked to a back window and flung open the curtains. The morning sunlight came flooding into the room as Alexander cautiously walked toward the window. "Well, was that your date last night?"

Alexander stood in shocked silence and beads of sweat began forming on his brow. He glanced under his bed and saw the corner of his medical bag peeking from under the comforter. "Oh, dear lord," he said as his stare returned to the ghastly scene two floors below in the alley behind his apartment. A young woman's remains were being inspected by a forensics crew. She was completely split open from her groin to her chin and her internal organs had been carefully removed and laid out around her blue, blood-soaked body. Alexander stared at her face while attempting to retrace his activities from the previous, drunken night. Her face was so slashed and torn that it was unrecognizable.

"Oh my, how utterly obscene," Alexander stated. "No, detectives. That poor unfortunate soul was not my date last night. My date wore a red dress. This young lady's dress, although quite red now, appears to have been blue. And my date was not Caucasian. My date was a lovely ebony. So, no detectives, I do not know who this person is."

"Well," Biggs pressed. "What time did you and your *date* arrive here and when did she leave?" "Ah, yes," Alexander began. "My whereabouts. Well, I had just finished having a nip of gin at a local pub with a new friend. Melissa. Melissa Bartlesworth. Perhaps you know her? She is associated with the Bartlesworth clothiers. Anyway, we finished our chat around eight last night and a nearby liquor store seemed to be calling me. As was a certain Black temptress standing outside. We arrived here around eight-twenty or so. We had a few drinks. A few laughs. And a bit of canoodling. I paid her and she departed my apartment at nine-fifteen. I showered, climbed into my pajamas, and fell fast asleep."

"Uh-huh," Biggs continued. "Didja hear or see anything last night? Anything out of the ordinary? Any suspicious figures or unfamiliar voices? Maybe around one a.m.?"

"No, I'm afraid not detective," Alexander answered. "I'm afraid that once I close my eyes, I am quite dead to the world. Especially after such activities. I am so sorry that I can not be of further assistance, but I simply haven't any information that I can share with you."

The disappointed pair looked at one another and gave a slight nod. "Alright," Anderson said. "Here's my card. If you think of anything, give us a call." "So," Alexander said as the detectives walked towards his door. "My little indiscretion will not be an issue then?"

"Naw, we're not vice," Biggs answered while staring into Alexander's black eyes. "We don't really care what the working girls do. Or their Johns. Unless those girls turn up dead. Then we are *very* interested in those girls. And we're even *more* interested in their Johns. So, you may want to find some other outlet for your, uh, you may want to find some other way to get laid. This is the second girl that we've found like this in a week. And when we find the bastard that did this, and we will, he's gonna *beg* for the death penalty. But he won't get it. Not in this ass-backwards state. Humane treatment, my ass. Just look at that girl."

"Well, barbarism does lead to barbarism, I suppose," Alexander responded. "But certainly, you must admit, sir, that there are significant flaws in the criminal justice system that has resulted in the execution of innocent…" Alexander stopped suddenly as he stared at the stone expressions of the detectives and decided to change course. "Understood, my good man," Alexander stated. "Yes, yes. Last evening was just a moment of mortal weakness on my part. I promise that it won't happen again."

Alexander closed the door behind the detectives and let out a low chuckle as he muttered to himself, "Oh, but we know that was a bit of a fib now, wasn't it? Well, I won't be damned to hell for that. No, not for *that.*" He went back to the window and watched as the forensic crew was sullenly zipping the remains into a crumpled body bag. "No. Not for telling a little fib. A fib about the *actual* woman that was here last night. A Caucasian woman in a blue dress. What a pity. She really was quite charming. And speaking of little fibs, I mustn't be late for my position at the perfumery. Yes, yes. I must be on time for my special customers. Oh, how I do hope that they come back. I have the most perfect scent for them. And the most wonderful little fib."

"Why yes, young man," Alexander stated to his customer as he placed a small bottle of perfume into a neon pink paper bag. "I believe that this scent will be perfect for her. It is quite understated, but a perfectly recognizable blend of lilac and rose. Yes, and how thoughtful of you. A little gift for the girl you will have dated for thirty days. I remember a time when young men and ladies would perform their dance for months if not years before finally committing to a life with one another. It is so refreshing to find a young couple who are reviving this time-tested ritual of romance, what in this age of swiping left. Or is it right? Oh, I do not understand the modern methods on those contraptions that everyone is obsessed with. Just walking around staring at their tiny screens while ignoring the beauty of this world. If they were only to look up, they may find what they are searching for staring back at them. Ah, well. I do hope that she enjoys your gesture, young man. But just a bit of advice from an old man who has experienced lost love. Do not take her for granted. There may come a day when you are not enough for her. There may come a day when another catches her eye. A day when he swoops in and takes her from you. A day when she will break your heart and ruin your life. A day when…oh, but what am I saying? You are just beginning your exhilarating dance and here I am dredging up the memories of an old fool. Enjoy your dinner with her tonight. And enjoy every moment with her. Thank you for stopping in."

The confused young man nodded and exited the perfumery. Alexander grinned widely when he heard a pair of familiar voices enter. "Yeah, Bro, that was a totally cool podcast. He's totally right, Bro. Men have become total pussies. All emotional and crying and shit. We're cavemen, Bro. We provide for our women and our women are to provide for us. No questions asked. Hey, Bro, I wonder if that Black bitch is working. I'm ready to show her my club, Bro."

"Oh yeah, totally Bro," the other replied. "I don't see her, but there's that old (derogatory term omitted). Hey, Nancy-boy! That Black bitch working today? We got something for her!"

The grinning Alexander reached under the counter and retrieved a small bottle that momentarily glowed dark red. "I am most sorry my young friends, but no. No, she has the day off. But look at what I have for you, just as I promised. It has just arrived. Imported from a, um, much warmer climate. Now, just a dab on your chest, and you will get all of the feminine attention that you so rightly deserve. Just a dab, mind you. It is quite strong. You wouldn't want to have to beat the women off with your, uh, clubs now, would you?"

"Oh, hell yeah, Bro," one of the men said as he sniffed the open bottle. "We're gonna be fuckin' chick magnets, Bro!" "Yeah, Bro, we're totally hitting the clubs tonight. We may not even need our special drops. Chicks'll just drop their panties for us, Bro. Might be nice to fuck a conscious bitch for once. We're gonna be drowning in pussy, Bro. Alright you old pansy. How much?"

"Well, this product is quite new," Alexander answered. "Quite new indeed and we are looking for young men such as yourselves to try it out and tell us if we should stock it permanently. So, no charge. On the condition that you let us know how this worked out for you. Yes, I will be quite anxious to hear about how this little bottle may change your fate. Deal?"

"Yeah, alright Nancy-boy. You got it. We'll be back to let you know. And we'll let that Black bitch know too, right Bro?" "Oh, yeah, totally, Bro. We'll be back tomorrow, Nancy."

The pair left and Alexander's face darkened before saying to himself in a deep growl, "Well, I do not anticipate seeing your faces in here tomorrow. Or ever again, for that matter. But the young lady who works here? Yes, I believe that you may see her tonight. Yes, I believe you both deserve that. But be careful what you wish for. You want pussy? Well, then pussy you shall have…Bro."

"Oh man, Bro, this is gonna be awesome!" One of the young men said to the other in the bathroom that they both shared. "Yeah, Bro! But let's not just put a little on. Let's use the whole bottle, Bro!" "Totally, Bro!" The pair poured the contents over their glistening, muscular chests and began rubbing it into their taught flesh. They stared at one another in an awkward silence as they felt the crotches in their pants tighten. "Uh, watcha looking at, Bro?" "Uh, nothin' Bro. What are you looking at?" "Yeah, nothin' Bro. Let's just get to the club, Bro. We need some pussy. Like now, Bro."

"Bro, this chick's totally all over me!" one of the young men exclaimed as a young blonde was gyrating against his leg to the rhythm of driving beats of the nightclub. "Yeah, this one too, Bro!" the other exclaimed with sheer delight. "They look familiar, Bro. Aren't these the chicks that we, uh…" "Yeah, totally, Bro! We put something in their drinks a month ago. They must not remember us! This'll be so much more fun with them awake, Bro!"

The foursome was joined by four other scantily clad young women, who began grinding against the men in a passionate daze. Their tight sequined party dresses swayed to the robotic music as they lasciviously groped and kissed their formers rapists. Another woman's voice was heard from behind them. The young woman from the perfumery was standing in her black party dress, fishnet stockings and six-inch black pumps. She lustfully licked her full lips and said, "Hey there, boys. Still interested in *me*? Why don't we all go get a room and have ourselves a little party."

The pair of young men dropped their jaws at the tantalizing sight, high-fived one another, and yelled out, "Broooooo!"

The seven women shoved the pair of exuberant young men into the cheap hotel room. The entranced women giggled as they threw the pair onto the bed and began tearing off their shirts and pants. The men's engorged members were standing at attention as the perfumery clerk sauntered toward the bed. Her dark brown eyes were glazed over as she said in a near whisper, "You boys have been *very, very* bad. But that scent you are wearing is making *us* want to be *very, very* bad too. I wasn't even going to go out tonight, but then I detected your scent. Your cologne. And I knew it was *you*. I knew I had to *find* you. I knew that I needed to *have* you. So, I slipped this little number on and tracked you. I tracked you to that club where you were playing with my new friends. Are you ready for *us* to be *very, very* bad?

"Oh, fuck yeah, baby! We're gonna take turns with all of you, right, Bro?" "Oh yeah, Bro! One after another. We're gonna let you be as bad as you wanna be. And you're gonna like it."

The seven women began laughing hysterically before the perfumery clerk said, "Oh, we're going to like it alright. But just so you know. *These kittens have claws.*" The seven women began emitting a high-pitched growl as fur began bursting out of their skin. Full tails emerged from under their party dresses and their perfectly manicured fingernails became razor-sharp claws.

The shocked men squealed in anguish as claws and fangs began slicing their bodies apart. The merciless onslaught caused sheets of blood intermingled with bits of flesh to splatter upon the ceiling and walls. The unrelenting attack continued as the shrieking clowder of rape victims purged their minds of their crippling trauma. The men's torsos, legs, and arms were gushing blood from the deep, torturous lacerations. One of the women took her claws and sliced off one of the men's penises. It flung across the room, bounced off the wall, and landed on the crimson-coated floor. She pounced down on it and began batting it about before joining her sisters in their macabre frenzy of retribution.

The seven women woke up from the identical bizarre dream. They were now sipping drinks together around a circular booth. Their party dresses had been replaced by blue jeans and casual tops. They looked at one another and began laughing before the perfumery merchant said, "Wow. I have no idea how I got here, and I've never seen you ladies before, but it's like I know you. Like, we have some sort of special bond. Like, we've done something important together. It's just so weird."

"I know what you mean," another young lady said while cleaning an unknown red substance from under her fingernails. "I've totally lost track of tonight, but it's like I know you all. And truly love you all. And not only that. I feel like a huge weight has been lifted from off of me. I have this weird feeling that something heavy that I've been carrying around with me is just gone. Like we've all righted a wrong somehow. I feel happy. I feel free."

The seven smiling women nodded at one another as a gentlemen approached their table. "Why, hello there ladies," the older man said through a devilish grin. "I am quite sorry to bother you, but I am just so entranced by your obvious sisterhood that I would like to pay for your drinks this evening. Yes, it certainly looks as though you seven have something to celebrate. But ladies, a bit of a warning. Watch your bartender very carefully as he makes your drinks. And never leave your drink unattended. There are many nice men in this world, but there are also many scoundrels who have absolutely no sense of decency. No, anyone who would take a woman against her will is purely evil. And I pray to my lord that it never happens to any of you. But if you *do* find yourself in such a situation, just remember. You have claws for a reason, my dears. Now, I must be off. Just have the barkeep put your libations on my tab. My name is Picklesbee. Ta, ladies."

"Oh! Hey there, Bros!" Satan yelled out from his perch on his stationary bike. "I'll be right with ya. Almost done with my workout. Those fuckin' mean-girl cheerleader bitches said I was getting' pudgy. I gotta get back in shape. Alright. That's enough for today. Three minutes on this thing will really work up a sweat. Oh, and well, it's also hotter than hell down here. Get it boys? Hotter than hell? Because you *are* in fucking hell! Welcome home, Bros! So, you just had to hide your true nature by raping women and being all homophobic and shit, huh? Yeah, in my experience, bros who are homophobic are really using that as a cover. They're ashamed of who they are attracted to and who they truly are. So, instead of just sucking cock like their good lord intended, they bash those that have rightfully embraced their true nature. Don't you see? There's nothing wrong with any form of sexuality! It's fuckin' nature! You can't control that any more than you can control your eye color or height or anything else! Dumbasses. And what's worse is you take your unnecessary shame and use it to harm others! In your case, trying to be overly macho and raping women. Now, shame in and of itself doesn't get you an invitation to my sultry little abode. But raping women? That gets you a one-way ticket to my fucking hellish paradise.

"But you're in luck! You get a chance to finally be at peace with who you truly are! You like sex? You got it, Bros! You like cocks up the ass? Well, you got that too! For all of eternity. Yeah, there are some demons down here that are really gonna like your toned, sweaty bodies. A bunch of 'em. And they are going to give you what you have been craving. Over and over and over until your little bungholes explode! Then, we'll do it all over again. And boys, these fuckin' demons are *hung*. I mean, *insanely* fucking hung. So, enjoy! Now I gotta work on my biceps. Where did I put my five-pound weights?"

CHAPTER 10

LETTERS

Melissa rubbed a light spray of her new perfume onto her wrists, then on her supple neck. She gazed at her swooning eyes in her bathroom mirror while reliving her previous evening's encounter with her new friend. Her heart swelled as she thought about his elegant words that dripped off his tongue in his refined British accent. Her heart then sank as she thought about watching him solicit a lady of the evening outside of a liquor store. Her soul was consumed by jealousy as she imagined what he may have done with this White temptress in her slutty blue dress. She was not worthy of receiving his passion. She was nothing more than a common whore who was put upon this Earth to be exploited by brutal men. She was not intended to be with a man as refined as her Alexander. She was intended to be in a much darker place. Her trance was suddenly broken by the voice of her fiancée.

"Hey! You about done in there? I gotta go, bad!" Robert Jackson yelled. "Yeah, just a sec!" Melissa responded. "Keep your pants on!" She hastily exited the bathroom and stormed past him into the bedroom.

"Yeah, I'll keep my pants on!" Robert angrily replied. "There's really no point in taking them off, now is there? I mean, I've hardly seen you the past couple weeks. Like last night, for example? Where in the hell were you? What time did you finally drag your ass home?"

"Oh, feel the need to track my every move?" a fuming Melissa answered. "What? Controlling where we live, what we eat, who our friends are, and the fucking remote not good enough for you? Now you want to know my whereabouts every minute of every day? Do you want me to record my every movement in a spreadsheet and send it to you? Or better yet, why don't you just put a tracker on me? That way you'll know everything that I'm doing in real time. That work for you, Ace?"

"Hey, hey, hey," a backpedaling Robert replied. "Listen. What's with the hostility? I just haven't seen much of you recently. You seem distant. Like, even when you're here you're not really here. And this can be a dangerous town. I just asked where you were, that's all."

Melissa shook her blonde head to relieve her anger and said, "Yeah. Okay. Sorry. You're right. I have been distracted lately. And to answer your question, I had a few drinks with a friend, um with friends, and I just lost track of time. No big deal. I'm not sure what time I came home. Last night is a bit of a blur."

Robert desperately wanted to ask who her companions were but diplomatically decided to let it go for the moment. "Yeah, sure. We've all been there, right? You need an aspirin or something? And why are you wearing your old jeans and sweatshirt? Aren't you going to work today?"

"Uh, no thanks on the aspirin, I'll be fine," Melissa answered as she put on her old tennis shoes. "And yes, I'm going into work. Well, sort of. I'm not going into the store. Dad wants me to go into our attic and look for old photographs or newspaper articles about our family's business. He wants to put up kind of a museum telling the history of our family and the shop. So, I'm going to spend my day going through a pile of old dusty boxes looking at ghosts."

Robert instinctively started chuckling and said without thinking, "Well, you might want to be careful which newspaper articles that you put up on those walls. I mean, your family has a history of embezzlement, money laundering, tax evasion, and buying off politicians. Hell, even rape. And who the hell knows what else your ancestors were up to.

I mean, it's *your* family. You know all the rumors better than I do. All the rumors about murdering their competition or anybody that crossed them. Hell, it's even rumored that your Great-Great-Great-Great Grandfather murdered his father-in-law so that he could take over his business. So, I'm just thinking that *those* types of artifacts might not be the best for business, babe."

Melissa's anger crept back, and she clenched her delicate fists while glaring at the man that she had loved not so long ago. "What the fuck do *you* know about it? Yeah, my family may have a bit of a past, but who doesn't? I bet if I looked into *your* family's past, I'd find all kinds of twisted shit."

"Yeah, I bet you would," Robert volleyed back. "Yeah, all kinds of twisted shit. Twisted shit about how they were chained and forced to come here as slaves. Twisted shit about being whipped and raped. Twisted shit about how they were treated even in the North after they broke free from their shackles of slavery and came here. Twisted shit about being forced to live in slums. Denied their rights. Being passed over for promotions because of the color of their skin. And on and on. Hell, *I* still have twisted shit done to *me*. Racist comments at coffee shops. Little old ladies who clutch their purses and cross the street when they see me. Cops pulling me over and searching me for no fucking reason. Yeah, go ahead and dig around. You'll find some twisted shit. But not twisted shit that *my* family had ever done. Twisted shit that was done *to* my family by people who looked like *you*."

The seething pair stared at one another in a frigid silence before Melissa said, "Yeah, whatever. Just stop talking shit about my family. I'll see you later tonight. Probably. And don't call me 'babe!'" Robert jumped as the front door slammed behind Melissa.

"Oh, my lord," Melissa lamented as she surveyed the cluttered, dusty attic. "This is going to take forever. Has this place *ever* been cleaned out? Well, just one box at a time, Melissa. We'll get through this. I guess I'll start with this one." Melissa began going through the boxes and marveled at the portraits of her ancestors standing in front of their clothier store. The paintings turned to photographs as her family's history unfolded in front of her enthralled blue eyes. The men wore beaming smiles while standing proudly in front of their store. And sometimes there were rather nefarious looking men standing alongside them. The final picture that Melissa retrieved from the box and placed in her 'keep' pile was of her father and mother smiling in front of their grand marquis. "Wow. I haven't seen a picture of my mother in so long. I never really knew her. She died in 2001 when I was only two. I've been told that she had the most wonderful laugh. If Dad doesn't want to use this one, I think I'll keep it."

She gasped as she then opened a box labeled 'RESEARCH' and found another set of pictures of her mother. "Oh, dear lord," Melissa quietly stated as she flipped through the police photographs of her mother's decimated body that had been found in a dumpster behind their store. Her mother's face was completely swollen and nearly unrecognizable and her torso had been ripped open, fully exposing her lacerated internal organs. Melissa fought back her tears while peering at the ghastly images.

"Oh shit," she said as she closed the box and pushed it into a corner. "I'm glad Dad didn't include *those* in his family memoir. That was too painful to look at. And Dad has never given up on finding her killer. But maybe he should. Maybe he should just let it go and let her rest. She is in a better place. A place where she can be loved and respected. A place where she can be at peace. Perhaps her killer did her a favor. Maybe she is better off being an angel. Far too many women are exploited and treated harshly in this damned world. And speaking of being damned, here's a box labeled 'FAMILY INDESCRETIONS.' Probably not good for the wall of fame, but what the hell?"

As Melissa sifted through the voluminous amount of yellowed newspaper articles about her family, she said to herself, "Yeah, well, maybe Robert has a point. This *is* a sordid past. Tax evasion. Bribery. Dealing with foreign spies. Money laundering. Suspicion of rape. Suspicion of murder. None of them were ever convicted. It helps to have friends in high places, I suppose. But I know all about this. It's all in Dad's book.

And definitely not going up on a wall. Okay. I think I have enough stuff to at least get us started."

She stood up and dusted off her worn blue jeans before noticing something in the corner. "Huh, that chest looks really old. Wonder what's in that?" She kneeled in front of the large, aged wooden chest and opened it. A thick plume of dust rose from inside causing her to violently cough. She waved her hand sending the heavy particles flying throughout the room and began delicately removing the belongings of one Virgina Smith. "Oh wow. This is my Great-Great-Great-Great-Grandmother's stuff. This is wild. This might be worth a fortune. Or not," she concluded as she lifted a moth-eaten garment from the chest. "Well, *this* has certainly seen better days. As has this. And this. And here's some cracked plates. And…a locket. Oh, how lovely. It looks to be solid gold. Any pictures in here? Yep. Wow. Virginia looked just like *me*. I mean, we could be *twins*. Well, I wouldn't be caught dead with that hair style, but…oh, sorry about that Grandma. I'm sure it was all the rage in your day. No disrespect intended. And who is this on the other side? Why, this man looks just like…like…Alexander?"

A loving warmth swept over Melissa as she placed the locket around her neck and continued her inspection of the chest's contents. "Hmmmm. *These* look interesting. Old letters. Between her and…you've got to be kidding me. A man named Alexander. Weird. Man, this script is hard to read. Let's see here. What's his last name. Alexander, um…no way. Picklesbee?"

Melissa began voraciously consuming each letter between the long-forgotten pair. Beautifully written scripts professing his love for his Virginia floated into Melissa's romantic heart as she eagerly read each entry. His enthrallment over her descriptions of the wonders of America. His results on his medical school exams. His pride in her part in the success of her father's business. His horror at her descriptions of the dastardly American Civil War. His every detail of his life every day since their last correspondence. Then, in 1864, the letters stopped. "What the hell happened?" Melissa exclaimed as she felt around in the bottom of the chest. "Why did he stop writing? Did he find someone else? Did she? I mean, she obviously married the first Thomas Bartlesworth. But what happened to *him*? And could it be that *this* Alexander and *my*, um, Alexander are related? Wow, how weird would it be that I've fallen for, um, I mean, I've become friends with a man who is a descendent of one of my ancestor's lost loves? This is just too strange. And cool. I have to find out what happened. I have to…" Melissa stopped her thought the moment her hand pulled out another stack of letters. Unopened letters. Unopened letters from one Alexander Picklesbee.

Melissa pulled a scalpel from her purse and gently opened the ancient envelope. She carefully pulled out the letter and opened it with reverence. Her brilliant blue eyes widened as she began reading.

June 1, 1864

My dearest Virgina,

I received your letter informing me of your romance with another. I understand how such a distance can provide great strain upon the heart and how the temptations of another might be attractive for you. But I beg of you, my love. Please do not follow through with this man. I can make this right. I can set sail for America and conclude my studies there. You are my world. You are my life. Please, my love. Please write back and summon me. I shall be there in an instant. And I shall weep when I am once again in your tender embrace.

Your Love,
Alexander

"Awww, that poor man. My bitch great-great-oh, whatever, grandmother dumped him. That really sucks. What does this one say?"

December 25, 1864

Here I am alone on this Christmas evening staring at a lovely gift that I longed to send to you. I am hoping that my last correspondence became lost in the post. Please, my love, tell me what I can do to right whatever wrong I may have caused. I miss you so. Please write back. Please. The thought of you in the arms of another is driving me positively mad. I am lost without you.

Your Love,
Alexander

"Well, keep swinging for the fences, I suppose. Or just take a hint, dude. She isn't coming back. Huh. This one's dated much later."

June 8, 1865

Well, my love, I am sad to say that I have attempted to mend my broken heart by crawling into a bottle. Yes, I have acquired quite a taste for gin. And I have acquired quite a hatred of my dreadful studies. I am being discharged from school. I need your guidance. I need your love. I am lost without you. Please write back. If for no other reason than to tell me that you are well. I worry about you constantly. I have enclosed the present that I intended for you last Christmas. It is a locket. I do hope that the images of us together will rekindle the feelings that I know you must still have for me.

With Love,
Alexander

"Well, I guess enjoying a nip of gin runs in the family, huh? This is so sad. The suffering this poor man went through. Why didn't she open these letters? At least she must have opened the locket. I wonder if she ever wore it? Or just stuck it in this old chest. If only she had written him back, perhaps she could have alleviated his suffering. Or maybe she knew he'd be a long-distance creeper. Who knows. What's this one say?"

August 13, 1870

Hello Virginia,

It has been a while. I thought that I'd give you a bit of an update as to how my life has been going since you betrayed me. As if you care. I have developed quite the taste for gin. Yes, it is the only thing that can relieve my torment for a few moments. The torment that you caused by your betrayal, my dear. I was kicked out of that God-forsaken university and am employed as a traveling salesman. My employer sends me all over the countryside selling a variety of wares. But one day I shall once again use the skills that I learned at university. One day my hands will be used to heal. Or be used to wring your traitorous neck. I suppose we'll see, won't we dear? Until we meet again.

Alexander

"Well, *this* shit's taken a bit of a turn, now, hasn't it? Yeah, maybe it was for the best she didn't write back. Or maybe she should have. I mean, just open the letters and read them, bitch! How hard is *that*? You could have seen how hurt he was. You could have seen how his life was spiraling downwards. And because of you. You could have helped him. But you didn't. You just dumped him and went on with your life as if he had never existed. I can't really blame him for being pissed. Grandma was heartless, I guess. Maybe my family didn't get all of their misgivings from just the Bartlesworth side."

September 18, 1878

Oh, my Virginia, how I wish you were here to see this. Yes, my loathsome parents have finally kicked the bucket. And their bodies were so mangled that we couldn't even have an open casket for the visitation. Yes, it seems as though they were attacked by some ravenous animal. Perhaps an animal that had been harmed or wronged in some way. Perhaps an animal that felt he had no other choice but to defend himself against the tyranny of this world. They have not found this animal. Nor will they. My loving parents, of course, left me completely out of their will. It was just as I suspected, so I shall remain a penniless salesman for the rest of my days. But, if there is a God, they are looking up at my smiling face from hell.

Alexander

"Damn, he really hated his folks. He almost seems to be descending into madness. And this ravenous animal that he writes about. Seems as though he's on *its* side. Or is *he* the ravenous animal that will never be found? Has his hurt grown so much that he could have murdered his own parents? This is fascinating. And here's the last letter. Just a quick slice with my scalpel and all shall be revealed. I hope."

August 31, 1888

Hello, Virgina,
I am writing to you from my latest sales assignment. Yes, I must now trudge the dreary streets of White Chapel selling my useless wares. My life has become nothing more than drunken drudgery. But I did something tonight, my love. Something just for you. Something in your honor. Yes, tonight I finally used my hands for their true purpose. And as I was performing my task, the only image that I had in my mind was your beautiful face. The face that I love so dearly. The face that betrayed me. The face of a whore. Yes, a whore. You are all

nothing but whores who lure men then break them in two. You shatter men's psyches and their spirits. You torment us with your perfumed beauty and intoxicating words of love. But I have found a way to be at peace. I have found a way to exorcize your siren curse from my very soul. I have never felt so alive. So important. So powerful. You shall not hear from me again. You are dead to me. Bitch.

From Hell
Alexander

Melissa sat in a stunned silence as a warm throbbing encased her body. She felt an ecstatic shiver for a moment before regaining her composure. "Wow. That seemed just evil. I don't know what to make of that, but it kinda turned me on. And what *exactly* did he do? Was it something violent? Did he harm someone? Sure as hell reads that way. Whatever he did, that letter is creepy as fuck. And really interesting at the same time. And why does that date seem familiar? I'll have to ask Alexander about all of this. He probably has no idea about this guy, but it won't hurt to ask. He's just *got* to be related somehow. Same name. Same face. There *must* be a family connection. Ooooo, maybe he and I could explore this together. It would give me an excuse, um, I mean it would give us something to do together. This is simply fascinating. I can't wait to talk to him about it when I see him next week."

Melissa was descending the marble stairs of her family's provincial home when she heard a knock upon the door. She placed the box of treasures that she was carrying upon a side table and opened the heavy oak door. "Yes, can I help you?"

"Yeah, sorry to bother you miss," one of the two cheap-suited men said while flashing his badge. "I'm Detective Anderson and this is Detective Biggs. Your father said we could find you here. We just have a couple questions. Do you know a man named Picklesbee?"

"W-why yes, detective. Yes, I know a man by that name. Alexander. Alexander Picklesbee. What is it that I can help you with? Please tell me he hasn't been hurt."

"Naw, nothing like that," Biggs answered as his eyes focused on Melissa's expressions. "May we come in for a moment? This is just a formality. Shouldn't take long."

"Um, well, of course, detective," an apprehensive Melissa answered. "Won't you please come in?" The detectives entered the grand foyer that was highlighted with a marble staircase, dark mahogany floors, and a brilliant crystal chandelier. Detective Anderson looked around, whistled and said, "Wow. Pretty fancy-shmancy. I've never been in this joint before. A lot of my predecessors have been though. Yeah, Miss Bartlesworth, your family certainly has quite a history of being a bit, um, unruly. But not you. And not your dad. I think I read his book about your family's exploits about five times. It was fascinating."

"Um, thank you detective, we're all very proud of my father," Melissa replied. "Now, you said you had some questions for me?"

"Oh yeah, sorry," Detective Anderson said before Biggs took over.

"Now, Miss Bartlesworth…" "Um, Melissa," Melissa interrupted. "You can call me Melissa. No need for such formalities." "Very well, Melissa then," Biggs continued. "Such a lovely name. So, could you tell us about this Picklesbee character? What does he do for a living? How do you know him?"

"Well, we've only just met, actually," Melissa answered through a contrived chuckle that caused Biggs and Anderson to give one another a knowing glance. "I ran into him, I mean literally, a few days ago as I was rushing off to work. I wasn't paying attention and just ran right into his back. I felt like such a klutz and was so embarrassed by it. But he was so sweet and charming and understanding that I immediately fell, um, I mean liked him. He was so kind to walk me to my work. You know. Bartlesworth Clothiers. We had a lovely conversation and really hit it off. Then, a few days later I bought a record from him at the record shop. Mozart's Requiem. What an inspiring piece of work. Anyway…"

Melissa was cut off by Anderson. "So, Picklesbee works at the record store?" "Um, no, well, kinda," Melissa attempted to answer as her mind grasped for the right words. "You see, he's kind of a temporary employee. He just fills in whenever a local shop needs the help. I believe he worked at the perfumery today. I don't really think that he does it for the money. I think that he just enjoys being around people. He really is quite a people person. Why, we've only just met, and I feel completely comfortable opening myself up to him."

"Uh, huh, interesting choice of words," Biggs answered as he scribbled notes. "So, when is the last time you saw this Picklesbee character?"

Melissa frantically searched her mind for the possible reasons that they had for posing this question. *Why are they asking me this? Is he under suspicion for something? This is ridiculous. My man, um, I mean this man wouldn't harm a fly.* "Why? Is he in some sort of trouble? I can assure you detectives, that Alexander is a lovely, peaceful man. He certainly would not be involved in anything, um, nefarious."

"No, I'm sure not, miss," Anderson answered while being careful not to divulge the motives behind their questions. "As I said, this is just a formality. Just trying to scratch some names off the list. So, if you could please answer our question. When was the last time you saw him?"

"Well, *that* certainly is simple enough," Melissa answered with the same forced chuckle. "That would have been last evening. We met at a tea shop and was there for a while, then decided to have something a bit stronger, so we went to a pub down the block and had, as he would put it, a nip of gin." Melissa laughed at her poor attempt at a British accent. The detectives did not share her amusement.

"Okay," Anderson inquired further. "How late were you at this pub?" Melissa thought for a moment. She knew what time they had left the pub. She knew what time it was when she watched Alexander walking toward his apartment with his bottle of gin and cheap whore in tow. And she now knew what to tell the detectives in order to free Alexander from any further suspicion.

"Miss?" Biggs asked. "Could you please tell us what time it was when you left the pub?" "Oh, I'm so sorry," the chuckling Melissa responded. "I was just trying to remember. I had, as I said, a nip of gin last evening. Well, more than a nip, actually. Anyway, yes, I remember now. It was around eight-o-clock when we left the pub."

"Alright," Anderson said. "Anything else?" "Um," Melissa hesitated before answering. "Well, yes. But I just want to make perfectly clear that Alexander and I are just friends. There is nothing, um, romantic going on. I have a fiancée, and he wouldn't look too kindly upon what I'm about to tell you, so I am asking for your discretion, detectives. I am here to assist you with whatever it is that you are investigating and want to be completely open with you, alright?"

"Of course, miss," Biggs answered. "You have our word. We just want to know his whereabouts, that's all." "Okay then," Melissa stated as she wiped the noticeable sweat pouring from her brow. "So, here it is. We left the pub at eight. We went to a liquor store where he purchased a bottle of gin. We then went back to his apartment, had a few drinks, and continued our conversation. After a while, I went home."

Biggs and Anderson shot another round of glances at one another before continuing their interrogation. "Alright," Anderson began again. "So, you went back to his place?" "Yes," Melissa answered. "And the two of you were alone? No one else there?" "Yes," Melissa replied as her heart rate increased. "Did you leave anything behind? Any, um, clothing or anything?" "No," a near-panicked Melissa answered. "Alright, and what time was it when you left his apartment?" "One-O-Clock!" Melissa yelled out.

"Well, you certainly are certain of *that*," Biggs stated. "How can you be so sure it was one?"

"Um, um," a scrambling Melissa responded. "Um, because I remember looking at my watch and it said one and I said that I had lost track of time and needed to get home. You know. Back to my fiancée. That is why. I am truly sorry, detectives, but I really am in a bit of a rush. Is there anything else that I can help you with?"

Anderson and Biggs looked at each other for a moment then nodded. They reluctantly closed their notebooks and smiled before Biggs said, "Thank you miss for your time. You have been quite helpful. If you think of anything else from that night, you know, just anything that seemed out of the ordinary to you, please give us a call. Here's my card."

Melissa closed the door behind the departing detectives and slumped to the floor. "Oh my," she said to herself as she willed her heart to slow down. "I hope I did the right thing. I hope they haven't already spoken to him. I need to talk to Alexander. But not tonight. They may be watching me. No, tomorrow morning. I'll find him tomorrow morning. After I call Dad and tell him that I'm still going through his attic, and I'll be late for work."

"She's lying," Biggs said to his partner as they threw their case files upon a beaten wood conference room table. "Yep," Anderson answered. "Well, either *she's* lying, or *he* is. Let's review their statements. It seems as though we have several possibilities. Either *he's* telling the truth and was alone with a Black prostitute. Or *she's* telling the truth, and *she* was with *him* until one and there *was* no prostitute. But why would he lie about that?" Biggs immediately answered his partner's query. "To protect her reputation? Maybe they're more than friends. Maybe he's trying to protect her by concealing their little tryst. We walk in. Her panties are on the floor. He needed to invent a story to explain them to protect her." "Yeah, yeah, or *maybe*," Anderson continued. "They're *both* lying. *He* was there. *She* was there. And the *prostitute* was there. Maybe their 'just friendship' has a kinky side. It's not like that shit's never happened before." "Yeah, could be," Biggs replied. "But here's another question. If there *was* a prostitute in his room that night, which one? The Black with the red dress? Or the White with the blue dress? We really shoulda found a way to confiscate those panties. A simple DNA test would prove who was there. Black prostitute? White prostitute? Or kinky little Melissa?" "Yeah, or all three," a frustrated Anderson said as he shook his head.

"And not only that," Biggs offered. "But we need to figure out if there's a connection. We now have *two* dead hookers on our hands. We have the one right outside of Picklebee's apartment and we have the one from a few nights ago. Another poor young woman who was found in another back alley in our Burrough. And also, not far from Picklesbee's place. We need to face it. We have a serial killer on our hands. And so far, Picklesbee is looking good for it."

"Well, not necessarily," Anderson countered. "Yeah, two dead hookers. Yeah, both found in back alleys. Yeah, both bodies were mutilated in the same way. But it could be a copycat. The condition of the first girl's remains was all over the news. The second one could be a copycat. We can't dismiss that possibility. We may be looking for *two* killers. But whether it's one or two, we definitely have a copycat. Whoever is doing this is using a very similar M.O. as Jack the Ripper."

"Oh fuck, that's all we need," Biggs said. "A fucking ghost to come out of retirement and start hacking women up. Wait. I just thought of something. What time did the coroner estimate the time of death of the most recent victim?" "Uh, let me look here," Anderson said as he skimmed through the coroner's initial report. "Between Twelve-Thirty and One-O-Clock. The same time that Melissa said she left Picklesbee's. Okay, okay. Hear me out. Picklesbee and Melissa and the White prostitute go back to his place. They play around, things get a little rough and...oops. Her death is an accident, but they need to cover it up, so they make it look like the first murder a few days ago to cover their tracks. Bingo! Not a serial killer! Two or maybe *three* different killers. One intentional, the other an accident that this pair tried to cover up. This is going to be easier than a single serial killer. Those bastards are clever."

"And this one has a bit of a humane streak," a woman's voice was heard saying. The Director of Forensics, Jessica Townsend, entered the room and placed another file on the table. She adjusted her white overcoat and sat at the head of the table. She brushed her dangling black curls from her brown eyes and said, "We just completed the toxicology tests. Our first victim had some pot in her system. No booze. Our second victim had gin in her system. Coincidence? Maybe. But they *both* had a heavy dose of an extract from a flower. A White Poppy. Coincidence? Highly, highly unlikely. No, gentlemen, both of these women were murdered by the same person. Or people. But our perp doesn't want his or her victims to feel any pain. Well, at least physical pain. They inject them with this extract that paralyzes the nervous system. The victim can't move. Can't scream. Can't feel anything at all. No, they don't feel it as their executioner cuts them open and removes their organs. One at a time. They just lay there and live with the realization that they are being meticulously and systemically torn apart. Until they finally bleed out and their heart mercifully stops beating. You are looking for someone with surgical skills or who is really good with their hands. Construction? Wood working? Tailor? Who knows. And they are somebody who is merciful and vengeful at the same time. Our perp doesn't want them to feel pain, but they want them to see their rage. In other words, you have a serial killer. And this motherfucker is one sick puppy."

Anderson and Biggs stared at Townsend for a moment. They looked down at their files when they noticed her wipe a tear from her caramel cheek. Biggs finally broke the morbid silence. "White Poppy. Why does that sound familiar? Let me look in the computer. See if we can get a hit on any victims that had White Poppy in their syst…" His voice trailed off as he stared at the screen. "What? What is it?" Townsend asked. "Hey, buddy, what did you find?" Anderson inquired. "Yeah, there's a hit alright," Biggs answered as he shook his head in disbelief. "Just one, though. One woman who was brutally murdered twenty-three years ago had the same extract in her system. This has never been solved. Completely cold. Anybody wanna take a guess on her name? Give up? Amanda. Amanda Bartlesworth. Wife of Thomas Bartlesworth the VI. Mother of one Melissa Bartlesworth. And certainly no connection to Picklesbee. Well, that we know of. But just come over here and take a look at these crime scene photos. Look familiar? What did we just say about coming out of retirement?"

Anderson and Townsend gasped as they looked upon the shredded body and scattered organs of Amanda Bartlesworth. "Okay, this just got fucking interesting," Anderson said as he rushed back to his case files. "Step One: We gotta figure out who is lying. Picklesbee or Melissa. Or both. That should be simple enough. Have vice bring in every Black working girl that hangs out by the liquor store. We find that Black prostitute in a red dress, then we can scratch Picklesbee off the list. We don't? He's still our prime suspect."

"Yeah, well," Biggs added. "We may want to start looking into who was in Amanda Bartlesworth's orbit around the time of her death too. I think we need to re-open this cold case and toss it in the mix. Was this Picklesbee around back then? Can't be Melissa. She woulda been a toddler. Unless she was a toddler sent straight from hell. If there's no connection between Amanda and Picklesbee, and his Black hooker can give him an alibi, then we can move on. But first, we gotta find that Black hooker. And get those fuckin' panties."

The following morning, Melissa waited for Alexander outside of his apartment. She wore a baggy sweatsuit, jogging shoes, and a ball cap over her blonde ponytail. Her heart leapt when she saw him leave his building and casually saunter down the sidewalk. She followed from across the street and watched as he stopped at a newsstand to purchase a paper. Several moments later, she crossed the street. As she passed the newsstand, she glanced at a blaring headline. SECOND "RIPPER" VICTIM FOUND IN QUEENS. "Aw shit," Melissa muttered to herself. "What have I gotten myself into?"

She continued watching from behind a light pole as Alexander approached the local liquor store. Her heart was bursting as she watched his dignified frame glide down the sidewalk. He wore an impossibly charming smile as he greeted his fellow passers-by. He stopped in front of the liquor store. Melissa's heart then wilted as he turned and smiled at a Black woman wearing a very revealing red dress. He came closer to her, stared directly into her eyes, and began whispering something.

CHAPTER 12

DEROGATORY

"Well, good morning, my dear, Alexander politely stated to a statuesque African American woman wearing a skimpy red dress. "Hiya, lover," she suggestively answered. "Lookin' for a date? Want to start your day out right?"

Alexander chuckled slightly then said, "Well, that certainly is an enticing offer, but I'm afraid that I will have to decline at the moment. But let me have one look at those beautiful brown eyes of yours." The woman's long, fake eyelashes batted over her mahogany eyes as she stared deeply back at Alexander. His eyes turned from a charming blue to pitch black as he whispered to her, "Yes, good girl. Just stare into my eyes for a moment. My name is Alexander. Alexander Picklesbee. You shall remember my name. And should anybody inquire, we were together two nights ago at my apartment. I met you outside of this liquor store and we went back to my domicile. We drank some gin and then canoodled. You do know what that word means, don't you dear? Yes, of course you do. I paid for your quite generous services, and you left my apartment around nine-fifteen. Oh, and you seem to have left these. I wish to return them to you now." Alexander reached inside the pocket of his pin-striped suit and retrieved the pair of panties that had been left by the blonde call-girl. "Here, my dear. These are yours, remember? And they are quite exquisite. I have laundered them for you so that you may wear them now, if you wish."

Alexander's eyes returned to their normal, inviting blue. The woman shook her head, looked back at Alexander and exclaimed, "Well, hiya big Al! Come back for seconds? Yeah, you know where to come for the good lovin' don't you sweetheart? I had such a great time with you the other night. The gin was wonderful. And thank you so much for returning my panties. These cost me a pretty penny. Well, actually, they just cost me a blow job on the teenage clerk, but hey, time is money. So, whadaya say there, big Al? Should we go for another ride?"

Alexander chuckled once again and said, "Well, that *is* an enticing offer, but I'm afraid that I am working at this liquor dispensary today. Perhaps another time, my dear. Perhaps we can get together again. Yes, perhaps very, very soon."

"Alright, love," the woman said with a suggestive wink before strutting down the street on her six-inch pumps. Alexander grinned after her and entered the liquor store. "Well, here I am, my good man. Just as we agreed. Enjoy your day off. And rest assured your fine establishment will be well cared for today. Ta, ta."

Melissa watched as the dazed liquor store owner left his shop. She clutched the locket that was concealed under her baggy sweatshirt and said to herself, "Oh, man. I hope he doesn't get upset with me," before entering the shop. Her heart began pounding as she watched him put on his bright, white apron behind the counter. She cautiously approached him and said, "Um, hey there, Alexander."

"Melissa, my dear!" Alexander beamed. "My, what a lovely surprise. Why, we aren't supposed to get together again for nearly a week. Is this coincidence, or have you sought me out?"

"Um," Melissa began answering while her mind whirled. "Um, no, I was, um, looking for you. Um, well, you see, these two detectives came to see me yesterday and, um,"

"Ah, yes," Alexander interrupted. "Detectives Anderson and Biggs, I presume?" "W-why, yes," Melissa answered. "How did you know?" "Well,"

Alexander replied. "Those two gentlemen visited me as well yesterday morning. Perhaps you haven't heard. There has been yet another murder of a local working girl. And her remains were found in the alley right behind my apartment. Isn't that ghastly? Such a horrific act committed right outside of my home. Why, it gives me the chills just thinking about it. So naturally, the detectives were questioning everyone in the building to see if we had seen or heard anything. I told them that I hadn't, and that was the extent of it. What was it that they asked *you*, my dear?"

Melissa's mind was flooded with thoughts as she searched for the appropriate response. She knew that he had been with the murdered hooker that evening. She had seen him with her. Should she reveal this to him? Should she reveal that she had developed a bit of a habit of stalking him? Should she tell him the fake alibi that she had told the detectives? Or perhaps she needed to just stay out of it at this point. And what about those letters and locket from a past Alexander Picklesbee? Are they related? She clutched at the locket that was under her sweatshirt while trying not to hyperventilate.

"Melissa, my dear?" Alexander asked. "Is there something wrong? You seem quite upset about something. Please. Tell me."

Melissa let out a deep breath and said, "Yeah, okay. Um, listen. These detectives came to my father's house yesterday. I was there going through old family photos and stuff for our clothier store, and I came across some letters that…no, that isn't important right now. Anyway, they asked me about you. You know, like how we met and stuff. And they also asked me if I was with you the previous night."

"I see," Alexander said while dusting bottles of cheap wine. He could feel the darkness rising in his soul as he tentatively continued. "And just what was it that you told these detectives, Melissa? I surely hope that you were truthful with them. Any sort of fabrication might, um, complicate things for me."

Melissa's body was saturated with sweat as she attempted to answer. "Um, well, listen. I, um, I lost an earring, and I circled back that night to try to find it and I just happened to see you with a blonde woman in a blue dress." Alexander sensed that she was lying about the earring. She had *not* lost an earring. No, she had followed him for some reason. The thought made his heart swell. "So, um, anyway, that woman I saw you with fits the description of the woman that was murdered. I, um, saw it in the newspaper this morning."

The newspaper? Alexander thought to himself. *That poor woman's description was not in the newspaper. No, the police are keeping a lid on that at the moment. And even so, she would not have seen that description before the detective's inquiry of her. What is my Melissa hiding? Should I search her soul? No. I'm afraid of what I might find. No, let her keep her secrets and let her fate be her fate. I want every moment with her to be a delightful surprise.*

"Anyway, I had seen you with her and I just knew that someone as charming and dignified as you could not have been involved so, I told them the truth. Then, um, well, I kinda fabricated a little bit of it."

"Do tell, my dear," Alexander stated while straightening bottles of rum. "Well," Melissa continued. "I told them that we went for a spot of tea. Hey, I think I'm getting your British accent down. Okay, not important. Then, I told them that we went to a pub and had some gin. We were there until around eight and this is where I kinda made some stuff up. I told them that we went back to your place. I emphasized to them that we were just friends and that there's nothing going on, of course, because I have a fiancée, but he might not look too kindly about me staying out with another man. They told me that they'd be, um, discreet. Anyway, I told them that I left a little after one. Oh, and they wanted to know if it was just the two of us, and I said yes. Oh, I hope that my little fib hasn't caused you more trouble. I just wanted to provide you with an alibi so that they didn't harass an innocent man. Please tell me that this will be okay."

Melissa's brilliant blue eyes began welling up with tears. The sight tore at Alexander's swooning heart. He gently wiped a tear from her perfectly pale cheek and said in a reassuring voice, "Now, now. Nothing to be upset about. This will be fine. Quite fine. I did have another, um, explanation of who I had spent time with following our time together, but that will be fine. I can clear this all up, quite simply. Yes, you and I went back to my place and drank a bit more gin. We were alone. You left a bit after one. I had not been completely truthful out of discretion and respect for your relationship with another man. Yes, that should take care of it. Nothing to worry about, my dear." Alexander's thoughts then darkened as his internal, demonic voice said, *no, nothing to worry about. Unless they find the Black hooker that I told them that I was with. This requires a bit of housekeeping.* "And one more item that I want to be quite clear with you about. Yes, I was accompanied home that evening by the poor soul who was ravaged in my alley. But I had nothing to do with her untimely, and rather brutal, demise. She left my home around nine-fifteen and I did not see her again until the next morning. In that rather unfortunate state."

A relieved Melissa smiled up at her kind friend and said, "Yes, oh good. Okay. Yes, I knew that you couldn't have been involved in something so horrendous. And that's our story then. Thank you for understanding. I'm so sorry that I lied, but…"

Alexander then cut her off. "Tut, tut, my dear. No need to apologize. And certainly, no need to thank me. It is *I* that should be thanking *you* for, how is it that the kids phrase it? Ah, yes. Thank you for having my back. A strange phrase of gratitude, but thank you, nonetheless. Is there anything else, my dear? Anything more that you need to tell me?"

Melissa continued to grasp the concealed locket before concluding, "Um, no. Well, there is *one* little thing that I want to ask you about, but that'll just give us something interesting to talk about next week. We are still on for next week, aren't we?"

Alexander briefly wondered what else Melissa was keeping from him before gleefully stating, "Oh, my yes, my dear. Same time. Same place. But perhaps we should skip the spot of tea and go right to the pub for a nip of gin? Yes, we are most certainly on, as you phrase it. Why, demons from the pits of hell could not keep me from an engagement with such a charming woman." He delicately lifted her left hand to his lips and gently kissed it. Melissa blushed and rapidly said, "Well, okay then. Sorry to rush off, but I'm late for work. You know where to find me if you need anything. Otherwise, I'll see you next week. Ta!"

Ta, indeed, a chuckling Alexander thought to himself. *I do believe I might be rubbing off on her. And she is so exciting and vibrant. Much more so than my Virginia. My Virginia, who betrayed me and caused me to do such vile things. My Virginia, who banished me to hell. If it weren't for her betrayal, I would never have engaged in such abysmal acts. And now, her descendent is within my grasp. Will she betray me as well? Is her heart filled with deceit too? No, my Melissa is not my Virginia. Just let go of your anger, Picklesbee. My Melissa is trustworthy. She is loyal. She is, how does it go again? Oh, yes. She has my back. Now, I really must arrange a date with that beautiful Black goddess. Yes, she has unwittingly become a loose end. A loose end which must be cut off. But not until after work. My lord needs a new plaything today. Now, who shall it be? No, not you. Nor you. Nor you. Ah, there you are. Yes, my lord does enjoy playing with bigots, heh, heh, heh. Come to the counter, my friend. I have a special liqueur. Just for you.*

Melissa's heart was racing as she left the store while hiding her blushing face under the brim of her ball cap. She looked up, and her heart went from euphoria to silent rage. *There you are, you whore,* she thought to herself as she glared at the African American call girl strutting up and down the pavement. *You think you're better than me? You think that you can satisfy my Alexander more than I? Oh, you poor, exploited thing. How is it that you have been relegated to a life of lying under sweaty, grunting, fat men just to pay your bills? I almost feel sorry for you. Almost. You lost my sympathy when you tempted my Alexander. Ah, there you go, slut. There's a new John pulling up. Looks like you'll be able to make rent this month, bitch. Wait. That's not a John. Why that's...that's...Dad?*

The unemployed White man exited the liquor store with a rare smile on his face. He took a bottle of vodka from his plain, brown bag and affectionately cradled it in his arms. "Yeah, I've never heard of this brand before. The new guy at the liquor said that you pack a special kick. That you'll make me relate to the world as my true nature intends. And that drinking you will get me what I deserve. I doubt that. I doubt that it gets me my job back. I mean, what the fuck? Everybody pilfers a little off the top here and there. It was just an excuse. Just an excuse to get rid of me so that they could promote that fuckin' (derogatory term omitted). Yeah, there's fuckin' discrimination in this country alright. Discrimination against us Whites! Against us *true* 'Murikkkans! All these fuckin' (derogatory term omitted), and (derogatory term omitted), and (derogatory term omitted), flooding into *my* country and taking *my* fucking job! The fuckin' government lets these fuckers infest our country and pays them to do it! Just so they can get their vote! It's all fuckin' rigged. Pay these fuckin' (derogatory term omitted) with my hard-earned tax dollars so that they can rape *my* women and eat *my* pets and take *my* fuckin' job! Here for asylum? Buuuuullshiiit. No, that's the fuckin' deep state. Made up of a bunch of rich elites that are building an army of fuckin' (derogatory term omitted) to take over the country. Yeah, but I won't let 'em. I'll take out as many of those fuckin' (derogatory term omitted) as I can. Just like I did a few nights ago. Hell, I probably did them a favor. Those two roaches are in a warm hospital getting free food and free health care. That I fuckin' paid for. The world is fucked up. I can't even use my food stamps for this booze. Naw, you won't give me what I deserve. But I sure as hell hope you can get me drunk. Yeah, there's a nice bench right under that tree. And right across from a bunch of (derogatory term omitted). Fuck you, motherfuckers. *My* tree, *my* bench, *my* fuckin' country."

The bigot adjusted his metaphorical tin-foil hat, sat down on the bench, and glared across the wide park sidewalk at a group of young African American men. He unscrewed the cap of his newly purchased vodka, looked adoringly at it, and took his first swig. "Damn, that *is* good," he said aloud. He took another swig, and a warmth swept over him. His perpetually tense body relaxed as his mind was freed from the shackles of inhibition. As was his mouth. He glared over at the group of five men, smiled at them and said, "Hey (derogatory term omitted)!..."

"Yeah, you probably shouldn't have said *that*," a smirking Satan said to the damned soul of his new arrival. "I mean, it's *one* thing to be a bigot, but you, motherfucker, took *that* shit to a whole new level! Wow. I mean, I thought that what you bigoted motherfuckers actually say was bad enough, but holy shit! The actual shit that is rattling around in your fucked-up heads that you *don't* say? Well, it nearly brings a tear to my eye. The way that you spew your needless hateful rhetoric is, well…you know what? I'm just gonna come out and say it. It's art. It is fucking art the way you motherfuckers detest other people. And if all that shit wasn't enough, then you got their mothers, sisters, and wives involved *too*! Damn. Nerves of fuckin' steel on this one. Too bad the rest of you isn't though.

"Yeah, those guys really enjoyed kicking the shit out of you. What was it first? The ribs? Damn, they just snapped! And through all your fat too! Then, your face. Fist after fist after fist just pummeling your lily-white mug until it was all swollen and purple and shit. And speaking of shit, you just kept talkin' it! Throughout the whole thing you just kept calling them racial slurs over and over. Which pissed them off even more, so they beat you harder and harder! Fuck, that was fun to watch. Oh! But the cherry on the fuckin' top of this beat-down sundae had to have been that Black cop!

"Yeah, he came by, saw what was happening, and your assailants just froze. They're standing over you with their bloody fists clenched and didn't say a word. They knew they were fucked. Until you had to open your big fuckin' mouth! You looked up at that cop with blood and drool dripping off of your ripped open lips and said, um, what exactly did you say? I wanna get this shit right. Oh, yeah! You looked up at him and said, 'What the fuck are you looking at (derogatory term omitted)? Why don't you go back to the fuckin' jungle and fuck your ugly ass momma up her ugly gorilla ass. I heard she likes it like that. Or better yet, why don't you be a good little slave and fetch me some chains to put on ya. Now get goin'. Boy.' Ooooooh snap, motherfucker! That cop was so pissed! He just looked at those five young men, smiled at them, and said, 'You gentlemen have a fun day in the park. Just clean up after you're done, okay?' Then he stood there laughing while those five guys beat the ever-living fuck out of you with *his* baton until your skull finally cracked open and your brains came tumbling out. Damn, that was fun. And well deserved. And now you're here.

"That's right, motherfucker! Welcome to hell! Your racist, bigoted ass is *all mine* for all eternity! But hey, why not use this as a learning opportunity? Lemonade out of lemons? Yeah, why don't we teach you a thing or two about history. About slavery. About the brutality of enslaving another human being. The torture. The whippings. The rapes. The endless hours of toiling under the hot sun with no food or water. Yeah, we're gonna make you a better person. You're gonna work in the cotton fields. Didn't know we had those did you? Well, we do! Where do you think China gets all of its cotton to make its cheap socks and underwear? From right fuckin' here! Yeah, from this point on, you are going to spend every moment of every day working in torturous conditions picking cotton. You will get no breaks. No food. No water. Your legs will feel like they're about to fall off, and your back will be near breaking. And if you slow down, well there will be plenty of my devilish little demons around to whip your little pink ass worse than those guys did up on Earth. And you're going to do all of this while wearing fifty-pound chains. Which reminds me. Go fetch me those chains. Boy. Heh, heh, heh."

CHAPTER 13

THE BEST FUCKING BOOK YOU WILL EVER READ

"What do you want to bet that this is the hooker that we've been looking for?" Detective Anderson said sullenly to the nodding Detective Biggs. "Certainly fits the description," Biggs answered while their uniformed colleagues taped off the cluttered back alley behind the neighborhood liquor store. "Young. Tall. African American. And a red dress. Or, at least what is left of it. Could be the one that Picklesbee says was with him the other night. Or not. There are a *lot* of working girls that fit her description. You notice anything missing?"

"Yeah," Anderson answered. "No underpants. Amongst other things. He's getting more savage. Her entire cavity has been cleaned out. The other two had their internal organs removed, but they were laid out neatly. If that's possible. This one? Just look at this mess. This was done in a fit of rage. The organs weren't just removed, but ripped apart and strewn everywhere."

"And the blood was used as ink," Biggs observed as they carefully stepped over shredded kidneys and intestines to inspect the far brick wall. "PRAY 4 THE WHORE. Huh. First message that he's left. So, we're supposed to pray for her soul but condemn her actions? Am I reading this right? He has both sympathy and rage towards her? Why do I get the feeling that we already know what's going to be found in the toxicology report?"

Anderson silently nodded while looking around the blood-soaked alley before saying, "Yeah. White Poppy extract. It's gotta be Picklesbee. Has to be. But why her? Why would he murder his alibi?"

"I don't know," Biggs replied while taking off his blue latex gloves. "So much doesn't make sense. *Is* she his alibi? Was she even with him a couple nights ago? Maybe it was her *and* the blonde that was with him, and he needed to shut her up? Or maybe this is the wrong hooker? But none of the other working girls recognized his description. Not that they're always the most reliable sources, but still. Or maybe *Melissa* is telling the truth and *she's* his actual alibi? But why lie about *that*? Well, somebody's lying and it's starting to piss me off. We gotta get this asshole off the street. These young women didn't deserve the life they were forced into and they sure as hell didn't deserve to be executed by this maniac. Torn open and ripped apart while lying there watching. Aware of everything that is happening to them until they bleed out. Then this asshole *really* goes to work on the corpse. I agree. Picklesbee is our perp. Has to be."

"Excuse me detectives?" a young officer interrupted. "I'm sorry to disturb you, but we've obtained some information from our neighborhood canvas. "Yeah, what do ya got?" Biggs asked. "Well sir," the attractive officer began as a tuft of brunette hair peaked from under her hat. "There were several witnesses that said that someone fitting the description of Picklesbee worked at this liquor store yesterday. Just him. The owner wasn't in. When we spoke to the owner, he said that he had no idea what we were talking about. Then he thought for a moment and said that he had no recollection about yesterday at all. He was just blank. So, *that's* weird. Plus, we've got that guy who was beaten to death in the park. We've tracked his movements, and he was seen here yesterday buying a bottle of something just before his death. Maybe no connection, but that's two murders yesterday that are connected to this liquor store."

"Yeah, well," Anderson interjected. "They do say that drinking will send you to an early grave. And those are two isolated incidents. Totally different M.O.'s. Totally different victims. Totally different investigations. Anything else?"

"Yes, sir," the officer replied while flipping through her notebook. "Two witnesses also saw a man matching Picklesbee's description talking with a tall Black woman wearing a red dress outside of this store."

"Alright, we got a connection," Biggs excitedly stated. "We have a dead hooker just a few blocks from his apartment. Another in the alley *behind* his apartment. And now, one that fits the description of his alibi found behind the *very store* that several people say he worked at yesterday. *And* that he was seen speaking with. I know it's all circumstantial, but it should be enough for a search warrant. And I want samples of everything. His fingerprints. Hairbrush. Toothbrush. Knives or anything that could be used to do…this. I'll call the D.A. and get them going on that while you get whatever forensics they find to Jessica. We're going to get this asshole."

"Um, Detective?" the officer interjected. "There's just one more thing. A woman fitting the description of our victim was seen getting into a car yesterday morning. It was the last time that she was seen. The witness is a bit of a neighborhood watch type. Well, actually, she's a bit of a prudish bitch, if you ask me, but she watches the girls get into cars and writes their John's plate numbers down."

"Oh, yeah," Anderson said. *"Mrs. Gallows.* We've heard from her. Repeatedly. And yeah, you're right. She *is* an uptight old bitch. Listen, I don't blame people for not wanting sex for hire on their streets, but this broad takes it to a whole new level. She actively shames these people. Puts up flyers. Calls the wives of the Johns and sends them pictures of their husbands in compromising positions. Takes pictures of the girls and puts them up with the word 'WHORE' across it and…"

Biggs and Anderson looked at one another with widened eyes for a moment. They then both started chuckling before Anderson continued. "Yeah, I guess everybody who uses that word is a suspect, huh? But not Gallows. She's pushing seventy and her hands are all arthritic and shit. Physically, she's not capable of something like this."

"She is in her heart though," a still chuckling Biggs replied. "It's ironic.

This woman that professes to be so pure and virtuous used to run one of the nastiest S&M shops in town. This wasn't just dressing up in leather and a little spanking. This was really depraved shit that she carried out. Whether her Johns wanted her to or not. There *was* no safe word. She got her money up front and tortured those poor bastards. She really got off on making them scream. And watching them bleed. And they, of course, never reported it out of embarrassment. No, that isn't something that you want to put into a public record. But one of her old Johns got even about thirty years ago. After she untied him, he broke her fingers. Every one of them. That's why they're crippled up now. After that, she was out of the S&M business. Well, kind of. She had been taking pictures and videos of all of her Johns, so the moment she got out of the hospital, she went from S&M to blackmail. Made a fortune. And a lot of enemies. Then, about five years ago she found Jesus, or some shit, and since then she has been a self-proclaimed crusader against the sex trade. Now she's just an old prude who wears clasped up collars on dowdy old dresses, clutches the Bible, and spews scripture. Whatever. If there's a hell, that nasty old bitch is going to end up there. For a lot of reasons. But she *is* accurate with her information. So just what did our dear Mrs. Gallows have to say?"

The officer shook her head in dismay before answering. "Yeah, we got the license plate number. It belongs to a Thomas Bartlesworth the VI. He's the owner of Bartlesworth Clothiers. I've also heard that he's a bit, um, connected. Do you know of him?"

Anderson let out a deep sigh then hung his shaking head for a moment. "Yeah, we know of him. Shit. All roads are leading to either Picklesbee or that damned clothing store, aren't they? Alright. First things first. Search warrant for Picklebee's place. Forensics. Then, we'll deal with the Bartlesworths. Thomas *and* Melissa. Now, what is your name, officer?"

The officer beamed at the inquiry as she stood at attention and proudly declared, "I am Officer Yun Song, sir!" "Alright, calm down there, Officer Song," a chuckling Biggs said. "This isn't *Platoon*. Anyway, nice work. Keep canvassing and report directly to us. And keep

Bartlesworth's name out of it for the moment. I don't want anybody else to know about his involvement. You know. To prevent leaks. Got it?"

"Yes sir!" Officer Song declared before returning to her squad car. "Ambitious little thing, isn't she? And kinda cute." a grinning Anderson stated. "Keep it in your pants, Anderson," Biggs scolded. "I'm not covering for you for that shit again. Especially what you did to that last girl. Come on. Let's catch this asshole."

"Thank you so much and do come again. I truly hope that you enjoy that book, young lady," A smiling Alexander said to a four-year-old girl while handing her a bag containing *Annamazing! Let's Be Friends!* "Oh, I'm sure she *will*," her doting mother said. "It just looks adorable. And it's *never* too early to start teaching our kids that it's wrong to be a bully. Thank you!"

"Yes, adorable indeed. As is your precious daughter. Ta!" Alexander said after them. His sparkling blue eyes turned black as he scanned the souls of the various patrons that were browsing the shelves of the independent bookstore. *Well, this is quite uneventful,* he thought to himself. *I really should have known better. Why would I choose a bookstore to hunt my prey? Most people who frequent independent bookstores are intelligent, civil, and freethinkers. Not the sort of lot that you would find toiling in fire and brimstone. No, for that I should have gone to an adult bookstore. I'm sure there's quite an assortment of depraved individuals who frequent those. I know that I certainly enjoy them, and I'm not exactly an angel. Quite the opposite, actually. Another day, perhaps. No, this may have been a failed experiment. Ah well. If nothing else, I have met some fine people here today.*

His heart, along with his body, suddenly jumped as a scowling woman slammed a 666-page book down on the counter with a loud thud. Alexander saw a pair of arthritic old hands before looking up and smiling at the woman. His smile was not only for customer service but also because of his joyous realization that his day had not been wasted after all. *Yes,* he thought to himself. *Why, you are perfect. What a black heart this old bitty has. What torturous acts she has committed on people. Both men and women. Both physical and emotional. She may not look like she is long for this world, but I can sense that her mean spirit will keep her on this earth for quite some time. Perhaps as long as there are roaches. Yes, my lord will enjoy having her. Perhaps we should accelerate her departure, heh, heh, heh.*

"Yes, my dear, what is it that I can do for you?" Alexander said while wearing his charming smile. "First of all," the glowering woman answered while adjusting her tightly buttoned collar on her dowdy dress. "You may *not* call me 'dear.' I am *not* your 'dear'. I am *not* one of your immoral playthings. Yes, I know what goes on in a man's soul. I know that your charming demeanor is nothing more than a ruse to lure women into your bed so that you can commit depraved acts to their bodies." *Well, that certainly is true,* Alexander thought. *But you do not know everything that is in* this *man's soul. But I certainly know everything that is in yours. Dear.*

"My apologies," Alexander answered. "How may I help you, um, miss?" The old woman snorted and replied, "If you *must* refer to me at all, you may refer to me as Mrs. Gallows." "Ah, Mrs. Gallows," Alexander replied. "Very well, then. How may I be of assistance to you, Mrs. Gallows?"

"This…this…book," she answered with a sneer. "I am here to return it. I have the gift receipt. I do not know why anyone would think that I would enjoy such…such…utter trash." Alexander looked down at the thick book and read its title. *Revenge of the Downtrodden. The Hanging Chads Omnibus, Vol. 1.* "I see," Alexander replied. "I do not see any problem with a refund for this mada…um, Mrs. Gallows. But may I inquire as to what you find objectionable? So that I may warn other potential customers."

Mrs. Gallows glared at him and snorted once again. "What do I find objectionable? Everything. Everything about this so-called book is a travesty. The profane language. The violence. The gore. The anti-religious messaging. The attempted pro-woke indoctrination. Everything about this pile of trash is offensive. And it was quite obvious that this supposed author did his own editing. Why, he has no idea how to use commas. And his sentence structure is laughable. This is pure, unadulterated, poorly written blasphemy and I *will not* allow it to poison my home one moment further."

"Understood," Alexander replied as his eyes began turning black. "Yes, Mrs. Gallows. Here is your money. And as a token of our appreciation of your refined tastes, I am going to give you *another* book. Free of charge, of course." Alexander could hardly contain his excitement as he pulled an ominously glowing book from under the counter. Mrs. Gallows took one look at it, turned up her nose, and said, "I do not want that book. That woman on the cover is a whore. Take it away."

"Ah but you do," the devilishly grinning shopkeeper said as he held the book up in front of her obstinate eyes. "Yes, you *do* want this book. It is by the same author. You want to give him the opportunity to redeem himself. Everybody deserves a chance at redemption, don't they? Yes, my dear. Not only will you read this book, but you will become infatuated by it. You won't be able to put it down. I have heard it is quite a, um, page turner, heh, heh, heh."

The book was lovingly placed into a plain, brown bag and handed to Mrs. Gallows. She awoke from her trance-like state and gruffly said, "Fine. I'll take a look at it. But I'm sure that it's trash. Just like all of his other books. I'm sure that I'll be back tomorrow to return it."

Alexander chuckled slightly as he watched the uptight, thin frame of Mrs. Gallows march out the door. *Oh, I do not think that I'll see you tomorrow,* he said to himself. *Not if that whore on that book cover has anything to say about it, heh, heh, heh.* Alexander's thoughts were suddenly disrupted by a seventeen-year-old girl screaming out, "Oh my God!" Alexander looked at the young lady who was holding the discarded copy of *Revenge of the Downtrodden.* "Oh my God! This is that book that Patty told me about! She told me that I just *had* to read it! She said that it was the best fucking book that you'll ever read! How much is it, mister?" Alexander looked fondly upon her excited, youthful face and said, "For you, my dear, it is free of charge. It is payment enough to see the appreciation on your lovely face. Yes, this author does enjoy spreading his, um, *messages,* heh, heh, heh. Please take it and enjoy."

Mrs. Gallows set her cup of freshly brewed tea on her side table and sat in her creaking, hard wood rocking chair. She could feel the dowels of the back of the chair pressing into her aging flesh as she took her new book out of its wrapping. She glowered at the impossibly sexy image on the cover and ridiculous title. "*Sin.D.*," she scoffed before attempting to throw the book into her raging fireplace. The book remained in her hands. She began fighting against her crippled fingers that were opening the book against her wishes. She tried to look away from the opening pages and stare at the ceiling, but a strong force pulled her eyes down upon the dastardly ink printed on the paper. Word after word, sentence after sentence, paragraph after paragraph, page after page, and chapter after chapter, bombarded her pupils and became implanted in her brain. With each repugnant scene, her heart rate and pulse quickened. Her blood sugar would drop, then spike to impossible heights. Her crippled hands ached for relief. And the words depicting vile carnage continued to batter her brain and become imbedded in her soul.

"Oh! This is utterly reprehensible!" she cried out as the repugnant passages penetrated her fixated eyes.

"No, you won't," Cindy arrogantly replied as she put on a sheer black robe. "You need me to do this. You need me to eat and drink and fuck and murder. You need me to be at full strength so that I can go down to Earth and save your precious little piss ants. Speaking of which, where the fuck is my sacrifice? And my Black cocks? I can fill my mouth with the pizza but I'm not jamming it up my snatch! Hmmmm, actually that gives me an idea. Hey, is that crust foldable?"

A blood-covered Cindy was sitting on the drenched lap of a shivering, but still alive, sheriff. Blood dripped down her attractive, enthralled face and metallic minidress as she threw her head back laughing while tussling the sheriff's fading purple hair. Entering the room from an adjacent restroom came an equally crimson-coated Zale. She was giggling uncontrollably as she sauntered into the room modeling her latest outfit. She had intestines wrapped around her tiny shoulders and neck as though they were boas. On the top of her head, she wore the dark-purple scalp of one of the deputies. Blood dripped from the scalp and into her delighted, aqua eyes as she floated into the room. Covering her body from her neck to her knees was the long purple skin from the torso of another of their victims. The grisly flesh clung to her petite body by the sticky blood of its tortured contributor. On her little webbed feet, she was wearing two lower jaws that had been strapped on by someone's removed tendons. The devilish pair looked at their newly arrived colleagues and burst out once again into uncontrolled laughter.

"Oh, dear Enlightenment!" Harmony exclaimed as the final bit of Janet Tompkin's arms were being chewed and swallowed by her suffering husband. "I don't think I can stand anymore of this! I'm gonna...I'm gonna..." "Nice, Harmony," Cindy stated. "Real fuckin' nice. I knew this would happen. I think the word you were looking for is 'ralph.' Wow. What a mess. But good news for you, counselor! A little side dish. Zale, go get a really big spoon. And a funnel. Waste not, want not, right counselor? Wow. What the fuck did you eat, Harmony? It's all chunky and shit. Okay, open up the hangar. Here comes the airplane. Oh right. You don't have those. Just fuckin' eat it."

Harmony's vomit shot back out of the Magistrate's mouth as soon as it slid down his throat, showering his abused wife with a warm, putrid coating. "Goddammit, counselor," Cindy admonished. "I told you not to do that. Now we gotta start over. Zale. Spoon and funnel again, please. And this time, keep it down you fat fuck."

"Wow, nice flyin' there, Ace," Cindy sarcastically stated. "Where the fuck did you get your flight wings? A Cracker Jack box? Whatever. We're here. Open the door. Hey! Anybody out there seen Hank? What do you mean who's Hank? That tall pink fucker with dicks all over him! What? His name's Jebidiah? Whatever. Close enough. Now where the fuck is Hank?" Cindy looked around the landing dock and saw a large, pink, snail-like being with multiple phalluses dripping off of his blobby body. She squealed with delight and shouted out, "Hank! There you are motherfucker! Man, are you a sight for sore eyes! And sore thighs!" She went running up to him and locked him in a tight embrace while showering what was thought to be his head with kisses. His drooping phalluses immediately became

erect and began shooting black ooze. Cindy was coated from head to toe in black gooeyness as she began laughing and said, "Oh yeah! That's the stuff! Tastes just like licorice! Don't waste it all! Come on! Let's go to my room!" A trail of black slime and sticky footprints lead out of the dock and onto an awaiting elevator.

Mrs. Gallows was clutching at her heart and gasping for air as the final grotesque images from the immoral text pierced her psyche. Her tortured mind screamed out for release as her frail, shocked body mercifully succumbed.

"Well, well, well," a gleeful Satan said while stroking his broad, red chin. "Now what do we have here? A hypocrite! Awesome! A fucking bitch who has committed all sorts of evil bullshit against undeserving people who now tries to hide behind Jesus's fucking skirt! Hey, bitch! How did that work out for ya? What did all of that judgmental posturing and scripture reading and insincere praying get ya? Here's a hint! Fucking nothing except a one-way trip to hell! Oh, I think I love receiving assholes like you more than anyone. Oh sure, the serial killers of innocent victims, and the rapists, and the child molesters are a good time. I just love passing judgement on them. But they already know that they aren't going through the pearly fucking gates! They already know which ticket they've punched! But not you assholes. You *actually think* that being judgmental and hating people and oppressing people is God's jam. But guess what? It fucking *isn't*! He fucking *hates* people who oppress others in his name! Maybe more than anything! Well, maybe not as much as *Long John Silvers*, but don't fool yourself. Doing mean shit in his name is *waaaay* fuckin' up there on the list. Oh, and the look on you asshole's faces when you first realize that you've done fucked up. It's priceless. It really is. It's what gives me the motivation to get up each morning. All right, initiation's over. Let's get down to business. Your eternal punishment.

"Hey! I got an idea! Since you liked that book, *Sin.D.*, so much, how about I make *your* eternal fate the exact same one as the evil fuckin' villain in that book? Yeah, what was his name again? Wechuge! That's it.

Kind of an odd literary choice for the name of the villain but, whatever. Not my problem. *I* didn't write that shit. Yeah, so here's what we're going to do. Just like what happened at the end of that book to Wechuge we're gonna…wait just a fucking minute here. We got some fucking looky-loos who are trying to find out how *Sin.D.* ends. Hey! Reader! You wanna find out how it ends? Don't be a fuckin' cheap-ass and go buy it yourself! SHEESH! Some people, am I right?"

One of the observing mean-girl cheerleaders stopped snapping her gum and said, "Sin.D? Ohmygaaaawd! I tooootally read that book! It was, like, the best fucking book I've ever read!"

CHAPTER 14

PUPPY

"Oh dear, what now?" Alexander said aloud as he answered his apartment door. Standing in front of him was a stern-looking Detective Anderson surrounded by several forensic officers. "Yes, hello Detective Anderson," Alexander greeted as he adjusted his tie. "How may I be of assistance to you?"

"Got a search warrant, Picklesbee. And a whole lot of questions," Anderson answered as he pushed Alexander to the side and waved his troops into the small apartment. "Why, Detective Anderson," Alexander protested. "What is the meaning of this? Ah, yes. I believe that I know. My dear friend Melissa told me that you paid her a visit the other day. And now you know that I may have told you a little fib. Please, detective, allow me to clear this matter up."

"Alright Picklesbee," Anderson answered while folding his arms. "But first, open your mouth. Wide. We're taking a swab. Good boy. Now you told us that on the night our blonde hooker was murdered and left in your back alley, that you did not know her. You hadn't seen her, is that right?"

"Quite right," Alexander answered as he watched his personal belongings being carefully placed into plastic evidence bags. "But, detective, I really must…" He was cut off by a follow-up question. "And you said that you were with an African American escort who wore a red dress. Would *this* be her?"

Alexander's face went pale as he looked upon the decimated face and body of the Black escort that he had spoken with outside the liquor store. "Oh dear, that poor soul," he said sorrowfully. "No officer, that was *not* the woman that I was with that night. I was not with *any* working girl that night. I was, in fact, with Melissa Bartlesworth. She was with me until around one am. Although we are not involved romantically, I wish to remain discreet about our friendship. You see, she is engaged, and I have no intention of complicating her life. We are friends, but perception can become reality in the minds of some. So, yes, on the night of the blonde's murder, I was with Melissa. May I inquire as to when I can expect to get my belongings back? Or should I just plan on purchasing a new hairbrush, toothbrush, and other personal items?"

"Hard to tell," Anderson answered. "If I were you, I'd buy new stuff. We may have this for a while. And who knows. Maybe you'll get new ones provided by the state. So, Melissa just happened to leave her panties? Kind of an odd thing to remove in a friend's apartment, wouldn't you say? And just where are they? We'd like to take those along with us as well."

The panties, Alexander thought to himself. *My penchant for souvenirs may be my greatest downfall.* "Ah yes, the underwear. I would love to give them to you, but I discarded them. Actually, I gave them away. To that unfortunate woman in the photo. I was not with her on that night, but I had a temporary employment opportunity at the liquor store two blocks down. I laundered the underwear and gave them to that lady who was standing outside the store. My intention was to throw them away, but I thought that a lady in her profession perhaps could use them, so I gave them to her. That was my only interaction with that particular woman. And, you must already have those panties in your possession, because I had given them to her."

"Nope," Anderson said. "We don't have them. *She* didn't have them. There weren't any panties found on the body or anywhere around the crime scene. You wanna try again?" Alexander's face turned ashen as his mind struggled to find an explanation. He took a deep breath and said, "My dear Detective Anderson. I do not know what to tell you. I did, in fact, give those panties to that particular woman yesterday morning. I do not know what may have become of them after they left my possession."

The forensics team continued their meticulous activity while Anderson thought. "Alright. You were with Melissa. You weren't with the blonde hooker, and you lied about being with a Black hooker. You just happened to talk with a Black hooker yesterday morning and you just happened to give our missing pair of panties to her. And now, she has just happened to turn up dead. Doesn't look real good for you, does it? And, you *still* haven't told me who those panties *do* belong to."

"Very well, Detective," Alexander conceded. "They are indeed Melissa's. But it is such an innocent explanation. I spilled a drink on her lap. She removed her underwear to dry them out and they must have fallen on the floor at some point, and she left them here. We had, as I have told you, been drinking a bit. I had intended on returning them to her, but felt as though that might be awkward, so I decided to discard them. I had told you that she wasn't here and that I was with a Black hooker in a red dress. So, as I was entering my employment, by the grace of, um, my lord, I suppose, there was a beautiful Black call girl in a red dress. I asked her to provide me with an alibi, and I gave her the panties. And I did it all in order to protect my Melissa from any embarrassment. I do understand how this may look, detective, but there really is a reasonable explanation for all of this."

The room turned silent as a forensics officer fished a worn medical bag from under the bed. He opened it, looked at its contents, and carried it over to Anderson who peered inside. Anderson looked at Alexander with a wide grin and said, "Yeah, you got an explanation for everything. But do you have an explanation for *this*? A bag full of scalpels, knives, bone saws, and just about everything needed to rip somebody apart? What *is* this, the Jack the Ripper starter set? Well, Picklesbee, how about an explanation?"

"Well," a perspiring Alexander answered. "Yes, I suppose my having that bag and you having several dismembered victims in this neighborhood does not look good. But again, it is merely a coincidence. Collecting old medical equipment is a bit of a hobby of mine. Go ahead and test the items in that bag. I assure you, you will not find any links between your unfortunate victims and anything that you have taken from my apartment. Additionally, detective, do you really think that Jack the Ripper would leave his sadistic tools just laying around for anyone to find? Of course not. He would have found a discreet location to store his wares until they were needed. Are we about finished here? I do not wish to be late for my position at the pet shop."

"Yeah, or maybe he's just a fuckin' idiot," Anderson replied through his light laughter. "Well, we'll see now, won't we Picklesbee. We'll see. But one more thing. You're working at the pet shop today? And from eyewitness accounts, you have been seen working at a hardware store, toy store, record store, perfumery, the bookstore, and the liquor store. You seem to just work there for a day. But the funny thing is, the managers of these joints have no recollection of you. None at all. Not even the manager of the bookstore and *she* remembers *everything*. What a mouth on her though. Wow. Anyway, now, why would that be?"

"Well, Detective," Alexander began explaining. "I am not surprised that they deny knowing me. This truly is quite simple. I am retired, but I do enjoy serving the public. So, I offer my temporary services to the managers of local shops to give them a bit of a respite. They do not wish to go to the trouble of having to complete cumbersome employment paperwork, and I do not wish to go to the trouble of declaring this meager income. I am but a temporary employee who is paid under the table as the saying goes. There really isn't anything nefarious. A simple financial arrangement for services provided. It is a win-win for all involved. I am sure you understand, detective." Alexander's eyes blackened for a moment as he peered into Anderson's soul. His eyes quickly returned to their natural azure as his lips curled up into a wicked smile. "Yes, I believe you understand taking undeclared payments. And you understand brutality. That is what makes you so good at your occupation. Yes, I believe that our paths may cross again, detective, at a time when I am employed by one of the local shops. In fact, I am quite sure of it. And I am so looking forward to seeing you there."

A sharp chill ran down Anderson's spine just before his phone rang. "Yeah Biggs, what do ya got? Finished collecting stuff from Bartlesworth's place? Good. Did he cop to knowing her? Yeah? Admitted that he hired her for a quickie but doesn't know anything else? Figures. All right. We're just wrapping up at Picklesbee's. I have a feeling our little mystery is about to be solved. One way or another." He ended the call, turned to Alexander and said in a threatening tone, "I don't know what all that creepy shit was about, but don't you *ever* talk to me that way again. And you might just want to watch yourself. We've got eyes all over you." "Oh, I'm sure you do, detective," a calming Alexander replied. "We *all* have eyes on us. Always. I am looking forward to receiving my possessions. Good day, detective. I'll see you soon."

"Excuse me, sir?" the voice of a small girl was heard above the disharmonious orchestra of mewing and yapping in the pet shop. Alexander peered over the counter to find the angelic faces of two eight-year-old girls. One had curly red hair, freckles, and wore a flowered sweater, faded bell-bottom dungarees, and Birkenstocks. The other had dark brown skin that was framed by long, black braids. He could not help but chuckle as he looked at her bright pink anime costume.

"Well, hello there young ladies," Alexander greeted with his charming smile. "How may I be of service to you?" "Hiya," the smiling red-headed girl answered. "Well, sir, my name is Josie, and this is my best friend, Anna, and you see sir, um, we were wondering if you could help us find her a home?" Josie bent down and lifted an eight-week-old German Shepherd puppy onto the counter. The playful scamp immediately began wagging her tail and licking Alexander's hand. "Well," Alexander responded. "I do not believe that it is the practice of this shop to take in strays. Why, there are tests and shots, and a myriad of things involved in ensuring a puppy is safe to find its forever home. I am so sorry girls, but I'm afraid I cannot help you."

"Oh, please?" Anna beseeched. "You see, Josie runs an animal shelter and finds forever homes for neighborhood strays. But her shelter is full, and this sweet puppy just came to her house, and her mom said that it can't stay. *Pleeease?*"

Alexander's heart began to melt as he looked into the pleading green eyes of Josie and said, "Josie. Josie. Now why does that name sound familiar? Oh, my. Are you the Josie from the flyer?" Alexander went to the front window and retrieved the flyer that had been taped there. He chuckled as he read it aloud.

THIS IS AN URGENT MESSAGE FROM JOSIE PARKER!!!!!!
BY JOSIE PARKER

Do you need to open your heart and your home to an adorable cat or dog? I have many loving pets who are looking for just the right person to give their love to in their new forever home. Could that lucky person be you? If so, please call the Joe Argento Pet Shelter and ask for Josie at XXX-XXXX.

"Yep! That's me!" Josie squealed out. "My, young lady," Alexander said as he returned the flyer to the window. "What a generous girl you are. It revives my hope for humankind." His eyes darkened as he explored the souls of the giggling pair. "Yes, hope indeed," he continued as his eyes returned to a peaceful blue. "You both represent kindness and humani-tarianism. It is a rare quality these days. And I can sense that you two have great power and are going to have some great adventures. But, my dears, please take the advice of someone a bit more, um, experienced than you. Great power has the capacity to corrupt one's soul. Please be mindful of that. And no matter what challenges and heartache this world may present to you, please always cherish the genuine kindness that is in your souls. If you promise me that, I promise to find a proper home for...for...what is her name?"

Anna and Josie looked at one another and began tittering before Josie said, "Well, she seems to have a bit of an ornery streak, so we named her

Bealzebuddy. But we just call her Bea, for short." Alexander gently lifted the puppy's furry face and stared deeply into its eyes. "Yes, I believe that may be an appropriate name. This one *does* seem to have a bit of the Devil in her. Alright, young ladies. I shall find a wonderful forever home for her with a deserving family. And you shall both preserve the innocence in your souls. Deal?"

The pair of girls shook Alexander's hand and said in unison, "Deal!" Anna then said, "Wow, mister. Your hand is really cold. Do you need some mittens or something?" "I'll be just fine my dear. As will Bea. Ta, ta."

A woman and her eleven-year-old son entered the pet store a short while later. Alexander could feel the physical and mental anguish of the pair as his eyes surveyed the myriad of fading yellow, blue, and purple bruises upon their arms and faces. He closed his eyes briefly and witnessed a heathen beating them repeatedly while they cried out for mercy. Years of torturous abuse flashed through his mind and became imbedded in his black soul. Alexander wiped a tear from his eye, forced a smile, and said, "Well, hello there. How may I help you?"

"Um, hi," the woman cautiously said as she protectively shielded her son. "Um, we are looking for a dog. A, um, big dog, for, um…" The boy then yelled out, "We need a big dog for protection! We had to kick my dad out and we're afraid he'll come back!" The mother placed her index finger upon the boy's lips and silently shook her head.

"I see," Alexander stated. "I believe that I may have the perfect pet for you. Oh, Bea! Come here, my darling!" Bealzebuddy came galloping into the show room with her tongue wagging out. She instinctively jumped up at the boy who showered her with the love and affection that she craved.

"Um," the mother began. "Well, she certainly is cute and sweet, but we're really looking for something a bit, um, bigger. And more, um, ferocious." "Yes, yes," Alexander countered. "I know *exactly* what it is that you are looking for. Please, my dear. Look into my eyes." The woman reluctantly raised her head until her healing eyes were locked upon his. "This puppy loves you. And you love her. And rest assured, no harm will ever come to you or your child again. Not as long as Bealzebuddy is around. And she is no charge. Just take her to your loving home. You deserve her. And if that scoundrel ever bothers you again, well, he will be quite deserving of Bea as well. You take care of her, and she will take care of you. Agreed?"

"Please, mom?" the boy begged. "Please can we take her? I love her!" The mother shook off her haze and genuinely smiled for the first time in years. "Of course, dear," she said to her son. "Of course we can. I think that she will be the perfect addition to our family. Thank you, sir. Thank you for your kindness." "It has been my pleasure," Alexander replied. "And before you go, please take a bag of dog food. Oh, and some chew toys. This one *does* enjoy chewing."

The mother and son huddled together on their ragged couch as they listened to the rampaging drunk outside of their door. "Let me in, bitch! Divorce? You're going to divorce *me*? Fuck you! I'm going to divorce your fuckin' head from your body!" The thin wood finally gave way and a scrawny man in a filthy T-shirt staggered into the room. He looked upon his shivering family, flashed an evil smile and began removing his thick, leather belt. From the corner came a high-pitched growl. "What the fuck did you get? An attack dog? Yeah, she looks really fuckin' tough. And what did I say about pets? Alright, well you asked for it. Right after I teach *you two* a lesson, I'm gonna teach *this* little bitch a lesson. Right in front of you. I'm gonna beat her until she can't walk. Then we'll see if you want any more pets."

He began trudging toward the pleading pair. The high pitch growl turned deeper. He looked around to find the innocent looking puppy begin to expand until she was fully grown. Bea's growls turned to snarls as saliva dripped from her exposed fangs. He stared into a smoldering pair of red eyes and began trembling. "What the fuck *are* you?" the man screamed out as eighty pounds of furry ferocity lunged at his throat. The battling pair fell upon the stained carpet as Bea clutched the abusive man's throat and chewed. And chewed. And chewed. Until the carpet was awash in his blood and he had uttered his final gurgle.

Several police officers ran up the stairs and stood aghast at the grisly scene. "What the hell happened here?" one of the officers asked. The mother looked up from the content puppy that was lying on her lap and said, "My husband has been beating me and my son. You, of course, should know this, because I've reported it multiple times. And you did nothing. I kicked him out and changed the locks. He came back about a half-hour ago and broke down the door. He came toward me and my son. And then, our prayers were answered. A ferocious dog suddenly entered and attacked him and left him like, well, this. Then, the dog left."

"Wow," the officer stated. "I've seen dog attacks before, but never something like *this*. His head is nearly chewed off. And that cute little pup sure couldn't have done anything like this. Okay, ma'am. Young man. We'll call the coroner and get this mess cleaned up. Why don't you and your puppy go to another room. We'll let you know when we're finished." "No, that's alright," the boy replied as he handed a bloody chew toy to the enthralled Bea. "We're fine. We want to watch you take our pain away. Plus, I think Bea needs to go to the bathroom, don't you girl?" Bea enthusiastically yelped, jumped down from the couch, and lifted her leg over what was left of the family's tormentor.

"And then that fuckin' dog took a piss right on your head! That was so fuckin' funny!" Satan roared through his non-stop laughter as vicious demonic puppies tore through the flesh of his latest arrival. "Oh, fuck. I could watch my little angels rip you to shreds for eternity. And I will! Because you're in fucking hell, motherfucker! Oh, some days I just love my job and…yeah, what do *you* want, bitch?"

Satan was interrupted by annoying tapping on his red, brawny shoulder. "Uh, yeah, like *totally* sorry to bother you Satan," one of the mean-girl cheerleaders stated while stretching gum from out of her mouth and twisting it around her scorched index finger. "But, like, I just heard sumthin' that, like, you may want to hear. I mean, like, I don't wanna be a *gossip* or anythin', but, like, I just *totally* heard from my friend's brother, who heard from his neighbor's cousin, who heard from a guy at the pool hall that there's like, a lot of dead hookers who are dying in Queens."

"Yeah, probably, what's your fuckin' point?" Satan dismissively replied. "Well, so, like, these hookers all work in the same neighborhood as that shopkeeper who used to run the convenience store, and like, these hookers are all ripped up and gnarly and stuff like that shopkeeper used to do and I just, like, thought you'd want to know. But, like, you *totally* didn't hear this from me. AwRight?"

"Aw shit," Satan mumbled as he held his horned head in his massive, calloused hands. "Godammit, Alexander. What have you been up to? And things were going so well. You get to hang out on Earth with the mortals and I get new damned assholes to play with. But if you're back to killing innocent women and sending more souls to fuckin' heaven, well, that defeats the purpose, now, doesn't it? Aw, shit. I'd better look into this myself. Can't trust anyone down here. That's the problem with lording over a bunch of damned souls. You can't trust anyone."

He raised his head and barked out, "Alright! Go get me my overcoat, wide-brimmed hat, and sunglasses! I'm goin' on a trip. And stop snapping that fucking gum!"

CHAPTER 15

Jack

Alexander blew the steam off of his rich, dark coffee and took a sip from his delicate porcelain cup. He stared at the cup's flawless pure-white veneer and began imagining the equally pure skin of his new friend, Melissa. He smiled slightly then scowled as the image of Melissa transformed seamlessly into that of his lost love, Virgina. His now-trembling hand placed the cup on his saucer, and he turned his attention to the screaming headline in the morning newspaper. 'LATEST RIPPER-STYLE VICTIM FOUND BEHIND QUEEN'S LIQUOR STORE.' "Ripper-style," Alexander said to himself while his Virginia's face continued to swirl in his tortured consciousness. "I like that. Yes, it is indeed a style. I suppose I *have* always been a bit of a trendsetter. There most certainly would not have been this long string of serial killers in our world if it had not been for me. Oh, I am quite certain that I wasn't the first, but I am equally certain that I was the first to gain such notoriety. I do so enjoy the attention that my little misdeeds created. And the letters sent them all into a frenzy. Yes, the letters. The letters addressed 'From Hell.' Also quite appropriate, as it turned out."

He got up from the table, took off his red-striped pajamas, carefully folded them, and placed them into his small wooden dresser. His tall, taught, perpetually fifty-year-old naked body made its way into the bathroom. He adjusted the water temperature of the shower and stepped in.

Alexander's tears mixed with the water droplets that were pounding onto his face as he placed a soggy letter into the post on the evening of June 1, 1864. He wiped his rainwater and tears from his beleaguered face, turned, and stumbled into a local tavern. *I just do not know what to do,* he thought to himself. He ordered a gin, removed his water-logged overcoat, and sat alone in a dark corner. His aching mind was oblivious to the drunken revelry that was on display around him. Laughing men were grabbing at painted ladies who laughed in return. For a price, they could be made available for much more than laughter. There was a slight scuffle as two inebriated men began shoving each other. The bartender picked up a hardwood club, yelled at them to take their business elsewhere, and threatened to call for the Bobbies. Alexander was oblivious to it all.

What could I have done wrong? What qualities does this other man possess that I do not? It is most certainly not love for my Virgina. No one could love her more than I. No one. We were perfect together. She showed me that not all women were like my insufferable mother. Always nagging. Always criticizing. Nothing is ever good enough for her or my heartless father. That dreadful woman has been my model for all women. Heartless. Cruel. Greedy. That is my mother, and I thought all women to be just like her. And then, I met my Virginia, and she showed me what true womanhood was. She is supportive. Kind. Generous. And the most beautiful creature to have ever walked this Earth. She is nothing like my horrid mother. No, this must be a mistake. Perhaps this cad has placed some sort of spell upon her. Perhaps I shall go to America and fight for my love. Yes, I shall set sail right away. Once she sees the smile upon my face all will be forgotten. And forgiven. But what if I am too late? What if this scoundrel has his hooks buried too deeply into my love's confused heart? What if my travels are all for naught? There I would be with little money, knowing no one, and in the middle of a war. No, I shall wait for her response. It is the gentlemanly thing to do. I shall pray for an answer. And I shall have another gin as I wait.

"Care for some comp'ny lad?" A woman at the bar offered while ensuring to amplify her protruding bosom. "No, no thank you," Alexander mumbled before ordering his next gin. "I am, um, I am betrothed to another. But thank you for the offer, just the same."

"My, he's a polite bloke, now it'nt he?" the woman said to another patron before bursting out in laughter. "Betrothed to another? Take a look around, lad! We're *all* betrothed to another. Doesn't stop us from having a bit of fun, now does it?" The entire crowd exploded into laughter at the novice's expense. Alexander returned to his lonesome, shadowed table and seethed. *Yes, laugh at me,* he thought to himself. *Laugh all you like. There will come a day when I will show you the meaning of true love. Yes, there will come a day when you will not laugh at me. No one will laugh at Alexander Picklesbee ever again.*

"It is a bit pricey, but nothing is too good for my Virginia!" Alexander exclaimed as he dangled a gold locket in front of his hopeful face. "Yes, I am quite sure that I shall hear from her right after Christmas. She shall open my present, then open the locket, and see our wonderful portraits together. She then shall re-open her heart to me."

"Where exactly is she?" the jeweler inquired as he carefully placed the portraits of Virginia and Alexander on each side of the locket. "Why, my love is in New York!" a proud Alexander replied. "Yes, and I fear our geographical distance may have created a distance in her heart. But once she sees my present, all of that will be settled. Oh, do wrap it in your finest paper and ribbons, my good man. I want this to be the grandest gift that she has ever received."

The jeweler stopped his work for a moment and looked into the hopeful blue eyes of his young customer. "Are you sure you want to spend this amount on this young lady? Perhaps wait until you hear from her again?" "I will not even consider it!" Alexander exclaimed. "This gift shall be my entry back into her heart. And the cost is no object. As long as I am enrolled in my studies, my parents shall continue to provide me with my meager allowance. So, wrap it up, my good man. I must get it to the post right away. It must be in her gentle hands by Christmas."

"She is lost to me," Alexander slurred on the soggy shoulder of a disinterested escort who was sitting beside him in his dark corner of the tavern. He guzzled his seventh glass of gin and continued his pathetic dissertation. "I know it now. It has been half a year since my last letter to her and I have heard nothing. I had bought her the most wonderful Christmas present. A gold locket with our faces inside. But I did not send it. I only sent a letter. Perhaps that was my error. Perhaps I shall send one more letter along with the locket. And if I do not hear back, then I shall be done with her and her treachery. Just as I am done with that dreadful university. They will rue the day that they kicked out their most gifted surgical student. And my parents will rue the day that they cut me off from my allowance. It is just as well. I hated my studies, and I hate my parents. All I need to do is find a trade until their horrible souls are gone and burning in flames. Then I shall live off of their inheritance and I shall drink and dance my life away. Perhaps I shall send for you on that wonderful day. Yes, perhaps we can celebrate their demise together. Thank you for listening. You have been most kind." "That's all right, love," the escort replied while filing her painted nails. "Any time. If you're done, how 'bout those coins you owe me."

"But, but," the pleading Alexander stated. "You *cannot* terminate my employment. Why, I have been your best salesman for the last eight years. After I, um, left university, I toiled at meaningless jobs until I found my true calling. I worked in shop after shop and finally realized that I was to be a man about the country. That I needed to travel and see all the grand sights that our nation provides. And finally, in 1870, I saw your advertisement. It was perfect. It was my calling until I could make my way back to my medical studies. But I never went back. I have enjoyed this position so. Meeting all of the various townspeople and selling our wonderful wares. Please. I must have this job. I have nothing left. My parents will not give me a morsel. I am barely invited to family events any longer. And I do not have my Virginia. My sweet Virginia who betrayed me and left me to toil under your tyrannical thumb. Oh, I did not mean that sir. Please reconsider. I am your best salesman."

The owner of the sales company blew cigar smoke into Alexander's pitiful face and said, "Yeah, your sweet Virginia. That seems to be the problem. That's all you talk about. I have received numerous concerns from our customers about how you go on and on about this Virginia. It makes the ladies unsettled, and the men just want to punch you in the nose. Especially when you show up drunk. Which is more and more frequent. Hell, you're drunk right now. And let's get something straight. You were never one of my best salesmen. You were just the one that I could give the worst routes to. You're always so pickled that you've never even thought about it. You just accepted the assignments and went on your merry little way. But your endless, drunken speeches about this Virginia is effecting my sales in even the small villages that have no other purchasing options. They would rather go without than allow you into their homes. No, Picklesbee, it's time to part company. Here is your final remittance. Now be gone. Go drown your sorrows…someplace else."

"Oh, deny me your support, will you?" Alexander said to himself while creeping around the woods of his parents' provincial estate. "Your only child, left to fend for himself in this hopeless, frigid world while you drink from your golden chalices and dine upon the finest cuisine. A mere loan. That is all that I asked for until I find new employment. And you denied me. Called me a hopeless, worthless drunk. Called me an embarrassment. Banished me from my childhood home. Very well, then. Banish me. And I shall banish you. Yes, I shall banish you and take your fortune. And I shall indeed be an embarrassment to your name. I shall spend your fortune on drink and whores until we meet again in hell. Yes, my medical studies shall come in handy this evening. Just a little of this potion on a piece of raw meat, and it will be nap time for one of the local wolves. And its nap should be over by the time my parents arrive home from their elegant dance and the servants have gone. Yes, they will retire to their bedroom and find a rather unpleasant surprise. A rather unpleasant and *hungry* surprise, heh, heh, heh."

Alexander stood laughing as he watched the flailing silhouettes in the second-story bedroom window being lunged at by the shadow of a ferocious wolf. He sipped at his bottle and gleefully slapped his knee as the silhouette of his father's decapitated head was seen flying from behind one picture window to another. His laugher intensified as he watched his mother's body crash against the thick glass of one of the windows.

Her thrashing body left bright red streaks upon the glass from the blood that was gushing from her throat, mouth, and torso. While he stared at the morbid scene, he could feel her fear and excruciating pain in his blackening soul. His knees went weak, and he fell to the ground while trying to catch his breath from his unstoppable laughter, as he keenly watched the wolf's bloody head emerge from between his mother's toxic breasts.

"Yes, yes, quite a tragedy," Alexander said to his parents' attorney while attempting to conceal his elation. "No one knows how that animal may have gained entry. It is speculated that perhaps one of the servants left a door ajar. Such a pity. My parents were such kind souls. I shall do my very best to live up to their expectations and carry their fine name into the future. Have the constables finished at the estate? I am quite anxious to reconnect with my childhood home."

"I'm sorry, Alexander, but there must have been some miscommunication between yourself and your parents," the estate attorney replied while surveying his clients' will. "You are not in their will. They did not provide you with one thing. The estate and all of its belongings shall be auctioned off. Those proceeds, along with their considerable amount of liquid assets, are to be donated to numerous charities." Alexander's heart began beating rapidly while his vengeful mind raged. His hopes were then lifted. "Well, I seem to have made an error, Alexander," the attorney said. "Yes, your parents *did* leave you with something." "Yes? Yes? What is it?" Alexander eagerly said. "Here it is. This bag. It was to be a gift to you upon your graduation from university. Well, Alexander, maybe this is a blessing in disguise. Maybe this medical bag that you are receiving from your parents will help you to find a new direction in life."

Alexander stared unblinking out the window. He watched as young men and women sauntered along the sidewalk with their arms locked. He glared at their hopeful, happy, smiling faces and said in a deep growl, "Yes, perhaps you are right. Perhaps this bag is all I need to find my true calling in this world. Thank you, counselor. You have been most helpful."

The prostitute was adjusting her skirts while listening to Alexander rant under the shadows of the 1876 Board School of Buck's Row. "My, it is now August thirty-first, 1888. It has been nearly ten years since my parents' demise. Ten years since I was denied my wealth. Ten years since I was once again forced to be employed as a travelling salesman. Ten years of blisters upon my feet. Ten years of no recognition. Ten years of owning nothing but the clothes upon my back and my medical bag. My medical bag that I must now sell just to find a roof in Whitechapel. Ten long years. But not as long as it has been since I was betrayed by my one and only true love. No, it has been twenty-five years since her treachery. Tell me dear, what is your name?"

"Um, Mary. Mary Nichols. Are you wantin' to do it, sir? I've got me skirts all arranged for ya." "Yes, Mary, I want to do it tonight," Alexander sneered as he retrieved a sharpened object from his medical bag. He went up to the woman and stared at her with his insane eyes. He lifted the knife and said quietly, "Mary is a beautiful name. But tonight, I shall call you Virginia." His face was showered with blood as the knife sliced through Mary's neck. Her twitching body slumped to the pavement. "Yes, leave your skirts just like that, you whore. Let the world see what you use to tempt and betray men. Let the world see you as you really are. A worthless whore. Ah, but I hear someone approaching. Good night fair lady. And thank you. For the first time in many years, I feel alive. Vibrant. Say hello to my Virginia when you see her in hell, won't you? Ta, ta."

"Don't fight it my dear," Alexander growled at Annie Chapman nine evenings later. "Stop fighting it. You are making my lacerations quite irregular," he ordered while slashing the woman's throat causing streaks of blood to splash across a nearby wooden fence. "Yes, there you are, my dear. Nice and quiet now. And let's just pull this up so that everyone can see your fine red stockings. There you are. Legs spread like the whore that you are. And whores aren't meant to bear children. *My* whore, Virginia, certainly will never bear *my* children. Nor will you. Not without your womb, heh, heh, heh."

Alexander was washing his face in a public bath as horrendous thoughts and images rampaged through his mind. The terrified looks upon the faces of his two helpless victims. The blood that gushed from their brutal wounds. His smiling reflection in their dying eyes as their lifeless bodies sagged to the ground. *This is utterly beautiful,* he thought to himself while combing his pencil-thin mustache. *Beautiful and exhilarating. No, I do not believe that I will be relinquishing my parents' inheritance any time soon. It has provided me with hope and strength for the first time in my life. For the first time, I am receiving what I so rightly deserve. Peace. Peace in my heart that has been shattered by every single person who has professed to love me. Just like these working girls. They profess to love me, but all they want is to use me. To take my money. To laugh at me. Just as that whore laughed at me so many years ago. Just as my mother laughed at me. Just as my Virginia laughed at me on her wedding night. I know that she did. But who is laughing now? This entire district is in a lather. Some are frightened. Some are intrigued. The police are baffled. And no one is laughing.*

In fact, in their own morbid way, they admire me. They admire what I'm doing. And I do so enjoy the attention. So, why not toss another log onto this fire? Why not add to the confusion and fear? And why not add to my newfound infamy? I believe that it is time to pen another letter. But not to Virginia. And I must write in a slightly different hand. Wouldn't want anyone to recognize my style of correspondence.

Now, what to call myself? Should I use my real first name, just for the excitement? No, I think not. I do not want to ruin my fun just yet. Not before my passage to America. Just a few more weeks, and I shall have the money to be free from this. My Virginia thought that she was free from me. She'll soon find out. What a lovely surprise she will be getting this Christmas.

Now, back to my name. Horace the Impaler? Noel the Knife? The Executioner? I rather like that one. No. Something simple. A very common name. William? Kent? James? No, Jack! Jack the what? The cutter? The murderer? The vengeful? Oh, I know. It is beautiful. As beautiful as my Virginia's ripped body will be, heh, heh, heh.

Dear Boss,

I keep on hearing the police have caught me but they wont fix me just yet. I have laughed when they look so clever and talk about being on the right track. That joke about Leather Apron gave me real fits. I am down on whores and I shant quit ripping them till I do get buckled. Grand work the last job was. I gave the lady no time to squeal.

How can they catch me now. I love my work and want to start again. You will soon hear of me with my funny little games. I saved some of the proper red stuff in a ginger beer bottle over the last job to write with but it went thick like glue and I cant use it. Red ink is fit enough I hope ha ha. The next job I do I shall clip the ladys ears off and send to the police officers just for jolly wouldn't you. Keep this letter back till I do a bit more work, then give it out straight.

My knife's so nice and sharp I want to get to work right away if I get a chance.

Good Luck.
Yours truly
Jack the Ripper

Dont mind me giving the trade name. Wasnt good enough to post this before I got all the red ink off my hands curse it No luck yet. They say I'm a doctor now. ha ha"

The city was shrouded in a blanket of dampness as Alexander strolled along his new hunting grounds on the early morning of September 30, 1888. He watched intently from the shadows as a man was attempting to pull a woman into the street. A second man seemed to have noticed the fracas and crossed to the other side. As did a third man. Alexander traced their movements down the dark corridor until they were out of sight. The woman cried out for help, and her attacker kicked at her and exclaimed, "Blimey! I thought you were up for a bit-o-fun! You don't hafta carry on like that! Fine, I'll just leave you be then!"

Alexander approached the sobbing woman and extended his hand. She looked up at him through the fine mist and smiled. "What an absolute brute," Alexander said as he lifted the woman to her feet. "And at a time such as this. Here. Let us go by this Educational Club so that you may collect yourself, my dear. There, there. It is alright now. Please. Tell me your name." The calming woman looked into the man's kind eyes and said, "Elizabeth. Elizabeth Stride, sir." "Elizabeth. What a lovely name. And you, my dear, may call me Jack."

Alexander stood over his latest corpse for a moment and watched the blood flow from the gash in her throat. *Why do I not feel more alive?* He thought to himself. *Why do I not feel more satiated? No, my work is not done tonight. This whore's blood has not been enough to rid me of my Virginia's taunting face. I need satisfaction. I need release. I need another.*

Perhaps I will get a bit more enjoyment out of performing my work closer to the police. Yes, perhaps there is a whore in Mitre Square that could use my attention, Alexander thought to himself as his long strides quickened.

"Good evening," Alexander said softly to a teetering woman. "Well, 'ello love," the woman said through her toothy smile. "Out for a stroll this evening? Might I join you?" Alexander inquired while retrieving a small bottle from the pocket of his black overcoat. "Why, I wouldn't mind bein' in the company of such a generous gentleman," the intoxicated Catharine Eddowes replied. Alexander's darkening eyes darted around the empty warehouses that surrounded the square. He smiled at the woman, took out a sharp knife and began slashing through her throat. "Yes, I am a gentleman," he said softly while pulling her skirt above her waist. "And you are no lady. Ah, you will be found soon. And soon there will be a manhunt. I believe that I'll head east. The opposite direction of where I came. And I believe that I shall relieve you of this," he said as he ripped a piece of her apron off and used it to wipe the blade of his knife. He carefully stepped upon the stone ground to prevent the echoing of footsteps, turned a corner, randomly discarded the apron, and disappeared into the dank London fog while police whistles careened around him. "Ah yes, time for another letter," he mused while avoiding the searching shadows of the police. "Or perhaps a postcard."

I was not codding dear old Boss when I gave you the tip, you'll hear about Saucy Jacky's work tomorrow double event this time number one squealed a bit couldn't finish straight off had not the time to get ears for police. thanks for keeping last letter back till I got to work again.

Jack the Ripper.

"This is so frustrating," Alexander said to himself in the squalor of his rented room in a Whitechapel boarding house. He was furiously scribbling his latest letter while lamenting his current situation. "My sales calls are becoming increasingly fruitless. Just a few more, and I will have enough to book my passage to America. I must refocus my energy upon that. It isn't like my late evenings have been very fruitful, either. It has been over two weeks since I succeeded in finding two victims in the same evening. Perhaps I was too arrogant. The people are quite cautious now and the police are always present. And the police are receiving letters from frauds. Unscrupulous people who are attempting to take credit for my work. Is there no civility left in this world? Ah, chin up, Alexander. We will find another lady to punish. If not here, then in New York. Our latest correspondence must suffice for the moment. My first two letters were sent to the Central News agency. That certainly stirred things up now, didn't it? I believe I shall send this one to the president of the Mile End Vigilance Committee, Mr. George Lusk. If the police cannot catch me, what hope does *your* little band of vagabonds have, you silly old sot? Ah, well. It is entertaining to play with you, Mr. Lusk. Now to place this kidney in the box and off we go. I do hope you enjoy the kidney, Mr. Lusk. And I must pick up another bottle of gin on my way back from the post. I have sucked this one dry."

From hell

Mr Lusk

Sor

I send you half the Kidne I took from one women prasarved it for you tother piece I fried and ate it was very nise I may send you the bloody knif that took it out if you only wate a whil longer

signed Catch me when you Can

Mishter Lusk"

Alexander stood anxiously while he was being paid for his latest sale. "Thank you so much, kind sir, for the business. I look forward to our next meeting," he said to the shopkeeper before exiting. His thoughts then turned darker. *Yes, thank you so much, although you will never see me again. I now have enough for passage to America. I shall leave at once. Tomorrow. November the tenth. I shall arrive by the seventeenth, procure housing, and begin searching for my long, lost love. My long, lost Virginia who is about to lose her beautiful little head. On Christmas. But perhaps I should leave a parting gift for my friends in Whitechapel. They have been such generous hosts, after all, heh, heh, heh.*

"It has been quite some time for me, my dear," Alexander stated to Mary Kelly as his foreboding frame stepped out of a darkened entryway. "Yes, nearly six weeks since I have felt tender feminine flesh. And yours is, well, exquisite. Your complexion is so fair. Your hair so light. You are quite beautiful, my dear. You remind me of someone. Someone very dear to me. Someone that I long to be close to. But alas, I cannot. Perhaps I could be close to you tonight? Just for a spell."

"O-of course, sir," Mary replied as she suspiciously eyed the medical bag that the man was clutching. "Would you like to come back to my room? It isn't far. Just around this corner on Miller's Court." "I would be honored," Alexander answered as a devilish smile appeared beneath his thin mustache. "Tell me, dear, how old are you?" "Twenty-five, sir," Mary answered. "Twenty-five," Alexander repeated. "Well, it is as though Old Scratch himself has destined for this to be. Perhaps my prayers have been received after all. Lead on, my dear." The pair entered the shabby room. Alexander looked upon his date's pretty face, smiled, and began opening his bag. "I just need to retrieve something, my dear. Something that will make my evening so much more enjoyable. Yes, you remind me so much of her. And for that, my dear, I'm very sorry that you will have to suffer."

Alexander whipped out a knife and slashed Mary's face from the bridge of her nose to the bottom of the chin. The shocked woman fell back upon the bed, and before she could scream, he had slit her vocal cords. Blood gushed out of her wounds, and she helplessly stared wide-eyed as the maniacal marauder sliced her breasts until they tumbled onto the saturated bedding. She was still alive as he ripped her abdomen open and placed discarded flaps of flesh onto a table. He smiled as she let out her final gasp. His smile broadened as he removed everything from her cavity and placed it around her stiffening body. He let out a morbid giggle as he repeatedly slashed and stabbed her perfect face while staring into her petrified, dead eyes. When he had finished, she was nearly unrecognizable as anything that had once been human.

"My, you are a work of art, my dear," he said as he wiped blood from his hands and face and put his overcoat on over his drenched clothes. "My greatest achievement. So far. A fitting farewell to this horrid place. And this will be a fitting introduction to the New World. Thank you my dear for rehearsing with me. Yes, I now know what I am going to do to my Virginia. And unlike you, I want *her* to stay awake for the entire hellish experience."

"Well, it certainly didn't take you long to take away the family business, did it?" Alexander said to himself as he looked up at the large letters that read, 'Bartlesworth's Fine Clothing. Providing New York's Finest With The Finest Since 1865.' "No, not long at all. But after my visit, you will have wished to have stolen some other man's girl. It has taken me a while to find you in this bustling metropolis but find you I have. And in two days, you will receive my Christmas present. And I am quite sorry, but there are no returns. All sales are final. Oh, that is quite clever. I need to remember to say that at some point."

Alexander began trudging back to his rented room while his maniacal plan rushed through his demented mind. "Yes, this shall be perfect. I have procured everything that I need. I shall knock upon their door on Christmas morning. My Virginia will answer the door. She will not recognize me at first. Not with my wig and beard. I shall say that I am there representing a customer who wishes to present them with his special Christmas cookies. She shall thank me and close the door. And I shall wait. Wait until they have eaten the cookies that have been made with my very own White Poppy extract. All of her friends and family will be paralyzed instantly. Then, I shall enter. I will stare into my Virginia's petrified blue eyes as I remove my disguise and reveal myself to her. I will stare into her blue eyes as I disembowel everybody in her household. Her friends. Her servants. Her children, if there are any. And lastly, her beloved husband. I will carve them up right in front of her and lay their putrid organs at her immobilized feet. And then, my love, parting will indeed be such sweet sorrow. I will lay her frozen body and stare into her eyes one final time as I rip her from her pelvis to her chin and dig out her cavity with my bare hands. All while telling her that I was *her* creation. *She* was responsible for what was happening to her. For what had happened to her loved ones. For what had happened to the women in Whitechapel. Oh, it will be so liberating to finally declare that it is I who is Jack the Ripper. And my heart will burst with joy when I tell her that *I* was created out of *her* cruelty."

Alexander was laughing hysterically as he began ascending the icy steps of his boarding house. His right foot landed awkwardly on a slippery slab of wood, and he tumbled backwards onto the frigid, hard pavement, cracking his skull. He laid there muttering to himself as blood seeped out of the back of his head, "No, no not yet. Do not take me yet. Not when I was so close." Alexander Picklesbee exhaled one final time as passers-by congregated around his deceased body. Virginia Bartlesworth would never become aware of his presence in her city. Or how close she had come to being sacrificed at the demented altar of Jack the Ripper.

"Well, well, well, looky who we have here!" Satan bellowed. "Gather around, kids. We have a goddammed *celebrity* in our midst. If it isn't Jack the Ripper himself! Oh, you're quite popular down here. The savageness of your crimes. The pure hatred for your victims. Your cunning in not getting caught. Oh, and the whole 'From Hell' thing on your last letter was clever as shit. Thanks for the publicity, by the way. Yeah, your last little act would have been quite the doozy, but I just couldn't let you do it. That's the problem with dealing with the Devil. I'm *always* gonna find some way to fuck you over. But hey! You had that final hot little British tart! You fucked her up good, man! And you were imagining Virginia the entire time you were hacking that poor girl up, now weren'tcha? Come on, you know you were. You can tell me. Still too confused to talk, huh?

"Well, I'll tell you what. Seeing as how you're kinda popular down here, and you have experience in sales, I think I'm gonna take it easy on you. Yeah, I've been thinking of opening a convenience store where I can get my coffee in the morning and maybe hang around and shoot some shit with the demons. Whadaya say? You wanna run it? I mean, you'll have to burn the fuck out of your hands every morning and every evening on the security gate, but other than that it's just keeping up on inventory, stocking the shelves, and selling shit. But listen, if you take this gig, you gotta promise me one thing. You see, there's this newfangled thing that was invented about forty years ago, that I just love. It's called chewing gum, and I just love that shit. So, you have to stock loads and loads of chewing gum in the store. Deal? What am I saying? Of course it's a deal. What choice do you have? You're in fuckin' hell! Oh, and do you think I could get your autograph? Wow man. Fuckin' Jack the Ripper in my mothafuckin' house. This shit's off the hook, yo."

CHAPTER 16

PUZZLE

Melissa was pouring over information that she had gathered from numerous historical websites while clutching the gold locket that hung from her vulnerable throat. Her flannel pajamaed body was lying on its stomach on the bed while she kicked her bare feet in the air. Her eyes were transfixed on the bright computer screen as she began putting the puzzle pieces together. *Okay,* her analytical, whirring mind thought to itself. *Who is this Alexander Picklesbee and how are you related to my boyfr... um friend? They absolutely must be related. The similarities are uncanny. Think, Melissa, think. What do we know about the past Alexander?*

We know that my great-great-great-great grandmother moved to New York in 1863. We know that she broke up with this Alexander in 1864 to marry my great-great-great-great grandfather, the first Thomas Bartlesworth. Virginia's father dies. She inherited his clothier store, and it became Bartleworth's. But through the years, this Alexander stayed in contact with her. But she never opened the letters. She just shoved them into a box. Okay, let's look at the letters.

His letter dated June 1, 1864, was him pleading with her. He still had hope for a reconciliation. His next letter was dated Christmas, 1864. He had bought her the locket but didn't send it. Same mushy, heartbroken shit. The next one is from June 8, 1865. He sent her the locket. I don't know if she wore it or not, but it had been opened. By somebody. He says that he's started drinking. Gin, no less. Well, there's a slight connection. He's been kicked out of medical school. And he still has hope. He signs off 'With Love.'

Then nothing for five years. August 13, 1870. And things take a turn for the worse. He's still drinking heavily and is employed as a traveling salesman. Huh. Sales. Another similarity. But this letter is threatening. This letter is from a man who is going mad. He threatens to wring her neck. And he says, 'Until we meet again." It isn't said in a very pleasant tone. No, this is a man who is planning on seeing her to seek revenge upon her. This man is dangerous.

Then nothing for another eight years. On September 18, 1878, he writes to tell her that his parents have been killed by an animal. He is joyous about it. Except for the fact that he was left out of their will. A final reason to hate them, I suppose. He is even defensive of the animal as though this beast was justified in what it did. He has a stronger connection to this mad creature than he does to his own parents. His hatred certainly burns bright and never goes away. This last line is intriguing. 'But, if there is a God, they are looking up at my smiling face from hell.'

One final letter. August 31, 1888. Why does that date seem familiar? I'll think about that later. This one is insane. He's now employed as a salesman in Whitechapel. But most of this is about something that he has done. I need to re-read this passage again.

'But I did something tonight, my love. Something just for you. Something in your honor. Yes, tonight I finally used my hands for their true purpose. And as I was performing my task, the only image that I had in my mind was your beautiful face. The face that I love so dearly. The face that betrayed me. The face of a whore. Yes, a whore. You are all nothing but whores who lure men then break them in two. You shatter men's psyches and their spirits. You torment us with your perfumed beauty and intoxicating words of love. But I have found a way to be at peace. I have found a way to exorcize your siren curse from my very soul. I have never felt so alive. So important. So powerful. You shall not hear from me again. You are dead to me. Bitch.'

He did something in her honor. Something to honor the woman he once passionately loved. That burning passion turned to hatred. He had threatened her in an earlier letter. He loved that his parents had been viciously attacked and murdered. And now, he has done something to honor his hatred of her. Something to pay her back. Something that gave him renewed confidence and self-worth. Something that has made his broken heart be at peace. But what is it? What did you do, Alexander? What did you do on August 31, 1888? And there's this line again, but this time, he signs off with it. 'From Hell.' From hell. No, it couldn't be.

In all of my research of him over the years, the name Alexander Picklesbee was never mentioned as a suspect once. His physical characteristics aren't relevant. There were so many conflicting eye-witness accounts of what he may have looked like that it could be anybody of pretty much any body type, height, facial hair style, or age. Okay, this is just silly to think that I may have solved a mystery from over one-hundred years ago. But in all of my research on the subject, with all of the various suspects, none of them completely fit. There are strong circumstantial reasons to include them all, and there are strong reasons to discard suspicion of each of them. None of them completely fit for one reason or another. And I'm quite sure that this particular Alexander Picklesbee doesn't, either. Let's get this out of my head and go through the timeline and evidence.

Surgical training. Heavy drinker. Hated women, especially Virginia and his mother. We know by his letters he was in Whitechapel from his letter of August 31, 1888. Oh yes! Now I know the significance of that date! That was the date of the first Whitechapel murder that was attributed to him! Is that what he did in his former love's honor? Murder a prostitute? And his use of the phrase, 'From Hell.' The same phrase that was used in the final letter from the killer. Okay, okay, calm down, Melissa. According to this old passenger registration I found, Alexander left England for America on November 10, 1888. When was the final Whitechapel murder? It was...it was...no way. November 9, 1888. And then there weren't any more killings that were attributed to him. His motivation lines up. His location lines up. The dates line up. Similarities in the letters line up. Then, according to this obituary, he slipped on some ice and cracked his head open on December 23, 1888 here in New York. Two days before Christmas. You were going to give your Virgina a final Christmas present, weren't you Alexander? But the devil took that chance away from you, didn't he?

Melissa excitedly jumped out of her bed and yelled out, "Oh my God! I think that Alexander's ancestor was Jack the fucking Ripper!"

"What's that?" Melissa's fiancé Robert Jackson said as he entered their home. "Are you back looking into that Jack the Ripper shit? I thought you were past that. That's all you did for months, with the books and podcasts and online research. I thought it had finally run its course. Listen, I love that you have a hobby, but you aren't going to figure out who did it. Nobody could figure it out at the time. Historians haven't figured it out. It's a mystery that will never be solved. And why do your hobbies always have to be so violent? All the blood and murder. I'm tellin' ya babe, it just isn't healthy. Why don't you take up a peaceful hobby? Like gardening. Your father seems to find escape and relaxation working in his greenhouse. Why don't you spend some time doing that with him?"

"Well," Melissa curtly responded. "A few points here, champ. First, I wouldn't *need* a hobby if you were actually around once in a while to spend time with me. Yeah, yeah, I know. Working late. I bet you are. Secondly, I fucking *hate* my father's greenhouse. I was never allowed to go in there when I was a kid and he completely ignored me when he was in there. Sound familiar? And *one more* thing. I'm nowhere *close* to being done with my fascination with Jack the Ripper. In fact, I've *just gotten started*. But you're right about one thing. I think I *will* spend some more time with Dad. In fact, I think I'll spend the *night* there. I'm sure you won't be lonely. Just go find one of your ten-dollar whores."

She stormed into the bathroom and collected a few belongings before re-entering to change her clothes. "Melissa," Robert began in a pleading voice. "Please don't do this. It was just the one time. I swear. I know I used to have issues with, um, certain fantasies, but that's over now. My therapist has really helped me with my infatuation with hookers. I swear, I don't *do* that anymore."

"Uh,huh," an unconvinced Melissa replied as she collected her overnight bag. "Whatever you want to tell yourself. Just the one time? We *both* know that isn't true. I caught you at least *three* times after we got together. Who the hell knows how many other times there were. Especially before we met. And why I agreed to marry you after knowing that shit about you is beyond me. I mean, the twisted shit you told me and your therapist that you would pay extra for. Tie them up. Whip them. Pretend to choke them. Hold a knife to their throat while you fucked them. I loved who I thought was the real you, so I supported you. But now, I'm wondering, who *is* the real Robert? Mild mannered, open the door for you, always polite, Robert? Or the one who is fantasizing about slashing my throat while we're fucking? You think *my* hobbies are fucked up? Take a look in the mirror, pal. Oh, and don't think that I haven't noticed you hoarding the newspaper articles about the slain hookers. You getting those pages all sticky, are ya? Whatever. Do whatever you want. Get a ten-dollar whore and whip her ass. Jerk off into the plants while watching torture porn. Whatever. But whatever shit you're going to do tonight; you'll be doing it without me. And don't you *ever* lecture me about my hobbies again. You've got *your* fucked-up extracurricular interests. And I *most certainly* have mine. Maybe I'll be home tomorrow night. Maybe I won't. See ya. Oh, by the way. There's a message from your therapist. He said you missed your appointment tonight and was wondering when you want to reschedule. I hope you have a better lie for *him* than what you tell *me* about your whereabouts. And while you're scheduling appointments, why don't you get a blood test. I'm not in the mood for any STD's you may have picked up."

Melissa slammed the door. Robert's hung face sobbed into his ebony hands as his mind raced as to how to make amends for his past transgressions. His mood suddenly turned from despondency to fury as he stood up and began screaming at a framed photograph of his Melissa. "What the fuck, bitch? What the fuck do you think that I've been doing? For me? For us? I've been going to therapy! I've been doing the work! But I'm not perfect! Yeah, maybe I've slipped off the wagon once or twice. Like tonight. But I'm trying! Why can't you just support me you… you…fucking bitch!" Robert ran into the kitchenette and grabbed a butcher's knife. He re-entered the living room and began pounding the knife into Melissa's portrait until her tender face was unrecognizable. "Oh, shit, it's happening again. The feelings are happening again," he said as he collapsed onto the couch while shedding a torrent of regretful tears.

At one in the morning, later that night, a sleep deprived pair of detectives somberly walked up a creaking set of wooden stairs to the shabby second story flat of a working girl. As they approached the door, a uniformed officer ran past them and vomited over the railway. "I guess he has a weak stomach," Officer Yun Song stated while shaking her head at her nauseated colleague. "Can't really blame him though. This is the worst one yet. I hope you haven't eaten anything recently."

The stench of torn-apart flesh and internal organs was suffocating as the gagging detectives held rags over their noses and entered. What was left of the torso was hog-tied on the bed. The tortured victim had been ripped from her rectum, up the back of her spine, and through the back of her neck. Her decapitated head was watching over the proceedings from a dripping bookshelf with a pair of wide-open pleading eyes. Her back skin was flapped open, and her internal organs were strewn throughout the apartment. Wide streaks of blood were freely flowing down the bare, cracked walls.

Detective Biggs felt something splash on the top of his head. He wiped it off and looked at his crimson fingers. He looked up and saw blood droplets that were straining against gravity to hold their position on the saturated ceiling. "Well," he said as his shoes made sloshing sounds toward the victim's head. "I heard of painting the town red, but this is fucking ridiculous. What's this in her mouth? Flower petals? Maybe used to be white? Anybody want to bet that it's from a White Poppy? Jesus. We'll have to wait for the forensics, but my guess is that this poor girl was drugged and was conscious while her body was being ripped apart. Just like the others. This is the work of our guy. Our madman. No question. Victim number four. Officer Song, do we have a report on Picklesbee's whereabouts tonight? We've had a tail on him."

"Um, yes sir," Officer Song replied as she dutifully opened her notebook. "Person of interest Alexander Picklesbee left his apartment at around nine this morning. He walked through the park for several hours. He then spoke to the manager of a make-up store. He went to a liquor store and was seen speaking with a known prostitute. As a sidenote, detectives, she wasn't our victim. We know who she is, and I personally saw her walking the streets a few blocks from here on my way over. Anyway, he spoke to her briefly then went home. He was seen leaving his apartment at eight-thirty this evening. He went to a movie theatre and purchased a ticket to the nine o'clock show. And that's the last they saw of him. They couldn't locate him in the dark theater, and he did not exit after the movie. Well, he didn't exit out the front, anyway. He is suspected to have gone out of the back emergency exit. The officers then waited at his apartment. He returned home at approximately twelve-fifteen this morning."

"So," Detective Anderson said while stroking his broad, stubbled chin. "Our primary suspect is unaccounted for between nine and twelve-fifteen. We got a time of death?" "Um, yes sir," Officer Song answered. "Their initial estimation of time of death is between eleven-thirty and twelve. And it is only a ten-minute walk from here to Picklesbee's apartment. Of course, they'll have much more information once forensics takes a look at her."

"Yeah, forensics," Biggs replied. "We're supposed to get their report on anything found on the other three sometime in the next couple days. We may as well throw this one on the pile. I wish I had that report right now. I'm ready to arrest this son of a bitch. And I'm ready to be a bit rough about it. Thank you, Officer Song. You're doing wonderfully. We may make a detective out of you yet. C'mon Anderson. I think the chili dog place is still open." Two more uniformed officers vomited upon hearing the suggestion.

"Naw," Anderson replied with a shrug. "This shit doesn't do much for my appetite. I think I'll just head home. See ya around ten. Good night." Detective Anderson entered his unkempt one-bedroom apartment. He kicked away discarded pizza boxes and empty liquor bottles as he made his way to his stained couch. He pulled out his phone and opened the pictures he had taken at the crime scene. His mind began to imagine the torturous hell that the innocent woman must have experienced earlier that evening. He began sweating and breathing heavily as he unzipped his pants and began masturbating at the horrifically obscene images.

Chapter 17

Tails

"This fuckin' tail won't stay tucked inside my overcoat," Satan lamented as he watched Alexander saunter down the street. "I'm gonna blow my cover. Jesus, I fuckin' hate coming up here. All the noise. All the bustling. All the pathetic sinful souls that I wish to take with me. No, I already miss my happy place. So snugly and warm. Being lulled to sleep by the pained screams of tortured souls. And the constant blowjobs. It's just so relaxing. Well, except for the gum-snapping of those teenage bitches. Why couldn't God have created yet *another* level lower than hell that I could toss *those* bitches into? Ah, well. Their gossiping did come in handy in this instance. Rumors of dead hookers right after Alexander showed up. Coincidence? Maybe. But not fucking likely. And I can't read his soul without peering into his eyes. And I can't do *that* because then he'll know that I'm here and it might piss him off and he'll stop sending damned souls to me before their time. So, for the time being I'll just wait. And watch."

At that moment a six-year-old girl began tugging at Satan's long overcoat. "Excuse me, mister?" she inquired while wearing a concerned expression on her freckled face. "Yeah, what is it kid? I'm kinda busy," Satan replied as he peered down at the young lass from behind his large sunglasses. "Well, I'm sorry to bother you sir," the young lady began again. "But I was just wonderin'…um…do you need some sunscreen or sumthin'? You look awful sunburned."

Satan adjusted his wide-brimmed hat over his horns, knelt in front of the girl and said in a kind voice. "Naw, I'm alright kid. But thanks for askin'. I don't get enough people who are concerned about me back where I'm from. It's just always take, take, take, from them. And the complaints. Jeez Louise, do they complain. Non-stop. Anyway, not your problem. Naw, I just have a bit of a skin condition. Or maybe I'm Apache or some shit. Sorry. That probably wasn't politically correct. Not something I have to worry about back home. But don't worry about me. I'm fine."

The girl's mother approached the pair and said, "Jenny, don't be bothering this nice man." Satan concealed his jagged teeth as he smiled at the woman through pursed lips and said, "Oh, no bother ma'am. Your daughter is a delight. She was just concerned about my, um, red skin and I was just explaining that it was just a condition that I have. Her concern was very welcoming." He then looked into the young girl's eyes and glimpsed into her future. He gasped and a single black tear fell from behind his shades. "Um, listen ma'am, um, I'm not supposed to tell you this. You know, I'm just supposed to let stuff happen. But I need to tell you something. Do *not* leave your daughter alone with your priest. Ever. In fact, you may want to find another church, since you're into that shit. But please, promise me, do *not* leave your daughter alone with him. He may not seem like it, but he's a *very, very,* bad man."

The mother leaned forward and lifted her daughter's face to meet hers. "Dear, have you ever been alone with Father O'Malley?" "Just once," the little girl innocently replied. "He wanted to play a game with me. He wanted to play dress-up. He was showing me his underwear and he took out a cheerleader uniform for me to put on. Then a nun came in and interrupted our game. That's alright, isn't it Mommy? It was just Father O'Malley, and we were just having fun together."

The shocked mother looked up at Satan's distraught face and said, "Um, no. No that isn't alright. Grown men should not be playing dress-up with little girls. You did nothing wrong, dear. *He* did. And I can't believe we live in a world where I have to explain this to a six-year-old child. But I see that I must. And we are going to report this. Not to the church. We can't trust them. We're going to the police, and I want you to just be honest and tell them what you have told me. Alright, dear?" "Okay, Mommy," the little girl answered. "But is Father O'Malley going to get into trouble?"

"I sure as fuck hope so," the mother stated through gritted teeth before mouthing *'Thank you'* to Satan. Satan tipped his hat slightly, turned around, and whistled down the street. *What is the obsession with fuckin' cheerleaders? Satan thought to himself. Man, if any of these panty wastes ever actually knew a cheerleader, they wouldn't be so hot to trot for them. So fucking mouthy. And non-stop gossip. They sound like a fuckin' machine gun as they talk shit about everybody in Hell. They even gossip about me. And I can put them through all sorts of hell. Literally. But does that stop them? Nooooo. Always, 'Ohmygaaaawd! Like have you heard what Francis did after dropping Stephanie off after the demon dance? Ohmygaaaawd! It's like, so totally unbelievable!' And on and on and on like that. For fucking eternity. I'm starting to understand why God named it Hell. Fuckin' mouthy bitches. Anyway, where was I? Oh yeah, Picklesbee. Well, well, it seems as though I'm not the only one who is tailing him. Well, hello there detectives. Believe me, there is nothing that you can do to him that even comes close to what I'm going to do if he's back to sending innocent hookers to Heaven. No, his ass will be mine.*

Huh. They aren't very discreet about their tail on him. They kinda suck at this, actually. Have you noticed them, Alexander? Yes, I see that you have. But you'll have to do better than duck into that make-up store if you want to lose them. Or not. I guess that worked. Now they're distracted by the hot dog stand. Extra mustard. Sure, sure, I guess that's important when you're trying to catch Jack the Ripper. And what the fuck are you doing? Oh, what a travesty. I have as strong of a disposition as anyone else, but I just can't watch this. When will mortals ever learn? Ketchup on hot dogs is doing it wrong! Ah, well. Come on out, Alexander. The coast is clear. Are you coming out? Oh, I know what you're doing. This is your latest little gig, isn't it? You're working there to provide me with my latest delivery, aren't you? Good boy. Poppa needs a new soul to play with.

Satan watched intently as three gum-snapping, haughty young women dressed in their cheerleader uniforms entered the shop. *No! Not them Alexander! Please! Please stop. No more fucking cheerleaders. I don't have the strength.*

"Well, good morning young ladies," Alexander greeted the trio of teenage girls. "I'm so sorry to inquire, but is it not a school day? What are you young ladies doing out this morning?" A beautiful blonde looked at Alexander, turned up her nose and arrogantly said, "What's it to *you* creep? Getting an eye-full looking up our skirts? And to answer your question, yeah, it's a school day. So what. We're cheerleaders. We have cute smiles, big tits, and wealthy daddies. We can do whatever we want. We *rule* that school. And if anyone gets in our way, we'll just shed our crocodile tears and tell the police how that perverted old man principal or old dyke teacher tried to have their way with us. Then, they get fired. At the very least. I've been personally responsible for three school offi-cials getting fired since I was in eighth grade. So, unless you want to end up like *them* and lose *your* pathetic little job, you'll just keep your ques-tions to yourself and serve us as you were intended to do.

"You see, old man, there are two types of people in this world. The gifted, and the servants. We, quite obviously, are the gifted. We are pretty and popular and have money. We can get away with anything. We can bully people into submission. Just spread a little rumor and ruin their lives. Just say that a teacher is acting inappropriately, and poof. They are fucking gone. Their marriage probably is too. Just provide our greedy little followers with the lies that they so desperately crave. Just provide constant pressure, or the threat of it, and these weak-willed little worms will bend over and take whatever it is that we want to give them. All of their so-called ethics or morals or whatever just disintegrate. Because they are weak, and we are strong. The strong, like us, just take whatever we want whenever we want. And we don't care how we get it. Just give it to me or suffer the consequences. And the weak always bend. Always. And those who try to stand up to us? Well, I've already told you about the consequences, now, haven't I? It's just sooooo easy to turn one of these self-righteous assholes into a social media pariah. Then their social life is over. Or their prospects for a scholarship. Their employment potential. Their love lives. Gone in an instant because they foolishly straightened their spine and stood up to me. And, as a result, I *smashed* their fucking spine. And all the pathetic weak ones praise me for it and give me even *more* power and influence over them. They are so hateful and fearful. They love watching me destroy others' lives and live in constant fear that I will do the same to them. Wash, rinse, repeat. Over and over and over. Until I control the entire fucking school. So yeah, you old perv. It's a school day. And I'll ask again, so fucking what?"

Alexander smiled at the megalomaniacal young lady and briefly peered into her black soul before saying, "You are, of course, correct. My apologies for my unsolicited commentary, miss. Now, how may I be of service to you this morning?" "That's better," the young woman answered as her friends let out a mocking laugh at Alexander's expense. "I need some face cream. Something to make sure my skin is always free of any blemishes. What do you have?"

"Oh, well, I believe that I may just have exactly what you are looking for!" Alexander excitedly exclaimed as he reached under the counter for a glowing jar. "Yes, I believe that this will do the trick. This is exactly what a powerful young lady like yourself deserves. Here, let me show you how quickly this will work. Do you see this slight discoloration on your hand? Let me just rub a bit on, and see? All gone. And this is not just a face cream. This can be applied to your entire body and your skin will be as flawless as your soul. Would you care for it, miss?'

"Wow, that was amazing. Yeah, I'll take it. I have a date tonight and I want my entire body to be perfect, if you know what I mean. How much?"

Alexander chuckled as he placed the jar into a bright yellow paper bag. "Oh, my dear. For someone as special as you, no charge. Let's just say that I would like to stay on your good side."

"Smart move," the pompous young woman responded. "Yeah, I *bet* you'd like to see my good side, wouldn't you, you old perv? At least you know your place. You know that you are just one of the weak who are a servant to the strong. A servant to me. Come on girls. Let's go strut our asses at school. I have a certain jock that I need to rev up."

Alexander's face darkened as he watched the cackling trio exit. "Yes, my dear. Do be sure to use that cream on your entire body. We want every inch of your skin to represent who you are underneath. And yes, I do wish to remain on your good side. But that is not a problem that I will need to address. Because you don't *have* a good side you vile, little bitch. And soon, everybody will be able to see that, heh, heh, heh." Alexander snapped out of his wicked trance as a middle-aged woman was saying, "Excuse me, sir? Do you think that this blue eye shadow would accent my eyes?" "Why yes, madam," Alexander replied. "This shade of dark blue would be absolutely perfect for you. That is what we do here. We match the perfect person with the perfect make-up. Yes, everybody gets what they deserve here. And *you*, madam, deserve to look fabulous. Now, may I also interest you in this rouge?"

Satan shook his head in disgust as he watched the young women leave the store. He reached into the pocket of his overcoat and retrieved his flip phone. "I really need to upgrade this thing," he lamented as his sharp nails carefully pressed the numbers on the phone. "Now, what's that number again? Oh yeah. 666-666-6969. Heh, clever. Yeah, it's ringing. Hey, it's me. Me *who*? Who the fuck do you *think*? Satan! The Lord of Darkness and all that shit! Jesus H., I haven't been gone *that* long. Do I need to do something to you so that you don't forget me? No? Alright then. I need to talk to Glen. Why? It's none of your fucking business why! Just go get Glen! Fuck almighty! Do I have to do *everything* down there? If those fucking Christians only knew the pressure that I'm under and all the shit I have to put up with on a daily basis, maybe they wouldn't be so quick to judg…

"Yeah! Glen! Hey, listen buddy, I'm going to be up here for awhile and I need to ask you for a little favor. What the fuck do *I* care that you're in the middle of watching your stories? I'm your dark lord, so just shut up and do what I tell you! Jesus, you fuckin' demons. Just try to be nice and look at what it gets me. Alright, now write this down. I don't want you fucking this up. Yeah, I can wait for you to get a pen and paper. You got it? Oh, fuck! The pens are *always* in the top left drawer! Always! Been that way for centuries! And no, don't write it on the back of that envelope! That was an important letter! Yeah, you got it now? Alright, listen.

"We're going to have a delivery tonight and there's nobody else I can trust with this. I saw Alexander reach under the counter and give this chick some hexed skin cream or some shit, so she's definitely heading our way. Here's what I want you to do. As soon as she gets down there, strip her down and put her in a sexy maid outfit. Yeah, she should have one. She's such a fucking slut. Then, I want you to round up twenty of the ugliest, and I do mean *ugliest* fucking demons that we have down there. Well, I *know* that there's a lot to choose from. Just pick twenty. Yeah, he's a good choice. And him. Yeah, you got the idea. Alright, then condemn this new bitch to waiting on these ugly bastards hand and foot for eternity. Well, yes, *obviously* she will have to fuck them. Gang bangs and fetching them beer for eternity. Stupid fuckin' question, Glen. Oh, and one more thing. She is to be unpopular. I want her to be the most unpopular damned soul in all of Hell. Yes, of course. Mocked and ridiculed wherever she goes. When is she arriving? Fuck if I know. Probably sometime tonight, so just be ready. Oh, and Glen, you might want to sit down for this last part. You sitting? Alright, I'm really sorry to tell you this but, um, well, she's another mean-girl cheerleader. I know, I know. It'll be rough on all of us, but if we all just stick together, we can get through this. Yeah, just break it to everybody gently. Yeah, alright. Thanks Glen. You're a real pal and I'll be back as soon as I can. Yeah, okay. Yes, I'll say it back. It's just that there are a lot of people around who might hear me. No, I'm not ashamed, it's just a little embarrassing, that's all. Oh Glen. Please. Don't be like that. Okay, fine. Love you too. Happy now? Bye."

Satan noticed a smirking businessman from the corner of his eye. The businessman approached him, slapped him on the back, and said, "The ol' ball and chain got you on a short leash there, buddy?" "Oh, fuck off," Satan growled before concluding with, "And I'll be seeing *you* in about twenty years, motherfucker. Now leave me the fuck alone."

The young woman stepped out of her piping hot shower and began drying her toned body. Steam billowed around her as she applied a generous portion of her newly obtain cream onto her near-perfect white skin. She poured herself into a short, slinky black party dress and looked at herself in the mirror. She wore a devilish little smile as she said to her reflection, "Yeah, I'm definitely not going to need panties tonight."

She entered a friend's party on the arm of her latest male conquest while wearing a conceited expression as the group of teenage revelers exploded into applause. Each one in turn began heaping praise upon her. She was bombarded with endless compliments about her dress and her hair and her figure and her face. And her face. And…her…face. Joyous facial expressions turned to horrified shock and vocal revelry turned to gasps as her face began growing blemishes. Then they began appearing on her arms. Then her legs. She could feel small welts growing on her posterior and her bikini area. The blemishes first appeared small and pink. Then they darkened into a deep red and began growing. And growing. And growing. Within moments her entire face and body were covered in inch-wide round throbbing zits.

Her friends could no longer contain their maniacal glee at witnessing the misfortunes of another and burst out into laughter. Cheers and grandiose praise had been replaced by uncontrollable laughter, pointing, and cruel jokes at the expense of the confused and distraught debutante. She felt the pulsing blobs on her face and let out a terrorized scream. Her quivering blemishes continued to expand until her eyes were swollen shut and her body resembled a vile creation from a sadistic imagination. Suddenly, there was a loud explosion.

A chorus of, "Eeeeeew!" "Gross!" Oh, God, it's in my eye!" was exclaimed by the partiers as they were covered in a wave of white pus and blood. One by one, the teenagers began vomiting as they looked around and saw every surface in the room dripping with the ghastly discharge. And lying on the floor in the middle of the repugnant chaos was the bleeding deceased body of a disgraced former tyrant. Her cancerous reign on Earth had ended. Her eternity of tortured servitude in Hell had only just begun.

CHAPTER 18

REVELATIONS

Alexander used a thin straw to swirl a lime around in his gin and tonic. There was a light clinking sound as the ice tapped against the chilled glass. He was lost in his thoughts while he awaited his newfound friend. *I do wonder what the police may have found so far with regards to these latest 'Ripper' killings. Such a shame. Vibrant young ladies cut down in the prime of life. And young ladies who have experienced a life filled with pain and servitude, no doubt. What a horrid way to make a living. But they do provide a much needed and highly sought service, I suppose. So, here's to you, my lovelies. I do hope that you have finally found the peace that you so richly deserve.* He raised his glass into the air to honor the fallen women and took a sip from his drink. He opened his blue eyes and immediately smiled at the vision that was now before him.

"Hello, Alexander," Melissa said. She removed her dark red tweed overcoat revealing an equally dark red tight sweater and blue jeans that were tucked into calf-high black leather boots. "It's getting chilly out there," she said as she took her seat in the circular red vinyl booth across the table from him. "Early November. November eighth, in fact."

"Yes, yes, I suppose it is," Alexander replied. "A bit of a nip in the air. But not so much as when I was younger. No, the climate is indeed changing. The planet is becoming much warmer. Because of mankind's ignorance and greed. Much more violent storms. So many more wildfires. Reduced snowfall. Drought. And higher temperatures. If mankind does not take heed soon, why they will create hell here on Earth. And that, I can assure you, is a fate that *nobody* shall benefit from. Ah well. Free will and all of that, I suppose. On a much lighter subject, you look absolutely beautiful, my dear."

Yeah, she does, Satan thought to himself as he hid behind a newspaper while listening from an adjacent booth. *She's fuckin' hot. And I should know. And she looks just like that bitch that broke his heart and turned him into the Ripper. Like identical. I didn't expect this. I didn't expect him to find a fuckin' Xerox copy descendent of his lost love. Is that it, Alexander? Is that all it took to send you over the edge once again? But there's something about this girl. Something unsettling. I do wish I could look into her eyes. Look into her soul. But I can't. Not yet at least. If she's meant to come to me, she'll show up in due time. Just like Alexander did. And may again, if he's fucking things up.*

"Thank you," a blushing Melissa replied. "So, did you talk to the cops? Did you give them our alibi? Are you off the hook for these brutal murders?" "Well," a chuckling Alexander answered. "Let me take each of your questions in the order they were presented. Yes, I did talk to the detectives. Yes, our stories are now consistent. But no, I do not believe that I am 'off the hook,' as you phrased it. The police have been tailing me for several days. In fact, there are three of them outside this establishment as we speak. They will know that we are together. Which is fine. It only serves to strengthen our original story. We are merely friends who meet on occasion and have a drink together. I see no harm in their having that knowledge. Nor do I see any harm in their following me around. In fact, I rather enjoy it. I rather enjoy playing games with them. Ducking down dark alleys or out the back exit of a movie theater. I will just stand across the street in a darkened doorway and watch as they frantically look up and down the street for me while scratching their confused heads. I know that I shouldn't enjoy such a thing, but I must confess that I do. Old habits die hard, I suppose."

"What do you mean by that?" Melissa inquired while their smiling waitress placed her gin upon the formica table. "Oh, nothing," Alexander replied playfully. "Let's just say that when I was a bit younger there were times when I drew the attention of the authorities from time to time. I became quite good at evading them. It was a game, and I always won. I never got caught for my, um, minor indiscretions. It's nice to know that I've still got it, as the saying goes."

Minor indiscretions? Drew the attention of the authorities from time to time? Gee, you fuckin' think so? Satan thought as he perused the sports page of the paper. *Well, if that isn't the understatement of the past two centuries. Yeah, he's enjoying playing his cat and mouse games again. But is he playing operation as well? And speaking of games, the Knicks really do suck. Hmmm. I wonder what the owner would do for a championship season. Would it be worth his soul? I need to make a mental note of that and pay him a visit while I'm here. Okay, don't forget to try to steal the soul of the Knick's owner. Don't forget to try to steal the soul of the Knick's owner. Don't forget to try to steal the soul of the Knick's owner. That should do it.*

"Sooooo, speaking of the past," Melissa tentatively stated while she clutched at the locket that was concealed under her sweater. "Um, I kind of have some questions for you. Um, about something that I found in my Great-Great-Great-Great Grandmother's old chest." *I would like to find something in that bitch's old chest,* Alexander thought to himself before saying, "Oh, well what might that be, dear?"

"Well, um, this," Melissa said as she pulled the locket from inside her red sweater. Alexander let out a slight gasp and his eyes briefly welled up in tears as he gazed at the shimmering object. "You see, I found this locket. And when I opened it, I found these two pictures. One of my ancestor, who looks *exactly* like me. And on the other side, um, a picture of *this* man, who looks exactly like *you*."

"Oh my," a taken aback Alexander commented. "Why, I have not seen that beautiful locket in so many years. Um, I mean I have not seen a locket as beautiful as *this* one in so many years. It must have cost a pretty penny in its time. What is your question, dear?"

"Well, I know this sounds kind of crazy," Melissa cautiously continued. "But I also found some unopened letters. There were several letters from a man from England named Alexander Picklesbee. Which is, of course, *your* name. So, I opened these letters and found out that *this* Alexander Picklesbee was dumped by my ancestor, and I think it kind of drove him crazy. He wrote about how much he missed her and wanted her back. How he started drinking and got kicked out of medical school. His meaningless sales jobs. Then, the loss of his parents, who it seemed he didn't care for much. The final letters were, um, almost threatening. Like he wished to harm my ancestor. So, I guess my first question is, are you related to him? Is he your ancestor? Do you know anything about him? I mean, he has the same name and looks just like you so, you have to be related, right?"

Alexander discarded the questions as his thoughts turned to an earlier point. His face darkened and his closed eyes turned black as he thought to himself, *So, the bitch didn't even bother to open the letters, huh? Well, that certainly explains her lack of correspondence. I do not know what is more hurtful. Opening the letters and ignoring them or not caring enough about me to read them in the first place. What a horrid little bitch she was. Oh, if only I had been the one to send her to her grave. If only my opportunity to slay her entire family in front of her treacherous eyes had been granted. If only I had been able to rip her body apart while her terrified eyes watched me remove her loathsome organs. If only Satan had not taken that from me. And yet, she did keep the locket. And the letters. I do wonder why.*

His thoughts were interrupted by Melissa's voice. "Alexander? Alexander? Did you hear me?" Alexander's face lightened, and his sparkling blue eyes opened. He smiled at her and said, "Yes, yes. I did hear you, my dear. Just got lost in my thoughts for a moment. But before I answer your inquiry, is there anything *else* about this Alexander Picklesbee that you know? Perhaps if *I* knew what *you* knew about him, that would help in, um, uncluttering my mind about this matter."

"Well, *now* this shit gets really weird," Melissa answered while fidgeting with the opened locket. Alexander's eyes were fixated on the twirling image of his Virginia that was floating only a few feet away from him as he listened. "So, I'm a bit of a, um, let's say history buff on certain subjects. And I, um, well…how exactly do I say this? Okay, I'm just going to come out and say it. By going through the letters I can pretty much guarantee that *this* Alexander Picklesbee was driven mad by being jilted by my ancestor. So much so that his letters became increasingly violent. He was joyous about his parents being murdered by some vicious animal. He became threatening. He hated women. He was selling stuff in Whitechapel at the same time as some famous murders. The last murder was on November ninth, 1888. He left for America on November tenth. Then, the Whitechapel murders stopped. I think that he came to America for a final showdown with my ancestor. He picked Christmas for some reason. But two days earlier, according to his obituary, he slipped on an icy step and bashed his brains out and died. Listen, I don't know this for a fact, but the motive matches up. The location matches up. The timelines match up. So, what I'm asking you is; are you related in some way to Jack the Ripper?"

Holy fuck! She figured it out! Satan thought. *Damn, she is a smart one. Well, Alexander, how are you gonna handle this? Tell the truth and have a shot at staying up here? Or lie to her and be swept back into my servitude in the convenience store from hell? Oh, I can't fucking wait to hear this. Oh, look at this. Decorative pillows are on sale. Maybe I'll pick up a couple for Glen. His place could use a pop of color.*

Alexander let out a loud belly laugh. He swilled the remnants of his drink and waived at the bartender for another. He took his handkerchief from the breast pocket of his pin-striped suit and wiped his dampening forehead. He thanked the waitress for his drink and took a sip before staring into Melissa's brilliant eyes and saying with a laugh, "Oh, Satan, you are a cruel son-of-a-bitch." *Yup. I sure as fuck am,* Satan thought as he leaned is left ear closer to the adjacent booth. *Come on, get on with it, Alexander. This is better than my soaps.*

Melissa's face was filled with confusion as she listened. "Yes, quite cruel indeed. I lost my true love and was denied the opportunity to punish her for her betrayal of me. Then, when I fall for her descendant, I am once again denied the opportunity to be in the arms of the one that I cherish so. Because, you see, my dear, I had two conditions when I was allowed to come back to Earth. One was that I mustn't re-engage in my previous, um, activities. The other condition was that should anyone figure out my true identity, that I must tell the truth. I must reveal my true identity to that person. Of course, I never thought that that would occur, so I readily agreed to Satan's offer.

"Melissa, what I am about to tell you will sound quite mad. But, as you have already ascertained, I *am* a bit mad, and I am quite sure that Satan's little prank will deny me of yet another's love. You see, for the past 136 years, I have been in Hell. Since my unfortunate death on December 23, 1888, I have been in Hell. Not some figurative hell, mind you. Actual Hell with the fire and brimstone and tortured souls and on and on. Satan and I struck a deal. He allowed me to return to Earth for all time if I provided him with sinful souls before they were due to arrive. You see, there has been an uptick in souls going to Heaven, and he was wanting to even the odds, as it were. Plus, he gets bored rather easily, and I must say, he is a bit unbearable when he is bored. Quite a whiner, actually."

Oh, I'm an unbearable whiner, am I? Satan roared in his own head. *I'll unbearably whine up your posh white ass, motherfucker! Who the fuck do you think you are, talking shit about me to strangers? This woman doesn't even know me! Now, she's gonna get a bad impression of me! This is worse than those fucking cheerleaders! I expect that shit from them! They have the maturity of a, well, a teenager! But you? You're a distinguished man of the world! You should know better! Be better! This is really hurtful, you English fuck.*

Melissa did not know whether to laugh, cry, or run away screaming as she continued to listen while twirling the locket. "Anyway, all of that isn't important. I, of course, agreed, and I joyfully went about my assignment. You see, dear, what I do is accept temporary employment from local businesses. Most of them have been in this area, but I did go to Boise once. Anyway, also not important. I don't accept these positions as much as I offer them. I essentially hypnotize the manager or owner of the establishment so that they allow me to work for them for a day. And they never remember me or our encounter. Once I am employed there, I search for sinners who are destined to go to Hell at some point. Once I find them, I sell them a cursed object that proves to be their ultimate demise. And then, off to Hell they go. I am not proud to admit this, my dear, but I nearly sold *you* such an object. A record. You looked so much like my Virginia and my hurt feelings came back and I momentarily lost control of myself. Fortunately, I calmed down and took the curse off of that Mozart recording. And what a fortuitous decision that was. That gave us the opportunity to get to know one another and you received an astonishing recording of one of the greatest works of all time.

"So, my dear, that is why I am on Earth. A deal with Satan to provide him with more souls. Now, as far as my relation to the man in the locket. I *am* the man in the locket. I can certainly go into more detail at a later time, but yes, that is me. Yes, that is me and my Virginia. Yes, she left me and broke my heart. Yes, it drove me to drink a bit too much, get kicked out of medical school, and to hate women. Yes, it drove me into the depths of madness. Yes, I drugged a wolf, dragged it into my parent's bedroom, and watched from outside their window as the beast tore them apart. That *was* an entertaining evening, I must say. Yes, I was dispatched to Whitechapel where my insanity and anger grew to the point where I murdered several innocent women. Well, perhaps not innocent, but they certainly did not deserve what I did to them. Yes, I traveled to America with the intention of butchering your ancestor and her entire family in front of her eyes on Christmas. Yes, I was denied that opportunity when I slipped and fell and cracked my head open. Which, I might add, has resulted in a terribly nagging headache ever since my unfortunate tumble. So, yes, my dear, it is true. Everything that you just said about me is absolute gospel, for lack of a better word. Yes, I am Jack the Ripper. Or at least I was. But, my sweet Melissa, as shocking as I know this must be, you must believe me when I tell you…"

Alexander was cut off by Melissa's trembling voice. "A-Alexander, I-I-I just don't know what to say. I don't know whether you are playing some sort of joke on me or if this insane story is true. I don't know whether to fear you or love you. Yes, I fell in love with you. And now, I don't know who you are. Just like my fiancé. I don't know what to believe or what to feel. I don't know whether to run from you, lash out at you, or hold you. I don't know whether to laugh with you or cry without you. If you are playing a joke, then you are not the man that I thought you were. And if you are telling the truth, then…then…I am confused. I am devastated. I'm sorry, Alexander, but I need some time to process all of this. I need some time to myself. Please don't contact me. Good-bye, Alexander."

"Huh, I wonder what he said to get her to rush off in such a huff?" Detective Biggs asked as he watched Melissa rush past them and onto the crowded sidewalk. "Musta been juicy," Detective Anderson answered before looking at Officer Song and saying, "And speaking of juicy, hey, Officer Song. Or is it, Yun? Can I call you Yun? How about you and me getting together for a drink when our relief shows up? Maybe we could talk about your, um, path for advancement. And maybe we could talk about some other stuff too. Y'know. If ya want."

Officer Song's eyes darted at Biggs who silently shook his head at her. "Um, thank you for the offer, detective," she answered. "But I really don't like to mix business and personal relationships. But thanks just the same."

"What do you mean?" an agitated Anderson responded. "This *would* be professional. Just two colleagues putting our heads or something together to figure out how to fast track that detective's badge for you. And hey, maybe a little re-training on the use of hand cu…"

Anderson was immediately cut off by Biggs. "Officer Song, thank you for your time tonight. Our relief should be here soon. Why don't you head home. We'll see you tomorrow at the forensics lab. We're finally going to see what the white coats have found. Good-night, officer."

Alexander sat alone at his booth as a large man who had been sitting next to him walked toward the exit. *Oh dear*, he thought to himself. *What a cruel joke, Satan. To be forced to tell my love the truth about my sordid past. I am quite sure that she will never speak to me again. Yes, Picklesbee, it seems as though you have been jilted by another. Perhaps it isn't so bad, though. Perhaps this is Satan's way of rewarding me. Perhaps I am to complete my unfulfilled promise to my Virgina. Yes, perhaps I was destined all along to complete my promise on her descendent, heh, heh, heh.*

Alexander looked at the clock as he entered his apartment. "Two in the morning, already," he said as he began removing his clothes and hanging them in the closet. He jumped as he heard a fleet of sirens and brilliant flashing lights fly past his building. "Oh my, what now? Never a dull moment on my street, that is for certain."

He changed into his pajamas and had just completed shaving the evening's stubble from around his tailored moustache when he heard a light knock on his door. "Oh, detectives, what do you want now?" he muttered under his breath. He then lost his breath as he opened the door and looked upon the angelic face of Melissa Bartlesworth. She silently entered his apartment, unbuttoned her black trench coat, and allowed it to slump to the floor. Alexander's heart pounded as he stared at the flawless naked flesh that he had longed to hold since he was a young man in medical school. Melissa approached him, enveloped his shaking body in a tight embrace, and whispered, "I believe you. And it makes me love you even more, Alexander. Or do you prefer to be called Jack?"

Chapter 19

Dots

"Estimated time of death was one this morning. Same lacerations. Same, um, carnage," Officer Song solemnly reported to Detectives Anderson and Biggs. "This looks to be Victim Number Five of the same killer. Forensics have worked all night lifting evidence. They said there's something in particular that they're looking for and may have those results when they arrive in a little while to give their report on the other four women. And, with all due respect detectives, before we get into the weeds of this case I need to say something. I need to get this off my chest. These were women. They aren't statistics. They aren't unimportant "working girls." They aren't some files of evidence locked up in some filing cabinet. These were women. Breathing, living women. They were human beings.

"But that's not how many men see them, now is it? No, many, certainly not all, but many men out there view women as less than. We are property. We are servants and sex slaves and subordinate little mice who were put on this Earth to please men. Brutal, uncaring, self-centered men. This is, of course, the norm in many societies around the world. Even in the year 2024. Women have to cover up so as not to tempt men's primal urges. They can't drive. Can't go to school. Can't participate in their own political fate. They are, indeed, property. In our country, women have made huge strides in becoming equal members of society. We, of course, have never achieved that true equality. Just look at the pay inequities. Just look at the comparative number of elected representatives at all levels of government. Look at the heads of Fortune 500 companies. And on and on. No, we still have great inequality, but great strides had been made.

"And I do mean *had* been made. Because this fucked up "Bro culture" with all of its misogynistic impulses is taking over. And, once again, it is open season on abusing women. Millions of women who don't even have control over their own reproductive health. Women being unwelcome in the workplace. Harassed. Passed over for promotions. Hell, some in this horrid movement of knuckle draggers have even suggested that we shouldn't be allowed to vote. They are winding the clock back to a time when women should just be a good little housewife, have dinner on the table, and give hubby a blowjob when he can't get his secretary to do it. I feel the change. We *all* feel the change. In our workplaces. Our schools. In restaurants and bars. We feel the lecherous eyes. We know what many men think about us. There is no respect in their smiles. No caring. Just lust. Lust and control. And I, for one, am not going to take this shit. So, detectives, what you may see as just another case, I see as an unfortunate end to these women. Women who I think of as my sisters. These murders are just a morbid extension of the true nature of many men. There are many men who would do this exact same thing if they thought they could get away with it. And again, not all. There are many men who are our allies and partners and friends and lovers. They are wonderful people. But there are many men who are not. Men who view me as their entitlement when I sit at a bar or buy groceries or go for a jog. I see them. I see how they see *me*. And it makes me sick.

"Which leads me to my final point, gentlemen. Detective Anderson, if you *ever* dangle a promotion over my head in exchange for my company again, you won't have to worry about Internal Affairs. You're going to have to worry about my fucking Black Belt. And your balls. Got it? Oh, and one more thing. Keep your fucking eyes off of my ass and tits. I hope that I've made myself clear."

Detective Biggs had to bite his lower lip in order to restrain his laughter and applause as he looked at his fuming partner. Anderson's beet red face was lowered as he licked the wounds that had just been inflicted upon his meek ego. He carefully contemplated every possible comeback. All but one contained terms such as "dyke" and "bitch." He suppressed his natural inclinations, looked up while flashing a fake smile, and said, "Yeah, alright. I'm very sorry Officer Song if I gave you the wrong impression. It won't happen again. Now, can we get to work? We have the murderer of five *women* to find."

"Yeah," Officer Song retorted. "That apology was fake as fuck, but as long as you know where I stand, I'll accept it. Next time, I won't be so generous. Okay, I thought it might be helpful to go through each victim and see if we have anything at all besides the possible forensics to tie any of our suspects to each woman. Would that be alright, detectives?"

"You know what?" Biggs answered. "Today, officer, we are following *your* lead. You have a keen analytical mind. And a pretty good read on people too, as it turns out. So, take it away, officer. The floor is yours."

"Thank you, detective. I appreciate your respect," Officer Song sincerely replied. "Let's get started, shall we? Victim Number One was found in a back alley in Queens. Her throat was slashed and her internal organs removed and laid out neatly around the body. White Poppy extract found in her system. She was found just a few blocks from Picklesbee's. But also just a few blocks from the apartment that Melissa Bartlesworth shares with her fiancée, a Robert Jackson. No eyewitnesses. Nothing to tie any of them, including Thomas Bartlesworth, to her. She was missing her undergarments. They have not been found.

"Victim Number Two was a young blonde. Found in the back alley right behind Picklesbee's apartment. Same lacerations and removal of organs all neatly laid out. Again, White Poppy extract. Picklesbee lied about his alibi. He said that he was with another escort that night. Melissa said *she* was with him. Then, after they had a chance to get their stories straight, he changed his story to match hers. This victim also did not have any undergarments. Picklesbee had a pair of panties in his apartment that he said was Melissa's. According to him, he spilled a drink on her and she removed them to dry them out, then never took them. He said that he gave them to a Black prostitute who he spoke with outside of a liquor store. No connection with Thomas.

"Which leads us to Victim Number Three. Black prostitute in a red dress. Matches the woman of Picklebee's first alibi. White Poppy extract. This poor soul was ripped apart. The others were done more, um, carefully. This was done in a fit of rage and her, um, parts were strewn everywhere in the alley behind the liquor store. Written in the victim's blood on the wall was 'PRAY 4 THE WHORE.' Picklesbee admits to speaking with her and giving her Melissa's panties. There were also corroborating eyewitness accounts of him speaking with her. No panties were found. Then, another twist. An eyewitness, who recently died of a heart attack, saw her getting into the car of Thomas Bartlesworth. We got a search warrant for Thomas and Picklesbee and we'll get those results at any moment.

"Victim Number Four is just too gruesome to even discuss. Found in her rented room. The most horrific scene. Hard to tell if any of her personal effects were taken. We had a tail on Picklesbee, but we lost him. His whereabouts are unknown at the time of the murder. Same is true of every other suspect. This one had White Poppy petals in her mouth.

"And our latest one. Victim Number Five. Tall, African American. Found behind the movie theater that Picklesbee has been at and is just a short walk from the bar he was at. Back to his original M.O. He was more calm with this one. Throat slashed. Internal organs removed and placed around her head in a heart shape. Is he sending us a valentine? Does he really love these women? Is it a message to somebody else? Or just a red herring? This was careful. Almost loving. Her face was not touched, unlike the others. But, like the others, her eyes were wide open. She was probably still awake when the attack occurred. Time of death, around one. Picklesbee was seen leaving the bar at twelve, gave our tail the slip once again, and arrived home around two. Same clothes. No appearance of blood, although it was dark. No connection to Melissa or

Thomas that we know of. And, of course, no eyewitnesses. This woman was probably drugged as well so she couldn't scream as he tore her apart. We don't have enough yet, but it all seems to come back to Picklesbee.

"Nope, try again," the Chief Forensic Officer, Jessica Townsend said as she entered the room. The metal cart that she was pushing contained five thick files. The cart's back wobbly wheel made a harsh clacking sound on the wooden floorboards as hopeful answers to the mystery came tantalizingly closer. She placed the five files on the long, battered conference table, sat down, and began. "Now, listen. I'm not saying that we can exclude him. All the circumstantial evidence points in his direction. What I'm saying is that we have no forensic evidence to link him to any of these women. And when I say we have no forensic evidence, I mean we have *no* forensic evidence. We have no samples. There was absolutely *nothing* on the items that you took from his apartment. No hair on the hairbrush. No saliva on the toothbrush. No stubble on his razor. Nothing. Not even fingerprints. The officer who took his prints swears that they were on the card. By the time he got them back to the lab, they were gone. Just flat smudges of ink with no discernible features. I can't explain it. Must have been an error of some sort, but that doesn't explain why he leaves no trace of himself on his personal effects. Nothing. No skin cells on his clothes. No stray eyelashes. And the items in his medical bag? Yep, quite a morbid assortment of medical tools, but completely clean. No blood. No fingerprints. Absolutely nothing on anything that he owns. It's almost like anything he sheds, instantly dies and turns to dust or something. But that's a mystery for another time. A mystery that we may not get a chance to answer, because I doubt that you're able to get another warrant on him. You see, we *have* found a forensic connection. Just not to him.

"The connection is with Thomas Bartlesworth. We found on all five women, including last night's, multiple hair fibers and skin cells that match him. He was with all five. It's under their nails, on their organs, on their bodies, or what is left of them. His DNA is all over each of them. And it's a perfect match. Now, you find a link to him and this White Poppy extract, which, yes, is also in the system of our latest victim, well, you've got an open and shut case. His DNA on all five. According to your interviews, he has frequently been seen in the company of prostitutes throughout his adult life. Oh, and one other thing. Don't forget that his *wife* was found in a similar condition with the White Poppy extract as well. We may have just solved *six* murders here folks. And to tie this up in a tidy little bow, as for Melissa, we didn't have any warrant on her, so no forensics to test against. We did, however, find the hairs of an African American male on the first victim, but not on any of the others. So, if you had any reason to look at Melissa's finance, that looks to be a dead end as well."

Officer Song's gaping mouth mirrored those of the detectives. She looked at them, smiled, and said, "Well, detectives, is that search warrant still valid? I don't think that we checked the greenhouse, did we?" Anderson and Biggs quietly got up from their rickety chairs, put on their overcoats, and waved for Song and Townsend to follow them.

"What is the meaning of this?" Thomas Bartlesworth VI yelled as he entered his provincial home. "I-I'm so sorry sir," the butler stated to his frantic employer. "I asked for them to wait for your arrival, but they showed their credentials and a search warrant, and I had to let them in." "It's alright, Raymond. I'm sure this is just a little mix-up. Detectives, today is a rather busy day for me, and I cannot leave Melissa alone to run the shop for very long. I have been *completely* cooperative with you. I admitted to seeing one of those poor unfortunate ladies. I have no idea who the other four are. Please, won't you…"

Detective Anderson perked up, flashed a knowing look at Biggs, and asked, "*Four* women? Why do you think there are *four* more women that we are investigating?" "Well, well, aren't you?" Thomas stammered. "Wasn't there another found last night behind the movie theater? I know it isn't in the news yet, but for a large city, this is a small town. Everybody's talking about it. I just assumed it was the work of…of…um… whoever it is you are looking for. Now, please detectives, I do not know how else I can be of assistance to you."

"I do," Biggs answered. "Show us the way to your greenhouse." "M-my greenhouse? But what on Earth for?" a sweaty Thomas answered. "Why, that is just my hobby. There isn't anything in there but my plants and gardening tools."

"Yeah, I bet they're *sharp* gardening tools," Anderson chided. "Come on Mr. Bartlesworth. Let's take a look. Probably nothing there. But I've always wanted to have a bit of a green thumb. I'm eager to learn. Please. Lead the way."

The overwhelming scent of the combination of lush flora greeted the investigators as they entered the sultry greenhouse. Chief Forensics Officer Townsend showed the six members of their forensics crew a picture of the flower that they were searching for. Anderson and Biggs stood on either side of the quivering Thomas as they keenly watched the crew lifting petals and leaves in the perfectly landscaped oasis. They trudged through the soil, being careful to not step on any of the luscious plants. From the back of the greenhouse, Officer Song's voice rang out. "Detectives! I think we may have something here!"

Biggs and Anderson each grabbed one of Thomas's arms and marched him to the very back of the greenhouse. They waded through entangled leaves and burgeoning flowers until they arrived at the sweating glass wall. "Why, why, how did *that* get in here?" a shocked Thomas exclaimed as his bewildered gaze fell upon a gorgeous White Poppy. "You mean, *you* didn't plant that? Care for it? It's in really good condition. Doesn't look like it's been ignored," Anderson stated.

"No, no, that isn't mine," Thomas answered. "I mean, I used to have a plant similar to that one many years ago, but I, um,…" His trailing voice was replaced by Biggs's. "So, you used to have a plant like this many years ago. Maybe twenty-three years ago, around the time of your wife's death? Alright folks. You got the pictures? Let's dig this thing up and get it to the lab."

Thomas continued his frenzied stammering. "B-but, I *swear*. I had no idea that this was here. It is way in the back in an area I rarely use. Perhaps a seed fell from my previous one? It makes no sense. I dug that plant up twenty-three years ago! I didn't need it any longer! I did not place this here!"

"I bet you didn't place *this* here *either*, did you?" Officer Song asked as she pulled a metal box out of the newly created hole. She brushed the dirt from its top and hinges and opened it. "Wow, Mr. Bartlesworth," she said as her eyes were fixated on the contents of the box. "This must be some new way of gardening. Do you use bloody bras and panties as mulch or something? Thomas Bartlesworth, you are under arrest for the murders of…"

CHAPTER 20

HERESY

Melissa was sobbing on her boyfriend's shoulder as the pair lay in bed together. He was tenderly stroking her golden hair as her tears were absorbed by his red plaid flannel pajamas. His mind whirled as he tried to think of just the right thing to say to relieve her of her anguish. *I must be careful,* he thought to himself. *I do not want to hurt her more or make her cross with me. It has been weeks like this. Ever since her father's arrest. She comes to bed and weeps unconsolably. It is quite painful to witness. I wish that I could take her pain away. I wish I could hold her and relieve her of this burden. I wish to see her smile again. But the evidence against her father is quite voluminous. We have been told by the detectives that his hair was found on all the victims. The White Poppy plant in his greenhouse. And, of course, the souvenirs that he took from each of his victims. Each of those poor unfortunate souls had an article of clothing in his lock box. No, he most certainly is guilty of these heinous crimes. And now, they are re-opening the investigation into his wife's murder. He is so distraught and frightened that they have placed him on suicide watch. No, I'm afraid my Melissa is going to lose her father one way or another. This is going to be a very sad Christmas.*

He let out a deep breath, lifted Melissa's eyes to his and said, "Melissa, my dear. I am so sorry for everything that you are experiencing. I do wish I could relieve your pain, and I am quite sorry to bring this up, but I must know. I do love being in your arms each night, but what about Robert? What about your fiancé? It really isn't fair to him to string him along like this, dear."

"Yeah, I know," Melissa replied as she sat upright and wiped her damp face with the pink sleeve of her pajama top. "But it's complicated. I've told him that I need some space. I need some time to sort all of this out. My father's arrest. My relationship with him. I need time. And has he given me that time? Fuck no! He blows up my phone constantly! You don't know him like I do, Alexander. He has a darkness in his soul. He won't let me go. I just know it. He'll keep stalking me and harassing me. Unless I handle this in just the right way."

Alexander chuckled slightly and said, "Yes, well, don't we *all* have a bit of darkness in our soul, my dear?"

"This is different!" Melissa roared back. "His darkness is aimed at *me*! He gets off on kinky sex. Tying me up. Pretending to strangle me. Real twisted, violent shit. And when I refused to play along, he'd find a hooker who would."

"Well, my dear," Alexander carefully replied. "You *do* realize that you are lying next to Jack the Ripper, don't you? I'm not exactly known for my stability. Especially when it comes to engagements with the fairer sex. In fact, as I told you, I nearly killed you by placing a hex on your record."

"Yeah, and *that* would have been a real dick move!" Melissa retorted. "Real nice. Murder me just because I look exactly like your lost love. You definitely need to get *that* shit together. I don't want to go around constantly wondering if I'm going to be murdered somehow by my teacup, or TV remote, or bath towel." Alexander's heart was then lifted as Melissa released her beautiful laugh for the first time in weeks. "Oh, I know that I needn't worry about that," she continued.

"I know that *you* would never truly hurt *me*. Sure, you might have murderous flashes every now and again. Like when I put your socks in the wrong drawer the other day. I saw it in your eyes. For a moment, you wanted to strangle me. But the moment passed, and you simply smiled and placed the socks in their rightful place."

"Well, Melissa," Alexander replied. "In my defense, every item has…" He was cut off by Melissa's giggling response. "Yeah, yeah, I know. Every item has its own space in this world. I know. You've told me like, a *bajillion* times. It wouldn't hurt to loosen that shit up a little bit though. SHEESH! OCD much? Anyway, I can live with that. I can live with that because I know that you will never *truly* harm me. You would never harm your soul mate. Yes, that is what we are. Soul mates. I felt it the first time we met. I was drawn to you. Your charm. Your elegance. That sexy little British accent. And your darkness. I felt it. And it turned me on. I don't know why, but I've always been attracted to bad boys. Maybe to get back at my father for…for…I can't believe that he's being accused of *that* as well. Anyway, for whatever reason, I've always been drawn to the outlaw. The renegade. The villain.

"All through high school, my boyfriends were always the tough kids from the wrong side of the tracks. Then, there's Robert who may *seem* very polite and respectful and docile but has all kinds of fucked up shit in his head. And all of those missteps have led me to you. The ultimate bad boy who is my soul mate. My Alexander. My Jack. When you first told me, I had to leave the bar. Not because I was upset. As fantastical as your story was, I knew deep down inside that it was true. Yes, I may have had a few moments of confusion, but that's not why I abruptly left. I had to leave because just *knowing* that I was in the presence of Jack the Ripper nearly gave me an orgasm. It was crazy. I was in love with a deceased damned soul from Hell who was guilty of the most abhorrent acts against women. A man who had just told me that he nearly killed me. A man who nearly slayed my ancestor and her entire family. What was I doing? My head told me to run. My heart was drawn to you. So, I walked around for a while telling my head to shut up while allowing my heart to lead me. And it led me right back to you. So, don't worry about Robert. I told him that we will get together on Christmas. At my father's house. I will finish it then once and for all. And then, my love, we can spend an eternity in one another's arms. Oh, and there's one *more* reason that I know you won't hurt me. Because if you do, I'll tell Satan and then you'll be in trouble. So, just mind your manners there mister, and don't murder me or else I'll tell on you. Got it? Good. Now, let's change the subject. I don't want to think about my father or Robert anymore tonight. Let's order a pizza and you can tell me some more of your stories. They're fascinating."

"Alright my love," Alexander replied as he got out of bed and went to his coupon basket. "*This* coupon is still good. Quite the deal. Two medium, two toppings for twenty dollars. Would you like a sausage, mushroom? And perhaps a pepperoni, onion?" "That sounds perfect," Melissa answered as she went into the kitchenette and began retrieving plates and napkins. "And a salad. With Italian. Oh, and some mozzarella sticks. And maybe some garlic bread. I have barely eaten in weeks! I'm starving!"

"Your wish is my command, my love," Alexander replied as he began dialing the number. "Well, it should be here in an hour," he said as he plugged his phone back into its charger. "I will never get over this modern world. All of this information right at everybody's fingertips. The knowledge of the world in the palm of your hand. And what do most people use it for? Cat videos and sex. Satan has always said that he would rule the world one day, and this contraption just may be the tool he needs to accomplish that feat. The more information people have access to, the more ignorant they seem to become. Willfully so, in fact. They shun actual information that can have grave impacts on their lives in order to post themselves eating. Or at the park. Or doing any sort of mundane task. They believe that they are so special that others will be interested in every facet of their lives. From the boring to the tedious. It *must* be interesting because *they* are doing it, and in their own minds, *they* are the most interesting people to have ever walked the Earth. It has become a very self-absorbed, narcissistic society. A society of immediate gratification. And that lust for immediate gratification diminishes their ability to critically think. To take in information and question its validity. To use information to see the larger picture. They make decisions that make them feel good at this exact moment and ignore the future consequences. All they care about is what will make them feel good, or satisfied, or powerful at this exact moment. And any warnings to the contrary are belittled and discarded. This self-absorbed willful ignorance has been true of every mortal who has ever made a deal with the devil. It seems as though at least half of the people in this nation have made that very same deal. Without even knowing it, they are sleepwalking into Hell. And it is *also* amazing that I can speak to someone on this contraption and in an hour, I will have a piping hot pizza delivered right to my door. Yes, technology certainly has its pros and cons.

"But enough of this gibberish. What tales would you like to hear about, my dear? What will place a smile upon your perfect face? Would you like to hear more details of the original Ripper murders? How I was able to evade detection? Or perhaps my plans for your ancestor's demise on Christmas 1888? Ah yes. The proverbial one that got away. That would have been a delightful massacre.

"Or how about something more recent? Would you like to once again hear about my exploits since I was granted my position here on Earth? The spoiled little girl and her licorice? The man hung by his toolbelt? The demonic little boy and his toy soldiers? That horrid doctor in Idaho? The teenage boy whose record betrayed him? No, perhaps not that one again. That one reminds me of nearly killing you, my love. I think it is best if we do not speak of that again. I do not wish to have to, um, how does the saying go? Ah, yes. Be in the doghouse.

"Would you like to hear about those wretched young men and their cologne? Oh, how I abhorred them. 'Bro' this and 'Bro' that. Complete imbeciles. And speaking of imbeciles, how about the bigot who was beaten to death in the park? Or that wretched woman who *dared* to speak ill of the *Hanging Chads* series. Of all the people that I have sent to Hell, she may just be the worst. Utterly blasphemy to speak in such a way about a treasured piece of art. Oh, I know. How about I speak once again of that delightful little puppy, Bealzebuddy. What an adorable little scamp she is. I do so enjoy seeing her playing with her forever family at the park and ripping the throats out of would-be assailants. She does enjoy her chew toys. Or perhaps that conceited little bitch who turned into a giant zit? I must admit, I am a bit proud of that one."

"Ew, no," Melissa stated while wearing a disgusted look upon her face. "Not *that* one. Especially before we eat. I mean, sure, I'll give you points for your creativity, but that was just gross, Alexander. No, I want to hear more about your time in Hell. What's it like? Do you have friends there? Any celebrities? Come on, baby. Gimme some dirt on Satan and his bad-ass band of thieves."

Careful, Alexander, an eavesdropping Satan thought to himself as he hovered outside of Alexander's second story window. *I'm still kinda pissed about what you said about me a few weeks ago. Best not to try me again. And who woulda thunked it. Thomas Bartlesworth was the killer all along. A minor character who was just kinda in the background turns out to be The Ripper 2.0. I do feel a bit bad for ever doubting Alexander. But, in my defense, it was quite the coincidink what with these poor women getting hacked up right after the arrival of Jack the Ripper. But no. It wasn't him. And yet, why do I still have this urge to be up here, watching? Why am I still drawn here? Why do I feel that this story isn't complete yet? Well sure, one reason is that it's only Chapter 20 and this asshole author's books are always 23 chapters. Always. So, there's that. But there's something more going on here. Plus, I don't want to miss the roast beef special at the diner tomorrow. I hope Ruth's working. I can get free soda refills from Ruth. Plus, she has a nice caboose. Too bad she's not going to Hell. I looked into her eyes the other day and, nope. She's going north. Which is what a lot of these dumbfuck Americans should be doing with all the shit that's about to go down up here. But they're stuck. Fuckin' Canadian immigration laws. Americans really should band together and form a caravan and...oh, he's about to speak. Yes, tell her all about Hell, Alexander. I'm all ears. And horns. But mostly ears.*

Alexander began laughing and sat at the end of the bed. "Come my dear. Sit on my lap and I'll tell you all about it." Melissa immediately plopped down on his lap and turned her head toward him. Her petite feet dangled to his side as her sparkling blue eyes gazed into those of her soul mate. "Well, there really isn't that much to tell. It really is exactly what you might think and is rather boring. Excruciating heat. Fiery brimstone flying all about the place. The never-ending screams of the tortured damned. *Always* the constant screaming of millions of sinners. Although sometimes, they try to harmonize with each other, just to add a bit of whimsy to the morbid proceedings. It's actually quite pleasant when they do that. Like a million tortured ABBA's all singing at once. I listened to one of their records while I was employed at the record shop. Quite pleasant and toe-tapping, I must say. They are no Mozart, but quite satisfying, none the less.

"Anyway, new arrival day is usually quite entertaining. We get to hear the sordid stories of the recently damned and then Satan usually puffs his chest to make himself look menacing before passing his torturous eternal sentence upon them. He needs to do that. The poor creature does suffer from an inferiority complex because of you know who. No, he is definitely not a big fan of Jesus. Quite jealous of all of the worshippers he has. But he *does* find it quite amusing that the majority of Jesus's followers end up in Hell. Yes, many of the uber religious are quite dastardly. Oh, the atrocities that they commit when they are not sitting in their uncomfortable pews and piously proclaiming their loyalty to their savior. Rumor has it that…well, no. Perhaps I shouldn't tell you this. It is *just* a rumor, and I wouldn't want to be a gossipy Gus."

"What is it? Tell me! Pleeeease?" Melissa pleaded as though she were a child begging for ice cream. "All right, my dear. I'll tell you," Alexander excitedly replied through his lighthearted chortles. "I've just been *dying* to tell somebody this for some time. Well, you did not hear this from me, but a little birdie told me that Jesus gets quite upset at those who bastardize his name. Those who pray to him every night and preach to others about his gospel right after raping a child or beating their spouse or worshipping their latest golden calf. This is quite upsetting to him. He doesn't like for this to get around because of his reputation for being forgiving and all of that, but he is a man, after all, and all men have their fallacies. Even him. I have heard that when those types are being judged at the pearly gates, that Jesus himself will come down. It is said that he is to always be called when one of *those* types of souls arrive. He's usually soaking wet and in a robe when he gets there because he spends most of his time playing with former prostitutes in his Olympic sized pool. That entity does have a soft spot for those ladies, I must say. Well, I guess that is a stone that *I* cannot cast, now, can I?

"And so many prayers aren't received by him because he can't hear them from under the water in his pool. I have heard that he is submerged quite frequently because he has a kink for watching women while they swim. It is said that he sits on the bottom of the pool and watches them as they kick their legs to and fro. I guess he's a leg man. Well, we all have our thing now don't we. And as such things go, I suppose this one is relatively benign.

"Oh, and once again, you did *not* hear this from me, but I've *also* heard that Moses is no longer welcome at the pool parties. One time, Jesus was trying to impress a newly arrived lady by doing a double back flip off the diving board. Just as Jesus was about to hit the water, Moses parted it, and Jesus landed on the concrete floor of the pool. I understand that he sustained a nasty concussion. But he forgave Moses because, well, he's Jesus. But *then* Moses turned all the water in the pool into wine and all the women became quite intoxicated and made a horrendous mess all over Jesus's mansion. There was vomit and urine and feces everywhere. I am told it looked like the American Capitol on January 6, 2021, after those unruly heathens occupied it. But that may be an exaggeration. I sincerely doubt that it could have been *that* bad. Anyway, from that point on, Moses was no longer invited to his pool. And I must say, who could blame him?

"Now, where was I? Oh, yes. So, Jesus goes to the pearly gates. Now, of course, this causes quite the ruckus. There is cheering and clapping and calling out his name and all of that nonsense. He usually allows a few selfies and signs a few autographs for the blessed ones. But then he turns his attention to his faux followers. He lectures them and makes them watch every scene from their lives that did not adhere to his teachings. Then, he strips them naked, straps them up to a splintery cross, places a ball gag in their mouth and whips them mercilessly. He then slips the guards a C-Note and tells them that they didn't see nothin', see? He's apparently an aficionado of gangster movies. The disappointed souls are then vanquished to Hell to await their eternal damnation. And without an autograph or selfie from their savior. It truly is quite sad when you think about it. Now, again, this is just a rumor, so don't be spreading it all over the place. But I heard it from some mean-girl cheerleaders who reside in Hell and their information is usually quite reliable. Well, not that regrettable episode with Nancy and Scott. Turns out they were just friends, and their reputations were needlessly sullied. But I digress. So, that's Hell. Nothing too terribly exciting. The heat, and fire, and anguished screams. Over and over. I really am quite thankful to Satan for this opportunity to come to Earth and provide him with damned souls before they are due to arrive. It has been a lovely respite for me. And I found my true love. This country may be becoming Hell on Earth, but it is nothing like the real thing, let me assure you.

"Oh dear, that reminds me! I'm so sorry, but you will have to eat the pizza by yourself. I have taken a few weeks off from my responsibilities and I nearly forgot that I am scheduled to be employed at an adult book-store this evening. You have become a quite welcome distraction, my love, but duty calls. Please. Make yourself comfortable. There is a black box that turns on that television contraption. I think. I haven't figured out how to work it. I am so sorry, my love, but I mustn't be late. Can I pick up anything for you?"

Melissa thought for a moment, looked up at her beau with a wide smile and said, "Yeah. Maybe some edible panties. And a ball gag. I'm feeling kinda Christian tonight."

Chapter 21

Plain Brown Bag

Sweat was flying from Detective Anderson's greasy, thinning brown hair as he was feverishly working his three-and-a-half inch member. His saggy right bicep was beginning to become sore from the most work it had seen since lifting a package of donuts into his shopping cart the night before. He looked pleadingly down at his bopping mushroom as though he was willing for it to work. He finally threw his hands up in frustration and bellowed, "Fuck it!"

His naked ass made a loud suction sound as he got up from his cracked vinyl love seat and walked toward the VCR. He ejected the tape in disgust, put it back into its graphic cardboard cover and tossed it into the corner. The tape landed upon a pile of often-used videotapes with a plastic clunk. He watched for a moment as the haphazard pile began teetering from the weight of the tape. "Ah, goddam it," he muttered with irritation as the entire pile gave in to the added weight and tumbled over onto the once-white, now brownish carpet.

"This shit just ain't doin' it for me anymore," he muttered to himself once again as he picked up a soiled pair of grey sweatpants that perfectly matched his torn and soiled grey tank top. His flaccid breasts swayed over his belly as he struggled to bend down to put his legs into the sweatpants. He pulled the pants up past his navel, pulled his tank top down and let out a labored cough. He wiped the sweat from his pockmarked forehead and lit a half-smoked cigarette that had been lying in an overflowing ashtray.

"Nope. This shit ain't no good," he began again. "Same fuckin' whores. Same fuckin' situations. Same fuckin' positions. Hell, even the *bondage* shit ain't doin' it anymore. I need somethin' new. Somethin' *real*. I need to see these stuck-up bitches get what they deserve for *real*. No more of this actin' shit. I need some snuff. And the assholes in the department made me delete all the photos I took at the crime scenes. Biggs. Internal Affairs. Always on my ass about something. What the hell is wrong with these people? Don't they realize it's a man's world? And what are *women* doing on the force? Like that uppity little bitch, *Officer* Song. Lecture me, will ya? Oh, I'm gonna see to it she *never* gets promoted. Not unless she plays ball with me. Or plays with my balls. Jesus, all I've been able to think about was her threatening me. Standing there with her nose in the air and threatening me! A fucking detective! She needs to be punished. They *all* need to be punished. Especially my ex. I have to live in this shithole because she and my brat kids get half my check. It isn't right. I need to get my frustrations out. The murder scenes got me off for a while, but now that Bartlesworth is in jail, the murders have stopped. I need something violent tonight." He pulled out the waistband of his sweatpants and looked down upon his sad body. Frustrated once again by the view, he reached his left hand into his pants and pulled his penis out so that he could see the tip as he said, "C'mon little guy, let's see what they got in the backroom of the shop."

Upon hearing the front doorbell jingle, the attendant behind the counter of the 'Open 24-Hours Pornatorium' looked up and gave a welcoming smile to the new customer that had just lumbered into the establishment. The kindly looking shop keep had silver, slick-back hair with a light grey pencil mustache resting just above his thin upper lip. On his tall, lanky frame he wore a white apron. "Good evening, sir and welcome to our 'Pornatorium'," the smiling attendant stated. "If there is anything that I can do to assist you, please do not hesitate to ask. I am at your service. We take a lot of pride in helping our customers achieve the happy endings that they so richly deserve." Alexander then recognized the man who had just entered and said with a hint of anticipation, "Oh, my. Well, hello there, detective. I *thought* that I might run into you while performing one of my temporary services. Yes, yes. I had seen it in your eyes. Now, what can I do for you detective? Are you here for business, or pleasure. Am I suspected of being responsible for the great jaywalking epidemic in this community?"

"Uh, yeah, pleasure, I guess," Anderson gruffly responded. "And don't act so fuckin' high and mighty. I've got a weird feeling about you, Picklesbee. Maybe you didn't kill those hookers, but you're up to something. I can feel it. I've got my eye on you. And nice fuckin' apron."

"Well, thank you so much for noticing my apron," the smiling Alexander replied. "Now, detective, I do not want you to feel the slightest embarrassment at our meeting in such an establishment. We are men and men have our needs, now, don't we? So, what is your pleasure this evening? Threesomes? Blondes? Brunettes? Asian? Or perhaps a bit of light S&M? Yes, with all of the pressures of your position, I can see S&M being just the thing to melt those frustrations away. Especially your frustrations that are caused by the fairer sex. Am I right?"

"Not quite what I'm in the mood for," Anderson shot back as his perverted eyes scanned the cornucopia of sexually explicit video covers and magazines.

"Oh, I can see that you are a man of discerning taste," the shop keep stated. "Yes, quite discerning indeed. You are a man that is looking for something that is real. And violent. Am I correct, detective?"

"Yeah," a confused Anderson answered. "But how the hell do *you* know that?"

"Oh," Alexander answered. "I make it my business to understand what people want. And what they *deserve* to get. I believe that I have a *little something* under the counter that *might* just be what you are looking for."

Anderson's tennis shoes made smacking sounds on the sticky linoleum as he approached the counter wearing an intrigued expression upon his greasy, scruffy face. He watched as Alexander pulled a plain brown bag from under the counter and placed it upon the glass display case that covered multiple versions of the same type of sex toy.

Alexander smiled at Anderson and said, "Here you are, my good man. And this is on the house. Call it a professional courtesy. If you like what you see in these pages, I'm *sure* that I will be able to locate similar… *ahem*…material. All that I ask is that you wait until you get home before you open this plain brown bag. We certainly wouldn't want such material to be in the view of a child's prying eyes. Agreed?"

"Uh, yeah, sure," Anderson replied as his imagination began flashing images of possible sadistic delights. "Thanks. But this better be good, or else I'll be back here and shove this right up your ass. I don't like wastin' time. Just remember who you're dealing with. You waste *my* time, and I'm sure I can find something on you to ensure you *do* time."

"Understood, my good man, understood," the ever-smiling Alexander responded. "I'm *quite* sure that you will find *exactly* what you deserve within the contents of that bag. And *do* stop and see me again."

Anderson nodded and grunted dismissively at the silver-haired attendant, grabbed his plain brown bag, and sauntered out of the 'Pornatorium'. The front doorbell clanged, and Alexander's face twisted into an evil little smile as he said softly to himself, "Yes. *Please* visit me again. If not here, then perhaps in Hell, heh, heh, heh."

Twenty-five minutes later, Anderson arrived at his apartment that was two blocks from the 'Pornatorium'. He dropped his sweatpants and left them in a heap on the filthy carpet. The loveseat let out a tortured squeak as he flopped his bare, rotund ass upon its cracked vinyl. He eagerly took out the magazine, crumpled up the plain brown bag, and tossed it upon the floor in front of the vintage nineteen-inch television set.

He began sweating in anticipation as he grabbed Lil' Anderson with his right hand and began working it while flipping the pages with his left. His heart began pounding rapidly as he jerked off to the grotesque images of real-life beatings, rape, and torture of innocent, bound women. He flipped to the next page and giggled as his lecherous eyes took in image after image of a woman's head being meticulously sawed off by piano wire. He released a scream of satisfaction as Lil' Anderson regurgitated his thick, sticky seed all over the picture of the woman's bloody, pleading face.

"Oh, fuck," he stated loudly while trying to catch his breath. "That was the best that I've ever had! That was so awesome! Even better than the crime scene photos! The look on that bitch's face as they were beating and raping and murdering her. Yeah! That's what life is *supposed* to be about! We are *men*! We should be able to do anything we want to these stuck-up bitches!"

The vinyl seat let out a sound of relief as Anderson's hairy, pimple-covered ass got up and made its way back to where his sweatpants were lying. He was snickering to himself as he struggled to bend over and lift the elastic waistband when he heard a woman's voice from behind him say, "*Blech*! Jesus, darlin'! Didja hafta shoot me in the *eye*?"

A dismayed Anderson turned around and watched in stunned silence as the blonde-haired form of one of the murdered women rose from the open pages of the magazine. Her body had deep, bloody lacerations and dark purple bruises as depicted in her final photograph.

"Whatcha lookin' at sweetheart?" the blonde, battered woman asked. "Don'tcha know that this is your lucky night? This is the night where all your dreams come true…well…sorta. C'mon girls, let's show this handsome man how to party!"

The blonde woman reached her hand into the pages of the magazine and pulled out a battered, naked brunette and the headless form of another. "Oops, sorry love," the blonde stated with a chuckle as she reached back into the magazine and retrieved an auburn-haired decapitated head. "Here, love. You're gonna need this," she stated as she tossed the disembodied head to its rightful owner. The red-headed woman placed her head upon her lacerated neck, pushed down tightly and said, "Ahhhh, man. What a fuckin' headache. So, who's *this* big lug?"

A frozen Anderson stood watching the impossible scene as the blonde licked her lips suggestively and said in a playfully sinister voice, "This? This is Detective Anderson. He's our *date* for tonight. C'mon girls. He's a cop. I bet he has all sorts of *toys* we can play with."

The blonde's beaten naked frame went over to the crumpled plain brown bag that was lying on the floor. Anderson could not help but let out a slight whimper of excitement as the blonde bent over and picked the bag up. She uncrumpled the bag, placed her right hand into it, looked into Anderson's anticipatory eyes, and flashed him a wicked smile.

"Oh, yessss, this is going to be fun," she hissed as she pulled out a black leather handle. She kept pulling until she had extracted a six-foot-long strand of razorblades that had been welded together to form a whip.

"W-what the *fuck*, bitch?" was all that Anderson could stammer as he felt the first lash of the razors slice through his protruding belly. Then came the second strike which sliced the left side of his face open. He began screaming and pissed himself as he saw his blood pouring out of the gaping wounds. His pungent urine dripped slovenly down his thighs causing the black hair to become matted in the thick yellow liquid refuse.

"Hey! Knock that shit off!" The blonde yelled out as her wounds began disappearing from her delicate, pale skin. "We're not into golden showers!" With a flick of her wrist, the whip split the man's less than impressive member down the middle making it look like a mini-hot dog that had been microwaved for far too long. "Okay, that was fun and I'm feelin' like my old self again! You're next, toots!" the blonde exclaimed as she tossed the plain brown bag to the battered brunette.

She reached into the bag with an eager grin on her face. She looked at the device, looked up into Anderson's tortured eyes and said, "Yeah, I remember when this was done to *me*. This is gonna be *fun*. On your knees, prick!"

The other two women forced his struggling body to his knees as the brunette put on the harness. She approached him wearing a sadistic smile and presented him with her treasure. Strapped between her legs was a twelve-inch metal spike that had iron nails protruding from around its entire circumference. She lifted his trembling head and said softly, "So, you like torture porn? Yeah? Well tonight you're in luck because I do *too*. Now open wide motherfucker."

Anderson's mouth was forced open by the other two women and the torturous phallus was violently thrust into the wailing man's mouth repeatedly. Blood and drool were flying out of his punished mouth as his screams were muffled by the constant thrusting of the jagged metal. "Yeah, you like to watch women get abused? Tortured? Murdered?" the brunette stated angrily as the wounds on her body began to disappear. "Y'know, it's *one* thing to be dismissive of us. Belittle us. Treat us as objects. That's been happening for ages. And we know how to *handle* that shit. And believe me, we are getting *better all the time* at handling that shit. But to beat, rape, and murder us? Just for your own amusement? Just so you can feel powerful because you're ashamed of your tiny little penis or the homosexual wet dreams that you have at night? Jesus Christ, man! That's fucked up! Don't drag *our* innocent asses into your fucked up complex! I mean, if you're wanting to suck a *cock*, then just fuckin' *do it*! Here! Let me accommodate you!"

The frenzied motion of the jagged phallus continued for what seemed to Anderson to be an eternity, until the brunette said, "Oh, I bet you've been dreaming of it up the ass too, huh? Well, okay, Detective! Face down and ass up! Let's get you over your homophobic bullshit!"

Anderson's face was thrust down to the floor by a pair of bare feet as he spit his remaining teeth fragments out upon the blood-soaked carpet. The brunette strutted around his wide body and placed the pointed tip up against his dark opening.

"P-wease, p-wease, 'op!" Anderson screamed out as best he could with his mangled mouth and tongue. "Nope," the brunette answered back. "I'm not completely healed yet. Now sit back and enjoy the ride." She fiercely thrust her weapon into his shaking posterior repeatedly until blood gushed from his mercilessly torn-apart anus. She let out an orgasmic scream as her final wound disappeared from her body and she extracted her phallus from the whimpering man's shredded posterior.

"Two down, one to go," the brunette stated with a hushed satisfaction. "Here ya go doll. Your turn," she concluded as she handed the plain brown bag to the red head.

"Oh yay! I wonder what might be in this bag for *me*?" she squealed.

Her squeals intensified as she reached into the bag and pulled out a long strand of piano wire. She looked up at her friends with thankful tears in her eyes and said, "Do you mean that I…?"

"That's right, doll," the blonde answered tenderly. "You get to finish this fucker off."

The red head sat astride Anderson's sweaty, hairy back and placed the piano wire around his flabby neck. She began cackling with glee as she feverishly pulled the piano wire back and forth, back and forth, back and forth until his head was completely severed from his neck and laid helplessly upon the roach-infested carpet. The final scar from around her neck disappeared as she got up onto her newly healed feet and began splashing in the geyser of blood like a giddy schoolgirl in a mud puddle. Her two friends joined her in the jubilant sloshing, and their naked frames became saturated in the blood of yet another of their many aspiring oppressors.

The women toweled off, hugged each other, and said their good-byes. For now. They stood over the blood-soaked magazine, held hands, and smiled as their perfectly healed forms were once again absorbed by the heinous pages.

"Jesus," Biggs stated to Officer Song as they surveyed the carnage in their former colleague's home. "Wow. I knew he was into some pretty sadistic stuff. The shit he used to force women to do was just heinous. He'd pull over an innocent woman and use his authority to threaten them unless they did what he wanted. And what he wanted was never pleasant. I'm disgusted with myself for having covered for him for so long. But I was brainwashed by that whole 'Brothers in Blue' bullshit. But I warned him. One more time and I would personally report him to Internal Affairs. And the way he treated you was just disgusting. I'm sorry, Officer Song. Sorry that I wasn't man enough to uphold the oath I took. To protect and serve. For years I protected and served *this* pig. And a number of innocent women suffered because of my ineptitude. As did our justice system. But karma's a funny thing, now, isn't it? I don't know who he ran into tonight, but whoever it was gave him what he deserved.

I don't know about you, and you can do what you want with this, but I get the feeling that this is case is going to go cold rather quickly."

Officer Song's emotionless brown eyes looked around at the streaks of blood on the floor and walls. She then glared at the wide-opened, panicked eyes of Anderson's decapitated head and said, "Yeah, if we ever solve this, I don't think they should be prosecuted. I think they should be given a key to the city and a fucking parade."

Satan intently watched from a darkened doorway as Anderson's body bag was placed into an awaiting ambulance. He pulled his flip phone from the pocket of his large black overcoat and dialed. "Come on, come on, pick up. Yeah, finally. Hello. Let me talk to Glen. Yeah, Glen. Oh fuck, not *this* again. Who do you *think* it is? How many people call down there, anyway? Oh, *reeeeaaally*. And all of them collect? No wonder the fuckin' phone bill has been so high! Whatever. I'll deal with it later. Just give me Glen. Yeah, hey buddy. Satan here. Oh, hey, before I forget, did you get those throw pillows I sent you? Yeah? Really brightens up the place? Great. You know, I saw them and immediately thought of you. Yeah? Already stained and soiled, huh? Well, I wouldn't expect anything less from a demon such as you. Anyway, we have another one coming down. And it's that Detective Anderson who was investigating Alexander! See? Toldja! Won *that* fuckin' bet! Yes, it *was* a bet. Yes, you *did*. You *totally* agreed to it. I said, 'I bet that detective is going to end up in Hell,' then you said, 'No, I don't think he will. He's a distinguished peace officer.' That makes it a bet. You *know* I wasn't fucking there to shake your hand, but it's *still* an official bet, so pay up motherfucker! Goddammit Glen. You're such a fuckin' welcher. Fine, whatever. Anderson's coming down, so just put him on the rack or some shit until I get back. I don't *know* when I'll be back! I'm still at work and I may be awhile, so stop nagging me! Yes, yes, I'll pick them up. Yes, and that too. No, I won't forget. Yes, I'll write it down. Okay. Talk to ya soon. Bye."

CHAPTER 22

IMAGINATION

A solemn Alexander and shocked Melissa entered his modest apartment. They shook the snow off of their respective black coats and hung them in the small closet. The damp garments' shadows concealed a black medical bag that was resting on the closet's floor.

"I can't believe that we've spent Christmas Eve at a funeral," Melissa softly stated as she put on a pot of water on the kitchenette's lone burner and reached for the box of tea. "I can't believe that we've spent Christmas Eve at my *father's* funeral. These last few weeks have felt like a lifetime. Everything was so normal just a few weeks ago. Well, at least in my family. I would go to work, kiss Dad on the cheek, and we would go about our day's business. We were great partners in that. He taught me so much, and yet I feel completely unprepared for running the shop on my own. I will need you, Alexander. I will need your support. Not just as my lover. I need you to help me at the shop. You will, won't you?"

"Of course, my darling," Alexander replied while wearing a forced smile. "I will be by your side in every aspect of your life that you desire. I realize now that we are indeed soul mates. Rather unconventional soul mates what with you being all of twenty-five and I being one-hundred-thirty-seven. Plus, the little detail of my being Jack the Ripper and a former resident of Hell, while you are very much alive. Vibrant, in fact. But I suppose it was our destiny to meet one another. To love one another. And yes, to unconditionally support one another. I am so sorry for your loss, my love. I wish that I could hold you and take your pain away."

"Thank you," Melissa answered. "I can't tell you what your support means to me. But, as strange as it might sound, I'm not in pain. I actually feel relief for perhaps the first time in my life. I now know what happened to my mother. His confession was very detailed. And gruesome. His infatuation with prostitutes. My mother finding out and threatening to divorce him and take me away. His fury and fear about that. His using a White Poppy extract to paralyze her. Then drag her into that alley and dismember her. His paying off one of his business associates for an alibi. The mob is good at keeping secrets. It wasn't until he started killing again and all that evidence was found in his greenhouse that he came under suspicion for my mother's murder as well. He had kept it hidden all these years. But why? Why start killing innocent women again? Why confess to my mother's murder but not the others? He was adamant up until the moment he hung himself in his jail cell that he was innocent of these recent killings. Why? Why not just unburden yourself completely? Especially when you know you're about to take your own life. Well, maybe Detective Biggs can find out someday. But not Anderson. *You've* seen to that, haven't you darling?

"It's all so confusing. The man who I adored my entire life murdered my mother. How do I reconcile that? I'm awash with rage and guilt and sorrow. Should I feel guilty about missing him? Should I just be filled with rage? I don't trust my feelings. I don't trust anything or anybody. Except you. My Alexander. My Jack. We are kindred spirits. And I trust you implicitly."

Alexander poured the perfect amount of cream into Melissa's teacup then responded. "And I trust you as well, my love. You are only the second woman in my entire lives that I have trusted. One betrayed me. You, I am quite sure, will not. And I am yours. Tonight and forever. Which is why I have decided to cancel my plans for this evening. I just want to hold you and be here with you tonight. I wish to share in your grief."

"No, don't do that," Melissa sternly stated. "Please. Don't change your plans for me. You have a damned soul to send to Hell. And they must be important if you are being drawn so strongly to Plymouth, Massachusetts. Go do what you need to do. I'll be fine. I'll see you tomorrow afternoon at my fath…um…at *my* estate. I will have completed my business with Robert by then. I am now free from these awful murders and tomorrow I will be free from him. Free to truly begin my life with you. Go now. Complete your deal with the Devil. I need some time to prepare for tomorrow anyway. Go and we shall have our first wonderful Christmas together. It will be the Christmas that you have longed for. It will be the Christmas that you *deserve*."

"Very well, my love," Alexander answered as he straightened his silver tie. "I must admit, I *am* a bit excited about trying something new that I have discovered. An additional ability. I can be called back in time exactly one year and witness a damned soul's demise. I cannot be the direct cause of the death, but I can observe it. And perhaps help it along a bit, but that is all. I am unable to curse any item, for I am merely a witness to an event that has already occurred. For several days I have felt such a strong pull from Plymouth on last year's Christmas Eve. I am quite intrigued as to what gloriously evil sights are awaiting me. Until tomorrow, then, my dear. I am very much looking forward to giving you your present." Melissa gasped as she watched the tall body of Alexander Picklesbee disappear into thin air.

"Well, I can't tell ya how much I appreciate this Mister, um, what was your name again?" the owner of the Sand Dollar asked. "Picklesbee," the man replied. "Alexander Picklesbee. And it is my pleasure to look over your fine pub while you spend this holiday eve with your lady friend. You just enjoy yourself, Vince, and do not worry about a thing. I will close up at ten and leave the keys in the lockbox. I doubt that it will be very busy tonight, anyway. Now go, my friend, and enjoy your evening."

"Uh, yeah, okay," a slightly dazed Vince replied as he put his coat on. He took one final confused look around his bar, shrugged, and exited into Plymouth's brisk salt air. "Well," Alexander softly said to himself while perusing the gin options, "I apparently am still able to put people in trances despite this being a past event. That came in quite handy." He was then interrupted by a demanding woman's voice at the end of the bar.

"Uh, hey Poindexter!" the woman roared. "Nice fuckin' suit! When were you born, the turn of the century? I mean, the *last* turn of the century, not the most *recent* one. Oh, whatever. You maybe wanna stop muttering to yourself and get me another drink? How 'bout some gin this time. And no cheap shit! I'm a top-shelf kinda gal."

Alexander chuckled at the irreverent young woman and said, "Yes, I'm quite sure that you are a refined lady. Here you are miss. May I put this on your tab?" Alexander's eyes then widened as the woman pulled her black hoodie from off of her pageboy styled copper hair. He began shaking as he peered into her glimmering green eyes and said in a trembling voice, "What on Earth are *you?*"

"What am *I?*" the woman yelled back. "I'm a paying fuckin' customer, *that's* who I am. Now are ya gonna set that drink down or what?" She was suddenly distracted by a new patron entering the bar. "And I'm *also* a woman who has needs. And I *think* I may have just found the perfect man to fulfill them, if you know what I mean, and I think that you do, heh, heh, heh. Yeah, I can tell just by looking at him. There's my mark, um, I mean *date*. Or sumthin'."

The well-dressed man took off his expensive overcoat and sat down. "Hey, where's Vince?" he inquired. "Oh," Alexander replied as he peered into the darkened soul of the patron. "He wanted to spend the evening with his lady friend, so I am filling in for him this evening. Now, what can I get you, my good man?"

"Uh, bourbon. Neat. No, not that one. The one on the very top shelf. Yeah. The $200 one. And make it a double. "Coming right up, sir," Alexander answered. *Oh my,* he began thinking to himself. *The atrocities that you have caused. The needless suffering of families. The unnecessary prolonged pain, and illnesses, and deaths. And all for money. All so you can drive your fancy swasticars, and dress in the finest clothing, and drink the most expensive liquor. If this were 2024, I would curse this glass of bourbon and I would send you to Hell myself. But it is not. It is 2023, and I have a feeling that this young lady may be providing you with your ticket to your hellish destiny tonight. Such a strange creature. She is alive. And yet, she is not. She possesses a soul. And yet, she does not. It is as though she is a living, breathing figment of someone's imagination. Much like myself, I suppose.*

Alexander then heard the man's smarmy voice say, "And just who are *you*, sweetheart? Why is such a ravishing little thing all alone on Christmas Eve? You maybe need somebody to keep you warm tonight? Maybe give you a present?"

Alexander could not contain his smile as he listened to the red-headed, green-eyed woman's response. "Who, lil' ol' *me*? Well, hiya. My name is Maddy Sommers. I'm here, um, visiting a *friend*, you might say. You see, I'm the creation of my author. Morgan Cabot. You know her? Doesn't matter. You see, she is a medium and can call vengeful spirits to do shit for her by reading some Latin shit out of this old book. She wanted to bring one of her animated characters to life, so she read an incantation to do that. And POOF! There was Larry the fuckin' Leopard. All bright yellow, and bouncing around, and rhyming and shit. He's annoying as fuck. But what she *didn't* know was that the incantation brought one of her *other* characters to life too. And that would be lil' ol' me! And I do what she writes. And what she has written most recently was me having a little fun with a health insurance executive. You wouldn't happen to be a health insurance executive, now, would you? Hmmmmm?"

The man began sweating in anticipation as he responded. "W-why, yes I am. And that is *quite* the vivid imagination you have. Perhaps we should go somewhere, and we can be, um, *imaginative* together. Now, I really can't take you home and I can't be seen checking into a local hotel. Again. But my car is nice and warm and, um, *spacious*. We could be imaginative together for a while and I can drop you off wherever your little heart desires. What do you say?"

"Weeeeell," Maddy replied coyly in a sing-song voice. "I *guess* that would be *okaaay*. If ya pay for my *drinks*. And *maybe* take me out for some *ice cream* after. You *know* how much I love *ice cream*…right, *daddy?*"

The man wiped drool from his mouth, jumped off his stool, and put on his coat. "Yeah, yeah, ice cream. Anything your little heart desires. Come on. My ride's out here." As the tittering pair walked arm in arm towards the door, Maddy looked back at a shocked Alexander. "See ya Poindexter!" she yelled out before giving him a knowing wink.

Yes, see me you will, Alexander thought to himself as he carefully washed the pair of glasses. *And yes, quite an imagination. For this Morgan Cabot. But this Maddy character is telling the truth. She is truly nothing but a character from someone's very vivid and disturbed imagination. I believe that I will need to close this establishment a bit early tonight. I simply must see this.*

Alexander's body appeared behind a large crane at a construction site near a shopping mall. He waited in anticipation as he saw the man's swasticar pull into the lot. Gravel crunched under the hideous silver behemoth before coming to a stop. Alexander closed his eyes and concentrated on the inhabitants of the penis-envy on wheels. He smiled as his mind connected with the activities within the cabin.

"So, it's plenty warm in here. Why don't you let me take a look at what you're hiding under that baggy sweatshirt?" Maddy stared at him with her intense green eyes as her thin, mauve lips curled upward into a twisted little smile. "Yeah? I bet you're just *dying* to see what I have concealed under here, aren'tcha? Well, okay. But just one thing…"

Maddy reached into her hoodie, took out a long butcher knife and slashed the man's throat wide open. "Be careful whatcha wish for motherfucker!" she cackled as her youthful face was sprayed with blood. "Awww, look at that. It seems as though I've made a bit of a sticky mess in your stupid fuckin' swasticar. But that's what you wanted, right? A sticky mess?"

The gurgling man looked at her with panicked eyes as he desperately clutched at his crimson throat. "Wow. That's a really nasty cut there, mister," Maddy stated with fake sincerity. "I'd really love to tend to your wound, but we seem to be having a little problem with your insurance. It seems as though they don't cover gaping fucking wounds in the throat of a motherfuckin' douchebag such as yourself. I'm sorry, but you'll have to wait in the waiting room, and we'll be with you shortly."

Maddy jumped out and ran around the swasticar. She opened the driver's side door, dragged the tormented man out, and threw him to the ground. The man was attempting to plead for mercy as she continued. "You know what? *Here's* something that your insurance will cover 'cause it's much cheaper than stitches. And we want to be all cost-effective and shit, now, don't we? You see, if we can get the blood to flow away from your neck, maybe we can save you. Let's see. Now, don't worry. Even though this is an experimental procedure, I'm sure it will be covered." She found a rusty saw propped up against a cement mixer and used it to slice through the man's right arm. The man screamed in agony as his appendage plopped in front of his terrorized face.

"Nope, that didn't work," Maddy said as she quizzically rubbed her chin with her blood-soaked fingers. "Well, how 'bout if you pass me that leg?" His screams intensified as the rusty teeth of the saw ground their way through skin, muscle, tendon and bone. "Well, motherfucker. *that* didn't work either," Maddy said as she picked up a sledgehammer. "I am stumped. And well, I guess you are too, heh, heh, heh. Get it? Stumped? 'Cause your leg is now a stump? Oh, nevermind. Nobody gets my great humor. Anyhoo, I got one final thing that I can try that's covered by your insurance. It's what you wanted anyway, so, hey! Win fuckin' win! How 'bout a little head?" The final image that the tortured health insurance executive saw was twenty pounds of steel pounding into his collapsing skull.

"*Die* mother fucker *die!*" Maddy screamed as she pummeled the man's head repeatedly. "This is for *every fucking person* who you tortured. Every single person that you took *thousands* upon *thousands* of dollars from, then denied them the care that they fucking *paid for*! Every single person who *died* so you can have your fucking second homes and yachts and fancy condos for your mistresses! This is for *every single person* who trusted you and you fucking betrayed! You and *everybody like you* are going to fucking hell! And I'll laugh my ass off as I send you there personally!" Shards of skull and streams of blood and brain matter coated the gravel drive around his obliterated, putty-like head as her laughter intensified with each subsequent blow. She paused for a moment and said to herself, "Now, why the fuck do I have *Psycho Killer* by The Talking Heads playing over and over in a loop in my head right now? Oh, yeah. Duh. Kinda on the nose though, don'tcha think?"

She took a deep breath and proudly looked down upon the man's decimated body. "This is so fuckin' cool," she admired to herself as her gleaming emerald eyes surveyed the macabre destruction. She then began jumping in a circle while laughing and clapping. "Oh, I feel soooo fucking alive!" she exclaimed. "Hey, how are *you* doin' buddy? Not so good? Well, can I interest you in our platinum plan? Sure, it costs a fuck ton more, but on the plus side, there's waaaay more shit that it won't cover. No? Not interested? Well, fuck you then. And fuck your worthless insurance."

Maddy looked around at her unfamiliar surroundings and said to herself, "Now how the fuck do I get back to Morgan's? No way I'm driving *that* ugly fuckin' thing. Only *assholes* drive swasticars. I wouldn't be caught dead in one. *This* douchebag would though, heh, heh, heh. Guess I'm walkin'. Fuck, it's cold. Why couldn't Morgan have written me as being all hot blooded and shit? I'm gonna have to talk to her about that. And I don't want these fuckin' freckles, either. And I should get to eat ice cream in *at least* every other chapter. Oh, and I also want…"

"Well, I must say, that was *quite* inspirational," Alexander stated to his empty apartment. "What an interesting creature. So vile and filled with rage. And yet, she is also filled with self-justification. She does not question the morality of her actions whatsoever. This Morgan Cabot created her to be a killing machine for justice and freedom. Quite more high-minded than *my* exploits, I must say. I would not mind if our paths crossed again sometime. Both this Maddy *and* this Morgan. Ah, but another thought for another time. I do need to get my Melissa's Christmas present prepared. I certainly hope that she has as much of an affinity for antique butcher knives as I do. I am so looking forward to giving them to her. The entire set. All at once, heh, heh, heh."

Chapter 23

Pardon Me

Alexander nervously cleared his throat as he clutched his carefully wrapped present and approached the door of the Bartlesworth estate on Christmas afternoon, 2024. He looked at a note that was written in his love's beautiful hand that had been fastened to the front door.

Welcome home, Alexander. Or do you prefer Jack. You have waited so long for the Christmas that you deserve, and I am now going to provide it for you. Please come in and follow the trail to my bedroom. I have a surprise for you.

A chill ran down his spine as he pondered what her surprise might be. "Well, whatever it is," he said softly to himself as a wry grin crossed his face, "I am most assuredly ready. And I have a surprise for you as well, my love." He opened the front door and was immediately greeted by a heavy stench. He looked around and his bewildered eyes were met with streaks of blood, entrails, and various bodily organs that snaked their way along the grey marble flooring and up the elegant winding staircase.

"Melissa!" he cried out as he began following the macabre trail up the stairs and down the second-floor hallway. "Melissa! Answer me this instant! Please! Are you alright!" he yelled as he ran past removed eyes, severed ears, and sheets of gruesome flesh. The trail ended with a thick pool of blood that was congealing outside of a bedroom door. Alexander let out a deep breath and said to himself, "No. Please, not again. I have already lost one opportunity at everlasting joy. Please, I beg of you sire, do not take this away from me again."

He cautiously opened the ornate oak door and stepped inside. His eyes adjusted to the dim light, and he focused upon a smiling Melissa lying in her bed. Her blood-soaked negligee clung to her slender, pale body as she sat upright. "Hello lover, and merry Christmas," Melissa purred while wearing a broad smile of self-satisfaction.

"M-M-Melissa," Alexander stammered. "What *is* all of this? What have you *done?*"

Melissa stretched and yawned and replied, "I told you that I wanted you to have a special Christmas. A Christmas that you deserved. And here it is. Please, no more questions. Not until you open your present. I do hope that you like it."

Her eyes trailed toward the foot of the bed where a perfectly wrapped square box was resting. Alexander slowly approached the bed and laid his present down upon the saturated comforter. He picked up the box and lightly shook it. There was a slight thud as its contents shifted inside the cardboard.

"Hey," Melissa playfully said. "No fair trying to guess. Just open it." "Very well then," Alexander dutifully replied. He carefully removed the tape on one end of the box and lifted the wrapping paper in one sheet. "I certainly hope you didn't go to too much trouble, my dear," he nervously stated while trying to gauge the weight of the package. "Oh, it was no trouble at all," Melissa answered. "In fact, I really enjoyed picking it out for you. Just open it."

Alexander's eyes widened in disbelief as he opened the box and looked down upon what remained of the severed head of Melissa's fiancée, Robert Jackson. He stared at the disfigured blob that had been liberated of its eyes, nose, and ears. There were deep lacerations and ebony skin flaps hanging mournfully off of the skull. "Oh, my dear, what have you done," Alexander's shaking voice quietly stated as a black tear fell from his eye. "What have you gone and done, my love. How could you? How could you possibly know?" He looked into her glimmering blue eyes and exclaimed, "How could you possibly know that this was my Christmas wish! Oh, how I hated this man. I was so jealous of him. I so wanted to do this very thing to him, but I could not. I did not wish to hurt you. Even though you had fallen out of love with him, I did not wish to be the cause of his demise or of your lingering sorrow. This is most magnificent, my love. Yes, the most special Christmas present that I could have ever received. I just knew somehow that you would like *my* present as well. It is not nearly as ornate as yours, but I do hope you enjoy it."

"Yay! Presents!" Melissa exclaimed as her knees bounced upon her mattress, causing blood droplets to spray across the room. "Gimmee, gimmee, gimmee!" she squealed out as she greedily ripped the paper open and unsealed the box. "Oh my, these are *perfect*," she said with wonderment as she looked at her bloody reflection in the steel blades of the butcher knives. "Oh, and are these handles made from real bone? Real *human* bone? Oh, just look at all the tortured souls that have been carved into them. And they all fit perfectly in my hand. Oh, Alexander. This is the most precious gift. I shall cherish them always. And I shall put them to good use, heh, heh, heh."

"Well, about that, my love," Alexander stated as he straightened his tie and began pacing back and forth across the sticky and stained marble floor. "I do understand that young ladies need their privacy and that we men are not privy to all that goes on in your pretty little heads. But I must ask you to explain just what has happened here. And what, if any, involvement you may have had in any other, um, nefarious activities."

"Yeah, okay, sure," Melissa replied while continuing to hold a menacing knife in her delicate palm. "Sure, sure. Confession time. You see, I've always had a bit of a, um, *mischievous* streak, shall we say. I always found pleasure in others' suffering. And, in some cases, I was the *cause* of that suffering. You might say that I was a bit of a mean girl. I guess it runs in my genes. My entire lineage is filled with all sorts of misanthropes. Liars. Thieves. Rapists. Murderers. Hell, even my great, great, great, great grandfather, the *first* Thomas Bartlesworth murdered his father-in-law in order to take over his clothier business. And he, of course, was the man who stole the affections of your first love, Virginia. Generation after generation committed all sorts of atrocities and my father wrote a book about it. He had claimed that by airing all of our family's sordid secrets, that he had finally broken my family's deadly curse and that the Bartlesworth name was one that could now be trusted and held in admiration. But he too was just another bad apple that had fallen close to our rotting family tree.

"It all started just a few days before we met. I was rummaging around in my father's personal safe looking for some financial records when my palm accidentally landed on a little switch. The back of the safe flopped open revealing a secret compartment. I pulled out the various items and my heart sunk at what I had found. Letters from my mother to him revealing how much she knew about his activities. All of the sordid trysts that he was having with prostitutes. How she felt lied to and betrayed. You could feel the anguish in her soul through the ink on the paper. Then, the night before her murder, there was another letter telling him that she intended to hire an attorney and file for divorce. And who could blame her? Him, I suppose. Because there was also a recipe for a debilitating toxin that was extracted from White Poppys. And a map of the area where my mother was found. I, of course, knew right then that it was my father who had brutally murdered my mother in that back alley. He had paralyzed her and mercilessly sliced her up. All out of pride, or to hide his little secrets. Or maybe just to keep all his money. The reason wasn't important to me. I was disgusted by him and vowed to get back at him for what he did to my mother.

"So, I planted a White Poppy in the very back of his greenhouse, hidden behind a bunch of other plants. I learned how to create the extract. I was going to murder my father in the same brutal, disgusting way that he had killed my mother. That was the plan, anyway. Until one night when I saw dumbass Robert leaving a cheap hotel with a hooker.

My blood boiled. It wasn't just the men who were to blame here. It was also the women who tempted them. I had lost my mother because of them, and now I was losing my fiancé. I hated them. And pitied them at the same time. I thought that perhaps I could save my relationship and maybe others by sending these prostitutes to their final resting place. And, since they lived miserable lives of servitude, I would actually be doing them a favor by helping them find peace. Of course, I've always had a bit of fascination with the legendary Jack the Ripper, so if I were going to do this, I wanted to do it in style. In *his* style.

"That was victim number one. The prostitute that I saw Robert with. And I thought that it might be more fun to frame my father for these crimes and let him rot in prison. So, I killed them the same way he killed my mother in order to establish a pattern and a link to her. Oh, and I also made sure to take a souvenir from the victims. A pair of panties. A bra. A ripped up stocking. Anything that might have their DNA. And would fit into a little metal lock box that I would bury under the White Poppy. I had really only planned on the one murder. But I must admit, I felt such a *rush* as I stared into her paralyzed eyes while slicing her open. I made sure to show her every organ that I removed. Until she bled out and then the fun was over. Then, just leave a few strands of my father's hair that I had taken from his brush, maybe a fingernail clipping or two, and some skin cells and stubble from his razor, and the police would have all the evidence that they would need to convict him. And then, as a bonus, I would inherit the business and finally get to modernize this operation. Jesus, he was sooo old-fashioned. I can't wait to tell you all of my ideas for the place. But that can wait. Maybe over dinner. I have a roast cooking. I hope you like it.

"Anyway, I really was going to stop after that first murder. And, although I am very sorry that you got entangled in all of this, it really is kinda your fault that my spree continued. When I ran into you, literally, it was like my entire world had opened up. The moment I looked into your eyes, I just knew that I had found my soul mate. I can't explain it. It was as though we were connected. Then, when I found the letters and the locket with Virginia's picture along with Alexander Picklesbee's, well, it just seemed that we were destined to be together. But you, just like my father and my fiancée, had a penchant for prostitutes and that just could not stand. So, every time I saw you with one, I would get really jealous and, um, well…you know. I'd drug them and cut them up. But it was all for the best! These women were relieved of their horrible existence, you were being further drawn to me, I got my jollies by killing them, and my father would eventually take the fall! That is what I call a win, win, win, fuckin' win!

"The closer I got to you, the more jealous I became. The more jealous I became, the angrier I became. And the angrier I became, the more brutal I became to those women's bodies. I could feel the rage flowing through me as I ripped them apart piece by piece as they were forced to lay there and watch. Then, you told me that you were, in fact, Jack the Ripper, and it all came together. It was like the final puzzle piece that completed my soul. I decided to kill one more time as a special gift to you. That's why I arranged the organs in a heart shape. I was telling you how much I loved you.

"Well, I guess it wasn't the *last* time. There was still Robert to deal with and I thought that since you were denied your revenge upon my ancestor so many years ago on Christmas, that this would be my special gift to you. His bloody head in your hands to show you my eternal love and commitment to you. You really should have seen the look on his face when I thrust the knife into his abdomen. I was dressed in this sexy little number, and he thought we were going to get back together. Well, surprise! Instead of *him* sticking something into *me*, *I* stuck something into *him*! Oh, it was so funny. He kinda stumbled backwards while he held his stomach and just kept saying 'Why', 'Why', 'Why'. Like he didn't know. He was such an asshole. I pushed him onto the floor face first, ripped open his shirt and started slicing the flesh from his back. Then, I lifted his head and cut off his nose. Then his eyes. Then…um…no wait. I did that wrong. First it was his nose, then his *ears,* and *then* I cut out his eyes. He was still alive and screaming as I carved up his face. There was blood *everywhere*! It was so cool. I flipped him over and was cutting him open from his dick to his neck when he finally died. I looked at the clock and realized it was getting late, so I quickly left the blood and organ trail from here to the foyer and cut off his head. Thankfully I was able to get his head wrapped just a few moments before you arrived. I can't tell you how nervous I was as I was rushing around getting your present ready. So, do you like it? Do you really?"

Alexander took Melissa into his broad arms. Dark red streaks were transferred onto his grey pinstriped suit as the pair tenderly embraced. "Yes, I positively love it. And I love you. All this time and I finally realize that we are indeed soul mates. Your story is fascinating, and I must say that you have never looked more adorable than when you were confessing to me. The smile on your face as you reveled in your exploits warmed my cold, dead heart. Now, why don't we just get this mess cleaned up, have a lovely pot roast dinner, and perhaps relax by the fire while watching an old Christmas movie? I have never seen one, but I have heard about one where a pour tortured soul named Mister Potter is harassed by the town's cruel do-gooders."

Melissa stared into the dark eyes of her love and whispered, "Yes. I always thought that the Baileys were a bunch of whiney assholes. Maybe we can discuss what *we* would have done to them if *we* had been in that movie. I know what we would have done to Violet. That would be the perfect ending to a most perfect Christmas."

"Well, well, well, isn't *this* fuckin' cozy!" a booming voice came from the doorway. The pair turned to look, and Alexander exclaimed, "Sire! What are *you* doing here?" The hulking red frame of Satan approached them as he cracked his calloused knuckles. He lifted his horned head and replied in an annoyed tone, "What am I doing here? What the fuck do you *think* I'm doing here? I'm checking up on your pasty ass. I heard how all these innocent prostitutes were being sent to heaven before their time. So now, Jesus has even *more* women to play with at his fuckin' pool parties. Man, those parties are legendary. But do *I* ever get an invite? Fuck no! Whatever. Not important right now.

"Anyway, I put two and two together. Innocent prostitutes being slaughtered shortly after I pardon Jack the fuckin' Ripper? Coincidence? I think not. So, I came up here personally to see if you had betrayed me.

And, I must say, I am pleasantly surprised that I was wrong about you, Picklesbee. My apologies for having doubted you. I guess it was *this* evil little bitch all along. Now, how about an introduction?"

"Well, of course, sire," Alexander obediently answered. "Melissa, this is our dark lord, Satan. Sire, this is my soul mate, Melissa."

Satan stroked his broad chin and said, "Soul mate, huh? Yeah, you two are certainly cut from the same cloth. You're both evil and looney as fuck. But Melissa, my dear, as delightful and charming as you may appear, I simply cannot overlook your murderous rampage. You are a damned soul, and you must be sent to Hell.

"No, please sire," Alexander began groveling. "Please do not take her away from me. I have lived two lifetimes searching for my one true love. I have done everything that you have requested, and I promise you, my lord, that I can personally guarantee that her malicious activities shall come to an end. Isn't that right, my love?"

"Um, yeah!" Melissa replied as she batted her blue eyes. "Please, Mister Satan, I *promise* to *never* murder a prostitute or anyone else that is innocent ever again. I was just, um, sowing my wild oats, y'know? But those days are behind me. *Please* don't send me to Hell and away from my Alexander. Please."

"Manipulative too, I see," Satan said while continuing to stroke his chin. "Well, that does give me an idea. So, you say you two want to be on Earth together for eternity, huh?"

"Oh yes, sire, more than anything," Alexander tearfully replied.

"Well, Picklesbee," Satan answered. "Maybe we can reach a deal. I do make the best deals. But there's only one way to get from here to there. You know what to do. Now do it. Or I will be forced to, and you can watch your dreams go up in a ball of fuckin' hell fire."

"Of course, sire," Alexander replied as he sorrowfully went to the bed. "I know what I must do. I am sorry, my love. This is the only way." He picked up one of the knives, grabbed Melissa by her golden hair and ripped her throat open in one savage stroke. Melissa's body slumped to the floor. She gurgled one final, 'I love you,' before being overcome by death's icy grip.

Her damned soul was suddenly scorched by towering flames and glowing fragments of flying brimstone. Her confused soul stood at a blazing altar. Standing next to her was her beloved Alexander. And between them stood the ominous form of Satan.

"Dearly damned," Satan bellowed. "We are gathered here today to… Hey! Shut the fuck up everybody!" One of the members of the demonic congregation yelled out, "We don't want to be here! Weddings are torture!" Satan slapped his forehead and forcefully responded, "Well, of course it's torture! You're damned to Hell! What the fuck did you think this was gonna be? A fuckin' vacation? Now just shut the fuck up and let me get through this! Me and Glen have tennis lessons at three!

"Now, where was I? Oh, yeah. Dearly damned. We are gathered here today to join the demonic souls of Alexander Picklesbee and Melissa Bartlesworth. If anyone has any objections, keep them to yourself. I'm not dealing with your petty shit. Now, Alexander, do you promise to live with Melissa on Earth and send me damned souls at a frequency of at least one per week and keep Melissa from murdering hookers for eternity?"

"I do, my lord," a beaming Alexander answered as his sweaty palms clenched those of his betrothed.

"Alright, cool," Satan continued. "And Melissa, do you…oh now what?" Satan said as he was interrupted by a severed head rolling toward the altar. "Would someone please stitch Robert's head back on? This shit's getting old. This is the third time since this fuckin' thing started. You got the thread and needle? Good. Now don't let it happen again! Sorry, dear. Let's continue. Melissa, do you promise to work alongside Alexander on Earth for all eternity to send me damned souls at a frequency of at least one per week? *And* do you promise to not murder innocent people, especially hookers? And I fuckin' mean it! And, *most importantly*, do *both* of you promise to take these fuckin' mean girl cheerleaders off of my hands and make sure they don't do anything to get them sent back here so that I once again have to deal with their mouthy, gossipy, gum-snapping asses?"

Melissa and Alexander looked deeply into one another's eyes, smiled broadly and said in unison, "We do." "Great!" Satan yelled out. "Now you two can go fuck or whatever and just as you both cum you'll be transported together to Earth and wake up in Melissa's bed. Oh, and once you get there, you still need to clean up Robert's mess and…oh fuck. Someone wanna take care of that? His head came off again. Jesus Christ, I'm surrounded by incompetence. Anyway, congratulations or whatever. I'm running late for my tennis lesson. Glen! Hey buddy, didja bring the tennis rackets? What do you mean you couldn't find them? They're in the hall closet next to the Thigh Master and that box of ceramic cat figurines. Oh, fuck it. I'll get them myself. Oh, and Merry Anti-Christmas all you fucked up bastards! Seriously. I can't believe you people read this shit."

THE END

Epilogue

───────────

"Alexander! Alexander would you *please* come up here?" Melissa screamed out from the second floor of their shared estate. "Yes, my love, what is it?" an out of breath Alexander inquired as he reached the top of the stairs.

"Would you *please* talk to them? I just don't have the strength today. I have to go to the bank and extend our line of credit, then try to negotiate lower prices with our Canadian and Mexican suppliers. Then, there's that pedophile over on West Fourth Street that I have to slice up and send to hell. Which reminds me. You haven't sent a damned soul to our lord in nearly a week. Do ya think it might be a good idea to get off of your British ass and contribute a little? I've done eight *already* this month!"

"Well, about that, my love," Alexander sheepishly replied. "There is actually something that I wish to speak to you about. I have an idea."

"Well, just save it until I get out of the shower. If it isn't all clogged up again with their fucking hair!" Melissa stormed down the hallway and slammed the bathroom door. Alexander let out a frustrated sigh when he heard her yell out, "Yep! Clogged again! Just look at all this hair! Where's the fucking plunger!"

He shook his head solemnly as he looked upon the various blouses, stockings, discarded bottles of make-up, and pom-poms that were strewn about the hallway. He walked several feet down the cold marble and lightly knocked on a bedroom door. "Ladies?" he cautiously asked. "May I please come in? I wish to speak with you."

"Yeah sure, why not," a female voice replied. Alexander grabbed the doorknob, then wiped his hand that was covered in chewing gum. He sighed once again and entered the room to find four teenage girls sitting in a heap of pizza boxes, soda bottles, soiled clothing, and teen magazines. "Yeah, what's up? You got our breakfast ready yet?" one of the young women asked without looking up from painting her toenails.

"No, I do not. I need to speak with you. All four of you. We have now been here for five weeks and not *once* have any of you lifted a finger to assist around our home. In fact, you four are creating quite the mess and I am here to tell you that your selfishness and laziness ends now. Your actions are placing a strain on our marriage and that, ladies, I simply won't tolerate. Now, you will get up, get dressed, and clean this home from top to bottom. I want to be able to see my reflection in the shined floors by the time I get home. Do you all understand?"

All four girls began laughing before one of them replied, "Oh yeah? What are *you* going to do about it? You can't send us back to Hell, 'cause, like, that'll piss off Satan. So, just go make us our breakfast and leave us alone old man. We're busy."

Alexander took a deep breath and exhaled heavily. His face darkened and his eyes turned black before he said, "Missy, Buffy, Sparkles, and Trish. Listen to me very carefully. You are correct. I am unable to send you to Hell. But, believe me ladies, I am *more* than capable of making your lives hell on Earth. Every moment. Every breath. Everything that you do will be met with excruciating pain. I can perform operations on each of you that will never heal and will provide you with an eternity of suffering."

The four young women rolled their eyes and went back to their primping. "Yeah, like we didn't experience pain in Hell. How original. Whatevs. Now go make us our breakfast." Alexander clenched his fists and began again. "Or, I can ground you. No more dates with the local high school boys. No more cheeseburgers. No more pizza and soda and potato chips. No more chewing gum. And no more of your internets. Now, as I said, you will get up, get dressed, and clean this home from top to bottom. I want to be able to see my reflection in the shined floors by the time I get home. Or do you really want to try Jack the Ripper?"

Missy, Buffy, Sparkles, and Trish stared at one another with widened eyes then looked at the determined face of Alexander. "Fiiiiiine!" they bellowed out. "We're getting up! Gaaaaawd! This is soooo unfair!"

Melissa emerged from her bedroom wearing a form-fitting, dark blue business suit. She smiled as she passed four sweaty young women who were placing clothing into laundry baskets, sweeping, mopping, and dusting. She entered the study to find her demonic husband sipping tea and reading the paper. "Nice job with the girls," she said as she poured herself a cup. "Thank you," Alexander replied. "I can be a bit persuasive when I put my mind to it. Which brings me to the topic that I wish to discuss. I know you are quite aware of what this nazi regime is implementing in this country. All the pain and suffering and death that they are destined to create throughout the entire world. So many souls who have been converted from the pious to the damned. Millions of them. And, of course, their corrupted leaders. They are all paving their road to Hell. So, my dear, I have just one question for you. Would you like to assist me in helping a few of them along on their journey? Would you enjoy sending some sadistic fascists to Hell?

Melissa took a sip of her tea, placed the porcelain cup on its saucer, and smiled. "I sure as hell would, my love. And I know just where to start."